What If? What If?

Some thoughts demand to be heard over and over again.

Suzanne B. Miller

Contents

Dedication

Since this will likely be the only book I ever write, I'm making the most of this space.

To my four wonderful book-loving children, thank you for lending your talents and encouragement. Hannah, for designing the cover; Paris, for your marketing skills; Eden, for your editorial eye; and Cooper, for cheering me on.

To my parents, Barry and Judi – thank you for instilling confidence for learning and creativity. Your support is mirrored in the parents of this story.

To my grandparents, thank you for lending me your story of extraordinary resilience and faith. Your words are woven into this story.

And to my husband, Todd, thank you for supporting me in all my interests, whether it's combing cemeteries, diving into family history, or buying peppermint chocolate for me.

To the people at my proofreading party – Mum, Paris and Huia, if we missed something, let's call it character.

And to my friends, thank you for your encouragement.

Now, finally, on with the story.

To the reader

This story explores a condition that is often misunderstood and misrepresented in the media and everyday conversation. While fictional, Jasmine's emotional struggles are based on real people who live with intrusive thoughts. Each person's experience is unique, and the 'what if' questions are as varied as those who live with them.

You'll notice Jasmine's condition isn't named at first. That's intentional. Many keep it hidden from friends and family. I want readers to walk beside Jasmine's secret before labelling what she's facing.

I hope as you follow her journey, you will gain greater empathy and understanding for those living with this condition.

Woven through the book is a second story, inspired by my grandparents' lives. It offers a glimpse into an era when mental health was often misunderstood.

This book is a work of fiction, set in New Zealand, where summer begins in December and prose is written in the style of UK English.

It is not intended to offer therapy or medical advice.

Thank you for reading, **Suzanne B. Miller**

Prologue

It's just a thought. It's not real.

But it's real to me.

Jasmine felt hot all over and could feel her heart beating quickly. She sat in her therapy session, staring at an image of a bridge stretched over a river. Her stomach churned.

She wanted to scratch the itch that would bring her relief.

Jasmine focused on her breathing, trying to shove the anxious thought away. *I am safe. I am safe.* But the thought slithered back with a familiar whisper: *What if you die crossing a bridge?*

What if?

The taunting.

She shifted in her seat, frustrated at the exercise, wishing she had just avoided the situation. Avoidance is easier.

Her therapist closed the image. 'You did well today, Jasmine. You were exposed for longer than usual.'

Jasmine nodded, but felt no relief from the praise. She knew that as soon as she left the session, she would reverse the experience in her mind.

She would do it all the way home if she had to.

And she would *have* to.

Chapter One

What if I get skin cancer?

Most people worry about big things. Jasmine could worry about anything: whether she'd remembered to say thank you, the food expiry dates, or if she might die.

Dying *is* a big thing. She didn't think about being dead – just about all the ways it could happen.

Today felt fine, though. Which was suspicious.

The November sun was already warm, streaming through her kitchen window and catching specks of dust drifting in the air. She waved her knife like a wand, pretending to swirl the dust. Glitter would be a nicer word than dust, she decided.

She caught her reflection in the kitchen window and gave her outfit an approving glance: dressy jeans, a button-up shirt, and trusty Doc Martens sandals. She smoothed her brown hair into its tidy high ponytail and checked that her earrings were secure.

She often doubted her attractiveness, and today was no exception. She wondered if her eyebrows were plucked enough, or if her lashes should be darker to make her green eyes stand out. She never felt quite sure. And yet, when she smiled, the beauty shone out of her.

She stood on tiptoes to get a better look in her makeshift mirror, rubbing her chin to blend her soft makeup. Then she tucked in one side of her shirt to accentuate her waist.

Jasmine's thoughts were interrupted as her flatmate, Paige, stormed into the kitchen.

'Six more weeks!' she announced, grabbing an apple in one hand and tossing bread into the toaster with the other. Her energy filled the flat, as did her tendency to leave a trail of chaos behind her.

'That's thirty teaching days, plus prizegiving, dress-up day, and zoo day – but who's counting?'

As a primary school teacher, Paige measured her life in school terms. She had exceptionally curly hair, which tormented her. She always wore a cap to keep it under some form of control, which doubled as protection from the harsh New Zealand sun. As she gathered her gear for the day, she applied moisturiser to her arms and legs while adding peanut butter to her toast, chaotically blending the two at times.

'See you tonight? Birthday party at your mum and dad's?' she asked.

'Yep, free dinner tonight, yay,' Jasmine stated while helping Paige carry a bundle of books and a drink bottle, farewelling her at the door. She watched as Paige ran along the concrete path of their townhouse, which sat in a row with four others on what had once been someone's home and back lawn. The simplicity suited the housemates; there were no gardens to tend to and a patch of grass so small it could be mowed in two minutes.

Paige was Jasmine's loyal supporter; their friendship was forged in high school and continued through university. Jasmine's teenage years were rough when the 'what if' thoughts started.

When Jasmine first started therapy, she was encouraged to give the thoughts a name, to help her see them as a separate force. Medusa won the naming rights, a villain with a head of writhing snakes, persistent, disturbing, and uncontrollable.

Now, at 28, Jasmine had far more control than she'd had as a teenager.

But control wasn't the same as freedom.

Jasmine grabbed her lunchbox, threw in fruit with pull-apart bread, and exited the flat. Driving through the early morning traffic, she passed the rugby stadium and rows of fast-food restaurants before finally parking in the city beneath leafy trees that would shade her car. As she locked the door, she glanced up, wondering what the chances were that her vehicle would be hit with bird crap by the end of the day. The arrival of spring birds and lighter evenings was an invitation for a bird missile attack.

Bird droppings could ruin the paintwork of her car. She had heard it could happen. She thought about the need to move her car. *No, you don't have to listen,* she told herself, crossing the street, sounding much like Dr Kris. She focused on the clouds to distract herself, trying to see if she could find a shape in them.

But the thought of her car nagged her; she glanced back at the large tree hanging over it and the car's vulnerability.

Agghh.

Quickly, she returned to the car and moved it a few spaces ahead, just enough to protect it. She was grateful the extra time didn't make her late.

Medusa sometimes made her late.

She hurried into the Council building, making her way to her office. Her desk was a controlled state of colour-coded files and sticky notes. Before she could settle in, her friend, Joel, wheeled his computer chair to her space.

'Jaz, you are going to love this,' he announced, grinning. 'I was listening to the radio on the way in, and they were talking about code names for your workmates, and it gave some good material.' He clapped his hands together. 'I've already started assigning some.'

Jasmine raised an eyebrow as she unpacked her bag onto the desk. 'Tell me.'

'Okay, so someone who's a 'Mastercard' is the person who always takes all the credit.'

Jasmine smiled. 'I assume you are thinking of Felicity in Comms. You haven't forgiven her for when she stole your idea for the 'Trash to Treasure' campaign.'

Joel pointed at her dramatically as if he were playing a game of charades, and she was nailing the clues.

Jasmine laughed. 'Okay, what else?'

Joel leaned in, lowering his voice, 'Wheelbarrow.'

Jasmine looked to the roof, thinking. 'Wheelbarrow? Let me guess. You have to lift them?'

'Close,' Joel giggled. 'They always need a push to get going.'

Jasmine laughed. 'Oh, that's great. I can see this game will get you through the day.'

Joel grinned, darting his eyes toward his office mates. 'Yeah, it's giving me something to think about when I'm bored.'

'Got any code names for yourself?'

Joel tapped his chin. 'Not yet, but give me an hour, and I'll have some bangers.'

'I have one,' Jasmine teased, quickly seeing the options. 'It has to be 'Echo'.'

'Ah, because I ensure important information isn't lost and I share it on social media?'

'Nope, you can't help but repeat what you hear.'

Joel clutched his chest as if he were mortally wounded. 'Offended,' he said.

Joel lived for the drama. In just a week, he would step onto the stage as the character Seaweed Stubbs in *Hairspray*, performing at a theatre on the east, over the river. He had been oozing with excitement for months, and now that opening night was approaching, his energy had reached a new level.

Jasmine hadn't told him she might not go; she unrealistically hoped the bridge-crossing problem would be 'fixed' by then. She would delay buying her tickets or be 'sick' that night. She desperately wanted to see him perform, but to cross the river would be impossible. Medusa told her so.

Standing up after faking his death, Joel leaned against the partition of Jasmine's desk. 'You want to have lunch together today? It's a nice day outside; I reckon we eat in Garden Place,' he asked, pointing out the window to the garden area four stories below. 'And, do you have any spare food? I'm living on cornflakes and powdered milk at the moment.'

Jasmine screwed up her face at the thought of the powdered milk.

'I *do* have a treat for us today for lunch,' she said proudly, grabbing an envelope off her desk.

'Ooh, Mama's Donuts?' Joel asked, knowing perfectly well there was no such treat.

'Nope, a 1930s diary I found in the dungeons; the Council doesn't need to keep it,' she replied, slowly revealing the envelope's contents.

'The dungeons' was the term Jasmine and her colleagues informally used for the Council's archival room, which housed city maps, donated photographs, and historical records. Jasmine, as the archivist, often preferred spending time in the dungeons rather than in her office. It was a perfectly temperature-controlled space where she could spend quiet time.

Joel looked suspiciously at the diary in Jasmine's hands. 'So, if the Council doesn't need to keep it, why don't you just bin it?' He paused, glancing over his shoulder at the staff member in charge of reducing waste, who might be listening to his flippant disregard. 'Or recycle it,' he corrected smoothly.

'Nah, I want to find out who wrote it and try to return it to the family. Come on, it'll be fun – a little detective work.'

'Well, I do love playing detective,' Joel said. 'I'll read it today, but if it's all about the Depression or war, I'm out.'

Jasmine smiled, replying, 'I'm impressed you know the Depression was at that time.'

'It was a guess,' he said, laughing as he peeked inside the envelope. 'But seriously, why do you want to return it? If someone got rid of it, they probably don't want it.'

'Well, the person who gave it to us probably wasn't the owner. It was in a pile of donated items from a historical home, given to the Council years ago.'

'If no one has asked for it in years, I reckon it's ready to be *recycled*,' Joel said, really emphasising his words for the benefit of his greenie co-worker.

'I'm not recycling it, Joel. We will preserve history and find its owner,' she smiled. 'And you *will* have fun.'

'Doubt that,' sighed Joel like a child.

Jasmine knew he would join her because he would want to share the pull-apart bread she had popped on her table as an incentive.

'You're so odd,' he said. 'No one else your age is into stuff like that.' He pointed to the diary and waved his hand around like it was offensive.

'You're probably right, but hey, there might be some gossip in there,' she suggested, trying to build it up.

'I guess it doesn't look like it's too long, I can probably manage it,' Joel said, defeated.

'Well, that's true. But FYI, it's the first book of many,' Jasmine explained. 'Just think of it as a book series,' she added, laughing.

Joel – all six-foot-six of him – slunk back to his desk, careful not to earn a new codename for avoiding work. Jasmine watched as he folded himself under the desk. His height was a constant source of commentary from strangers. He and Jasmine often turned it into a game, timing how long it took before someone mentioned it. It was even better when a stranger followed up the comment by asking if he played basketball.

Joel's response was always, 'Of course, I play for the Lakers.' He loved to watch them scroll their phones, looking for his face in the team. The best part of the joke was that Joel didn't even know who the Lakers were.

Jasmine's morning passed quickly with meetings with museum curators about an upcoming display; it was just the kind of project she thrived on. She hurried back to her office to collect Joel for lunch and found him waiting by her desk.

'I'm so hungry, I'm going to die,' he said.

'Yeah, I'm just going to put on sunblock; it's heating up out there,' Jasmine replied, reaching into her bag for her SPF50+.

'Not me,' Joel said, presenting his arm. 'This Ngāpuhi skin doesn't burn.'

'You know that's not true,' Jasmine said, rolling her eyes.

'It's true. I just get browner and browner,' he said proudly.

Jasmine wanted to present him with statistics on skin cancer in New Zealand, including for Māori, but instead, she just said, 'At least wear a cap.'

'What, and ruin this hair?' he said, running his hand through his dark locks.

'Okay, your life, your death,' Jasmine replied.

'Eww, morbid,' Joel gasped while secretly reaching for her sunscreen to smear on his face.

Joel and Jasmine made their way out to Garden Place, a large area outside the Council that sounded nicer than it was. There was a small grass quad in the middle of a large concrete area, but no significant garden.

Stores and cafés surrounded the location, and the courtyard housed a fountain that added some level of art.

The two friends positioned themselves on a bench under the shade of one of the few trees. Joel stretched himself out so his legs were in the sun and his body was in the shade.

Jasmine reached into the envelope and carefully removed the contents. She ran her hand over the soft red leather cover and delicately opened it. The writing inside was slanted, written with an ink pen, with occasional ink splashes on each page. Jasmine read aloud the first page.

To Evie on your 25th birthday, 1933. Love Mother.

Joel whistled. 'Whoa, that's super cool,' Joel said, surprisingly intrigued. He grabbed his phone and quickly pulled up the calculator, '2018 minus 1933,' he said, holding his tongue in the corner of his mouth as if he was solving the calculation. 'Eighty-five years ago! Whoa. Freaky.'

Jasmine inhaled the scent of the pages, asking Joel, 'Don't you just love that smell?'

He wrinkled his nose. 'What, old and musty? Nope.'

'It smells like history to me,' she said, clearing her throat to read the first entry in Evie's diary.

November 1933

Mother gifted me this beautiful diary for my birthday. I know it must have taken a great deal of saving to purchase something so lovely, and I treasure it deeply. Times are hard, with financial struggles impacting even our small community. I am fortunate to work as a typist at the Farmers Co-operative Auctioneers Corporation on Victoria Street. I thank the Lord daily for His blessings, as many of my neighbours are not so lucky.

Mother lives nearby, working as a housekeeper, and I lodge at the Harwoods' home in town. My sister Maple and her husband Clive are also close, living on Armagh Street with their three boys. Those boys feel like my own, and I spend much of my free time with them. When I can, I bike to visit them. I belong to a wonderful community at the Baptist Church, which I attend regularly.

Jasmine glanced up to assess Joel's reaction. The first entry was brief – even underwhelming.

Joel leaned back and crossed his arms. 'Hmm, it's not exactly the juicy diary you promised,' he said, disappointed.

'No,' Jasmine agreed, 'but it was just an intro, and we got a few bits of info.'

'Really? I got nothing,' Joel replied.

'Sure you did – what's one thing you can tell me about her personality?'

Joel thought for a moment. 'Well, I guess she's religious...and grateful and family-oriented. She's like one of those old-fashioned neighbours or the people you see on Downton Abbey, "It pleases me to meet your acquaintance",' he said, imitating Maggie Smith.

Jasmine smiled and asked, 'If you were writing an opening entry, what would it say?'

'Oh wow. Probably what I ate for breakfast, what I dreamt about, who I was into.'

'Real exciting stuff,' Jasmine said with a hint of mockery. 'She seems pretty modest, but people back then probably weren't used to shouting out about themselves.'

Joel laughed. 'Right, no Instagram stories back then showing off your new apron. Hashtag, so proud.'

Jasmine could see the irony of the social media manager poking fun at his industry.

Joel waved his hand in the air as if conducting. 'Read on.'

Jasmine turned to the next entry.

12 November 1933
A lovely surprise arrived in the post today: a letter from Mrs. Crabb, who is now at the Campbell-Johnson Ward, announcing the birth of her baby girl. Both mother and baby are healthy. The congregation will be so pleased. We've put together a baby package for her. Mrs. Douglas made a beautiful quilt, and I knitted white-and-yellow booties.

Mrs. Crabb used to work with me at the FAC but left earlier this year when she got married. I'm looking forward to visiting and meeting the baby. I'll ask Mr. Farrell, my neighbour, if I might ride with him the next time he visits the hospital.

'She's generous too,' Joel noted. 'Knitting something for someone and making care packages.' Jasmine nodded, flipping the page.

15 November 1933
Last night, I attended the Hamilton Girls' High production of Gilbert and Sullivan's Patience. The students performed with such confidence. Mr. Harwood's niece had a role in the show and did an excellent job. It was a delightful evening.

Joel perked up. 'Finally, something I relate to. Read on,' he prompted dramatically. Jasmine was surprised he was willing to continue. It wasn't riveting.

18 November 1933
The weather is warming up, and I've been enjoying my lunch breaks with a walk to Garden Place. The hill there is being removed by unemployed men using picks and shovels. It must give them a sense

of purpose while they cannot find regular work, though it looks like hard labour.

Joel sat up. 'No way! Has this place been called Garden Place for that long?'

'Apparently,' Jasmine said, looking around, trying to imagine a time when the space was still a hill.

Joel gave a mock shudder. 'A little spooky, sitting in the same place she wrote about. Feels weird.'

They continued reading, flipping through Christmas and the summer of 1933, with modest food entries and preserved fruit descriptions.

'See! She writes about food. I'm not so shallow after all,' Joel pointed out smugly, now sitting on a patch of grass, tossing clumps in the air. 'She mentions the weather *a lot*. The diary could be used for historical data for the Metservice,' he joked.

While she read, Jasmine paused to jot down any information that might help her locate the diary's owner.

'Did you write down that she is 25, lives in Hamilton, and appears single? Sounds like someone I know,' Joel pointed out.

'Along with half of Hamilton! It's not *that* much of a coincidence, and I'm older than her.' Jasmine defended herself.

'And you are not as holy. I don't hear you thanking God or giving service.'

Jasmine ignored the barb and continued making notes. 'Hopefully, these details will help me track her down and lead to descendants, if there are any,' she said.

Joel tilted his head in consideration of the project. 'A mystery and some investigation – two of my favourite things,' he said, perhaps warming to the idea.

'It's time to go back to work,' Jasmine said with a sigh, disappointed that the diary so far hadn't revealed any significant clues or story, but she felt happy that Joel seemed on board.

'Let's flick ahead and see what happens,' Joel suggested, sitting up with a glint of mischief.

'No way! That's like total spoilers. I'm not doing it,' Jasmine retorted firmly.

'Oh, come on. I need to know if it's worth investing in this story.'

'No,' Jasmine said, shaking her head. 'We're going to commit to reading this story in the order it's written, and we will love it.'

Joel rolled his eyes theatrically. 'Fine, but tell me what *this* is then,' he said, leaning over and pulling on an exposed corner of a photo lodged in the book. It was a black-and-white photo of a wedding with a bride in a Charleston-style lace dress and a groom in a suit. Both looked solemn, or was it regal?

Jasmine flicked it over and noted the photo was taken in Hamilton.

'Is this Evie?' Joel asked, holding the photo up for Jasmine to see.

'I don't know. Maybe it's her sister?' Jasmine said, peering closely at the image.

'Well, we'd better read on and find out,' Joel said with a grin.

'Lunchtime tomorrow?' Jasmine asked.

'Lunchtime tomorrow,' Joel confirmed.

It would be hard for Jasmine to wait until tomorrow; she wanted to discover whether the bride in the photo was Evie – and if so, who was the man by her side, a man who, so far, had been absent from her writings.

Chapter Two

What if I get Campylobacter?

Jasmine and Paige pulled into the driveway in tandem, laughing at their synchronised arrival. After a quick bathroom stop and outfit change, they began the familiar drive to Te Awamutu, their hometown, about 30 minutes from Hamilton.

The car ride was filled with their easy chatter and debrief of the day. Jasmine told Paige about the diary she was reading with Joel, offering to bring it home for some night-time reading.

'Hmm,' Paige mused. 'You're not selling it to me. Maybe bring me in if it becomes interesting.'

Jasmine tapped the steering wheel in time with the radio, her eyes on the winding road ahead. Paige, lounging in the passenger seat, scrolled through her phone.

As the car approached Te Awamutu, Paige commented on the large welcome sign at the edge of the town, 'Do you think anyone still calls it the *Town of Roses*? Or was that just one of those marketing slogans from the 1990s?'

Jasmine nodded. 'I'm sure we could come up with something more original.'

'Oh! A better sign might be, "You Better Be Home Soon," like the Crowded House song.' Paige beamed, proud of her idea. 'They're the most famous people from Te Awamutu.'

Paige hummed a few bars of the band's song. Then she glanced out the window, adding, 'You know, Te Awamutu has one other claim to fame – Tokanui Hospital.'

Jasmine's hands tightened slightly on the steering wheel, though she kept her gaze forward. 'Yeah, the old psychiatric hospital, right? I remember kids at school always mocking that if you did something weird, you would end up at Tokanui.'

'Yep,' Paige said. 'It was the biggest employer around for decades. It was like its own little village.'

Jasmine nodded. 'Back then, they called it a lunatic asylum, didn't they? I hate that term.'

'Totally,' Paige agreed, wrinkling her nose. 'Some people there had it pretty rough. There's even a cemetery with the people who died while staying there.'

A silence fell between them, the hum of the car filling the space. Jasmine finally spoke.

'Every time I hear about places like that, I think... if I'd been born a few decades earlier, I might've ended up there.'

Paige frowned. 'What do you mean?'

Jasmine loosened her grip on the wheel slightly. 'My *condition* wasn't well understood back then. They might've misdiagnosed it as something else – schizophrenia or whatever else they didn't know how to handle. It's scary to think about.'

'Hey, they might enjoy having you there with your archival skills. You'd have every patient's toiletries categorised before breakfast,' Paige joked, lightening the mood.

Jasmine cracked a smile. 'You're ridiculous.'

'I'm serious! Can you imagine yourself in a place like Tokanui? "Sorry, Nurse, the patient files aren't colour-coded. I simply can't have my breakdown in this mess",' Paige said in an exaggerated English accent.

Jasmine laughed and joined in with a Cockney voice. 'No need to give me shock treatment – I'm shocked by your lack of filing!'

'Exactly,' Paige said, wiping tears from laughing. 'Although I don't know why you now have a Cockney accent.'

Jasmine grinned. 'When I'm in Tokanui, I'm from London.'

They pulled into the driveway of Jasmine's family home, still laughing as they approached the door.

Paige read the sign to remove shoes posted at the entrance and nudged Jasmine.

'You know, most people put this up to protect their carpet. Your dad puts it up to protect his sanity.'

Jasmine smiled, knowing Paige wasn't wrong. It wasn't just the shoe rule; her dad, Cliff, also checked the car door multiple times after locking it. He always ensured the house was secured, like Fort Knox.

But none of the rituals seemed to bother him.

'Hi, Mum,' Jasmine said, slipping off her shoes as Gaye came to greet the two of them.

Gaye was wearing an apron and clearly in full swing, making dinner. Jasmine spotted her dad's favourite meal on the counter: sausages, gravy, peas, and mashed potatoes – every 67-year-old's dream. She also spied a jelly and a bowl of egg whites ready to be whipped for a rolled pavlova.

Jasmine's sister, Bree, had arrived moments earlier and was scooping up her daughters' belongings from the hallway. The kids were crawling all over Grampa, giving him butterfly kisses for his birthday.

Bree, as always, was immaculately dressed, wearing her designer clothing line, 'Breez'.

The contrast between the sisters was obvious. Bree's blonde hair and slight wave meant no one ever took them for siblings. Her carefree nature matched her name.

Bree's husband, Todd, sat engrossed in the sport on TV, muttering about the All Blacks rugby game and how he'd rearrange the team. Meanwhile, Cliff juggled several conversations effortlessly – rugby, his granddaughters' chatter, and greeting Jasmine and Paige.

'Girls, come help Nana with the pav,' Gaye called, prompting her granddaughters, Morgan and Aria, to scuttle into the kitchen, hugging Jasmine as they passed. Morgan's front tooth dangled precariously, and Aria looked like she'd grown since Jasmine last saw her.

The wee girls sat at the bench with Jasmine in the middle. She took a moment to stroke their hair and soak up as much aunty-time as possible.

'Can I lick the bowl?' Morgan asked, sticking her finger straight into the beaten sugar and egg whites. Aria, ever the rule-follower, reached for a spoon and reminded her sister to wait.

Jasmine jumped in. 'No, girls, wait until the eggs are cooked. You don't want to get Campylobacter.'

'Campy-what?' Morgan asked, frowning.

'Oh, nonsense,' Gaye said dismissively. 'Raw eggs never hurt anyone.'

Jasmine sighed, watching Aria lean back while Morgan and Gaye remained unconcerned. Paige nudged Jasmine with a look that said, *let it go.* Jasmine sighed and looked away. She hated imposing her thoughts on the girls, but facts were facts. She excused herself to chat with her dad in another room.

'Another year older,' Cliff said with a grin. 'And even better – 67 is a prime number.'

Jasmine smiled at her dad's quirky love of numbers.

'Tell me about work, how's it going?' Cliff asked.

Jasmine launched into a detailed update about digitising records, community projects, and her latest challenge of tracing the history of an 85-year-old diary. Cliff listened intently, asking her thoughtful questions about the process.

Just as she finished, Bree glided into the room. She didn't understand Medusa, believing Jasmine should just shake it off. She lived a carefree life, which Jasmine wouldn't admit annoyed her. Bree wrinkled her nose at the mention of the old diary.

'Soo...' she said, dragging out the word, 'it does sound like a bit of a yawn – scanning documents and reading about dead people.'

The words stung. In Jasmine's mind, the job was perfect. 'I love it,' she said, her tone sharper than intended.

Bree wasn't finished.

'Oh, come on, Jazzy. That's no life – hanging out with the dead and their dusty papers. I thought it was bad enough when you worked in a library. How are you ever going to meet someone?'

Jasmine realised this was Bree's actual attack. Jasmine was single and therefore lonely.

'Life isn't all about meeting people,' Jasmine retorted. 'And I see people. My life is very full, thank you.'

Bree wasn't backing down. 'Jazzy, you know your mind works best when it's busy. You need a job that occupies you.'

Jasmine felt anger boiling up inside. 'Bree, you don't know how my mind works. And you never will.'

Cliff cleared his throat, stepping in before the tension could escalate. 'As it's *my* birthday, I have one request: no fighting. The only person allowed to cry at this party is the birthday boy himself.' He softened, adding, 'You are both creative in your own way – one with fabrics, one with documents. I think Jasmine's work sounds fascinating.'

Jasmine nodded, feeling a little rude for how she had acted on her dad's special day.

'Now, let's go see what's happening in the other room – the food smells great,' Cliff insisted.

As they left the room, Jasmine felt a reassuring hug and squeeze from her dad. She rested her head on his shoulder to say thanks. She knew that it wasn't up to Bree to dictate how she should live her life.

Medusa demanded that. Every single day.

Chapter Three

What if vegetables grow in poison?

The following day, while sitting at her office desk, Jasmine's screen lit up with a chat message from Joel.

Joel: 11 o'clock, sensor light.

Jasmine glanced at her watch, which read 10:38 am. Confused for a moment, she realised he meant her 11 o'clock angle. She turned slightly and spotted a colleague toggling between online grocery shopping and work, and minimised the grocery tab when someone walked by.

Jasmine: Sensor light?

Joel: Triggered to work when someone walks past.

Jasmine: Haha, good one. Nothing gets past you.

Joel: Lunch at 12?

Jasmine: Sure, we can read the diary.

Joel: :(

Jasmine: I was thinking we could also read at home sometime. Paige might like it.

Joel: Probably not, but you can try and bribe her too.

As the two left the office, they met their work friend, Moana, who worked as a Human Resources leader. Moana had a pet name for everyone; staff lived in hope of being endowed with one, although she insisted she couldn't force it.

'Hey Jazz-a-Dazz and Jolly-bean, what are you up to?' she asked with her fun but caring voice.

Moana was always dressed immaculately and wore accessories that portrayed her staunch love of New Zealand. Today she wore long dangling earrings made from pounamu, greenstone. Jasmine wondered if the weight of them might tear Moana's earlobe. When Moana wasn't at work, she was cheering for her three kids on the sideline of a sports game or running a fundraiser for their teams.

Jasmine marvelled at how Moana juggled so much of life while also having the time to stop and make someone feel important.

'We're just heading down to Garden Place with a riveting diary from the archives,' Joel said, flashing a fake smile, then whispering, 'Save me, take me with you.'

Moana giggled, 'Naww, that will be fun. Wish I could join you, but can't stop; I have to buy oranges for the kids' training tonight.' She then explained that she would cut the fruit into smiles, hopefully earning her the 'favourite mum' title.

Jasmine was sure Moana would achieve the 'best mum' level, even without the oranges.

'Okay, I'm off, happy reading Jolly-bean and Jazz-a-Dazz,' Moana said, blowing them a kiss.

'She's one of the best people to know,' Joel sighed with affection. 'She has a heart of gold – literally!'

His expression was so sincere, Jasmine didn't have the heart to point out that Moana couldn't literally have a gold, beating heart.

Although Jasmine considered her work friends significant people in her life, neither of them knew about Medusa. Keeping that part of her life hidden gave Jasmine a layer of protection. She had mastered the art of covering up any compulsive behaviour. Plus, she rationalised, it wasn't even that bad anymore, so why tell people something insignificant?

'Another sunny day, another reading,' Joel declared as they found their way to their usual spot.

'And another free lunch,' Jasmine noted.

They shared her pasta salad, Joel pausing between bites to share about his upcoming show.

'Honestly, there's more drama behind the scenes than on stage,' he complained, sharing accounts of love triangles.

Jasmine laughed, genuinely enjoying his stories. Watching Joel light up when talking about his art always made her smile. Performing on stage – open to judgment on every note and movement – seemed like an act of vulnerability, yet Joel thrived on it. He brushed off criticism from tough-to-please audience members with humour.

The more time they spent together, the more impressive he became. Quick to put others at ease and always alert to people's moods, Joel had a knack for lifting a room. It made Jasmine wonder if that kindness was forged during more challenging times.

He didn't know who his father was and often joked that dating in New Zealand came with the risk of discovering a sibling. His mother loved him, but he'd spent years being replaced – shuffled behind whichever man took her focus next. More than once, Joel had picked up the pieces of her shattered life.

He liked to say he came through it all unscathed and wore the claim like a badge. But Jasmine wasn't so sure. The masks he wore, the jokes he made, were at times a facade.

She understood that.

Avoidance was her survival tool too.

She and Medusa were long-time experts.

Noting the time, she picked up the diary. 'Hey, we haven't even read yet, and we're almost due back.'

'Oh, shame. Never mind.' Joel joked.

'You have to earn that lunch,' Jasmine warned. 'We'll just read briefly and see if the man in the photograph turns up.'

Jasmine quickly read through more entries; the cursive handwriting became easier to read the more she interpreted words. Joel joked that the diary could be written in another language for all he could tell, the handwriting being so foreign to him.

Evie's story moved through a season, touching on women's rights and politics – topics she was passionate about. But still, nothing gripping.

Sensing Jasmine's disappointment, Joel offered, 'How about we dive into the next chapter of Evie's story tonight?'

'Don't you have a rehearsal?' Jasmine asked.

'Not tonight. Wednesdays are usually for my guilty pleasure, Married at First Sight. But I can catch up later.'

Jasmine was grateful. She enjoyed reading history, but the diary was more than that. It wasn't a clinical list of past events – it offered insight into a person who had lived there. She found comfort in reading about things that had already happened. It felt less frightening than the current news, which was full of the unexpected.

Jasmine suspected her friends supported her for the same reason, although they probably hadn't analysed themselves as deeply as she had. The past was just safer. And even if the diary led nowhere, it was a good excuse to hang out.

She flicked Paige a quick message to let her know there'd be three for dinner, followed by a diary reading.

***

Joel pulled up to their flat in his little hatchback, his tall frame folded comically into the driver's seat.

As he stepped inside the house, he and Paige began their usual banter. Jasmine thought the two acted more like siblings than friends. Tonight's debate was the movie *The Bird Box,* and Paige was launching into an attack on its merits.

'Netflix literally had to warn people not to blindfold themselves while using sharp objects,' Paige pointed out. 'That alone tells you how ridiculous it was.'

'I still liked it,' Joel said defensively. 'And if people need to have the obvious pointed out to them, they probably shouldn't be allowed to watch it.'

'Exactly!' Paige grinned, sensing victory.

'So, what happened at work today?' Joel asked, making peace.

'For the first time ever, I had to jump into the swimming pool – fully clothed – to help a panicked kid.'

'Oh, drama,' Joel said, nodding in approval.

Jasmine saw an opportunity for a small joke. 'You could use this experience to teach them their favourite kind of math – dive-vision.'

Paige groaned. 'Oh no. Was that a math joke? Or worse, a math-dad joke?'

'No, just a weird-aunty joke. I heard it on the radio,' Jasmine admitted.

Joel raised a hand as if in Paige's class, 'Miss, do you know what's *really* odd?'

Paige sighed. 'No. What?'

'Just every other number.' He mimed a drumroll for extra impact.

Paige rolled her eyes. 'Alright, that one's okay to share with the kids.'

Jasmine laughed. 'It's official. We are geeks.'

'No, we're not geeks,' Joel insisted, picking up the diary and pretending to read it. 'We're like the Scooby-Doo gang, solving mysteries.'

Jasmine grabbed the book back. 'We'll start that after dinner.'

The friends made New Zealand burgers. Beef, lettuce, cheese, beetroot and an egg, all layered between soft buns with sesame seeds.

'Perfection,' said Joel, wolfing his burger down.

When the kitchen was tidy, the friends retired to the lounge.

'So, what have I missed so far?' Paige asked, referring to the diary, while getting comfy on the couch.

Jasmine recapped. 'We have a diary written by Evie, surname unknown. She's single, living here in Hamilton during the 1930s, works as a typist, loves kids, and helps people. She lives near her mum and sister.'

Joel piped in, 'So, she bikes or walks everywhere and thanks to Wikipedia, I can confirm that the population of Hamilton in the 1930s was only 15,000.'

Paige and Jasmine nodded with genuine interest, and Joel, feeling supported by their acknowledgement, continued to share his knowledge.

'Hamilton was very reliant on the train system. New Zealand used the area to transport goods. However, the city had to survive with only one bridge, from Hamilton East to the CBD.'

Jasmine froze. What was Joel doing, talking about the bridges? Did he know that was Medusa's fodder? Was he taunting her?

He continued with his Wikipedia knowledge.

'It's hard to believe the city survived with just one bridge when now we have six, and it's not enough. We have more than ten times the population but not ten times the bridges.' Joel finished his account, clearly satisfied with his knowledge-sharing.

Medusa awoke.

Jasmine felt snakes rattle with each mention of a bridge.

She forced a smile and excused herself. 'Just a quick trip to the bathroom,' she said lightly.

In the toilet, Jasmine gave in to her compulsion by whispering the familiar chant that somehow cancelled the danger she and her friends were now in.

Cobham, Victoria, Claudelands, Whitiora, Fairfield, Pukete.

Cobham, Victoria, Claudelands, Whitiora, Fairfield, Pukete.

Over and over, she repeated the names of the Hamilton bridges.

She didn't know why those words worked.

Medusa told her so.

And Jasmine obeyed.

The exposure seemed worse than usual. Worse than in her therapist's office.

As she uttered the countermeasure, the anxiety around her chest slowly loosened. She took the time she needed to compose and remind herself she was safe.

When she returned to the lounge, she ensured her face looked normal, giving nothing away.

Paige glanced at her knowingly but said nothing. Jasmine offered a slight nod, a silent reassurance that said *all is well*.

But it wasn't.

It was tolerated.

***

Oblivious to Jasmine's moment of anxiety, Joel raised an eyebrow as she returned. 'That was a mission.'

Jasmine nudged him with her foot. 'Hilarious.'

Grinning, Joel picked up the diary and passed it to her. 'I tried to read some of the previous entries to Paige. I managed a few words, but I can't read that writing.'

Jasmine opened the diary to the winter of 1934. Joel and Paige settled into their favourite spots.

While Jasmine had been calming herself in the bathroom, Paige had made popcorn and placed it in a brightly coloured bowl on the coffee table.

Jasmine was grateful for her friends. She knew they were there for her, to support *her* hobby.

She began reading the next glimpse into Evie's world.

23 June 1934

The weekend passed in a flurry of small but satisfying tasks. On Saturday, I baked a batch of scones and took some to Maple's house for afternoon tea with the boys. They devoured them before they had even cooled! We have a new typist at work today. Her name is Awhina, and she is a Maori.

'Sidenote – no macron over the 'a' back then,' she explained. Paige and Joel nodded. Jasmine continued reading.

She's the first Maori person I've worked with. She's new to Hamilton from Gisborne, shy, and mostly keeps to herself. I hope I can help her settle in and meet others at work.

Next week, I'm attending a seminar with Esther James, who is touring the country. I might ask Awhina if she'd like to come, though I suspect she'll be too shy to say yes. Still, it might be nice to ask.

'Okay, okay,' Paige interrupted, raising her hands. 'I know I just got here, so sorry to be that person, but we need to Google some of this.'

Joel grinned. 'Yeah, who's Esther James? And are we supposed to believe Awhina was the only Māori person in that company?'

They took turns searching on their phones; Jasmine loved that her friends were joining in the chase.

'So, looks like Esther James advocated for buying New Zealand-made products and walked the length of the country in the 1930s to promote the cause,' Paige explained.

'An OG influencer,' Joel quipped.

They laughed when they read that it was reported she gained twenty pounds during her journey, thanks to generous farmers sharing their produce.

'Hardly newsworthy,' Paige commented.

'We could use an Esther James today,' Joel mused. 'She'd be all over Instagram, telling people to shop local.'

Jasmine nodded. Her thoughts turned on Evie's words about Awhina.

'You know what's different to today? Evie mentioned that Awhina was Māori. Today, no one would think to write it down or point it out.'

'Except my mother,' Paige said dryly.

'Boomers,' Joel retorted. 'I can just hear her pronouncing it the old way.'

Jasmine scrolled further on her phone. 'It looks like the Māori population in Hamilton was tiny in the 1930s – only 194 registered as living here in 1936. The fact that Evie made a point of mentioning Awhina shows how different it must have felt.'

Joel looked thoughtful. 'Whoa, I didn't know that. Okay, an interesting history lesson. Continue.'

15 August 1934

The rain and wind have been relentless all week, but today brought a bright spot. Maple and the boys visited at work while running errands in town. She's a wonderful mother, and her boys are always so polite. It was a joy to see them and introduce them to my friends.

Benjamin, the company's motor driver, stopped by the office between deliveries. He's a tall, quiet man with impeccable manners, and today, he brought along a red-haired boy, no older than six. I offered the child a peppermint and asked if he was unwell. Benjamin explained that it was the school holidays, and the boy, Albert, was accompanying him. I wondered if his mother was unwell or working, but asking didn't feel right.

Joel sat up. 'So – who's this Albert kid?

'Maybe this is leading somewhere,' Paige added, intrigued.

Jasmine flipped to the next entry.

2 September 1934

Spring's arrival has lifted my spirits, bringing longer, brighter days. Albert and I have become fast friends. He often comes to my desk for a peppermint, and yesterday, he sat quietly nearby while I typed, keeping me company while Benjamin went about his work.

I learned more about Albert today. Benjamin shared that he and his previous wife adopted the boy before their separation. Benjamin told me he first saw Albert at an orphanage and felt an instant connection because of the boy's red hair. Now, Benjamin is raising Albert on his own.

It's rare to hear of a man taking on such a role – the mother usually does so. It says a lot about Benjamin's character, and I can't help but admire him for it.

Joel stretched in the beanbag and interrupted Jasmine's reading. 'She's such a good egg.'

'She has that wholesome, classic charm,' Jasmine agreed. 'But you can almost feel her shock at the idea of a single man raising a child.'

Joel grinned. 'I can't believe people lived like this – no reality TV or social media; their drama is *literally* about the local delivery guy.'

He giggled before continuing, 'She's adding a lot of detail about this guy, I think he's Evie's crush. Ooh, maybe he's the guy in the photo, although, I can't tell if he's a ginge?' Joel commented while scrutinising the photo.

5 September 1934

The weather has turned, and the walk to work is pleasant again. I've invited Ben and Albert to Sunday evening's sermon at the Baptist Church on London Street. I thought it might be helpful for Ben to have someone with whom to attend church. Mother will also be there, and I'm sure she'll enjoy meeting them.

Joel laughed. 'So that's how they asked people out in the 1930s. *Let's go to church.*'

'I bet it was a hot spot back then.' Paige joked.

3 October 1934

I updated my details on the electoral roll at the post office today. Ben and I have had some wonderful discussions about the government and the social security system. He's very well-read on the subject, and I admire how much he cares about these issues. Albert is back at school now, so I don't see him at work anymore, but I enjoy seeing him at church. I miss their daily visits to the office.

I bought some vegetable plants for the garden, and Mr. Hargraves, where I board, has kindly given me a portion of his ground to plant summer crops. Ben offered to help and brought basic slag to nourish the soil. His kindness and practical knowledge are such a blessing.

Paige interrupted, 'Hey Siri, what is basic slag?'

Siri quickly replied: *Slag is formed as a by-product of basic steel-making processes. It is generally rich in lime and phosphates and used as fertiliser.'*

'Never heard of it,' Jasmine said, her mind jumping to potential health risks. 'Putting steel by-products on your veges sounds about as good as putting lead in your paint.'

Paige waved her hand. 'Keep reading! I need to know where this is going.'

25 December 1934

Christmas Day, and a truly beautiful one it has been. Everything has gone splendidly, and we've enjoyed ourselves immensely. Our hearts are warmed by the thoughtfulness of so many friends and relations who remembered us this season. We gathered at Maple and Clive's for Christmas dinner – a chook with all the trimmings.

Mother brought fresh strawberries, and I baked a sponge cake. I was especially pleased that Ben and Albert could join us. I was happy to know they had somewhere to go and didn't spend the day alone.

Albert seemed to enjoy himself, and Mother has kindly offered to look after him during the school holidays so that he won't need to accompany Ben on his truck rounds.

The friends continued reading, pausing now and then for tangents of discussion. There was something comforting about stepping away from the pressure of looking amazing and having the perfect home, immersing themselves in a time when life's worries were straightforward.

Jasmine read aloud about a picnic interrupted by rain and a river walk with the church group.

Paige sighed. 'Life sounds pretty simple, I'm a little jealous.'

'I bet they didn't have three million notifications to check, either,' added Joel.

'Well, that is your job,' Paige pointed out.

As the evening wound down, Joel stood suddenly, 'I have to go. Have you guys bought your tickets yet?'

'Not yet,' Jasmine said quickly. 'We haven't decided *when* to go.'

Paige shot Jasmine a quick look of surprise that her friend was almost lying.

Jasmine felt uneasy.

'Well, don't wait too long; it's selling out,' Joel encouraged them.

'I'll organise the tickets tomorrow,' Paige promised.

Jasmine forced a smile and a nod. She knew the best-case scenario would be that the show would sell out before Paige bought the tickets.

Again, Jasmine relied on the avoidance card. But she had a sneaking suspicion that this time, the card would slip from her hand.

Chapter Four

What if I get mercury poisoning?

Readings of the diary slowed once the show opened, with Joel occupied in the evenings. Jasmine used the extra time to research Evie. However, what should have been a straightforward search proved fruitless. Despite scouring databases, tweaking search terms, and trying different spellings, Jasmine hit dead ends.

'I can only assume Evie might have gone by a different name,' she explained to Paige one evening. 'We will have to read more once Joel finishes the show.'

'Speaking of, I bought our tickets for closing night,' Paige explained and put a printed copy on the fridge door as an incentive. From then on, Jasmine felt anxious each time she passed the fridge.

Paige tried to make a plan with her on how they could go to the show. Jasmine refused to speak about it, promising she would deal with it on the day.

The November days rolled from one to another, and before she was ready, it was the day before closing night. Jasmine chose to spend the day in the dungeon, avoiding the decision, and perhaps even avoiding Joel.

The dungeons held large compactors which reached the ceiling and slid on runners, holding documents and photos that were easily accessible. She walked down the rows of the folders and allowed herself time to appreciate the work she had accomplished. It was a far cry from the state she inherited it in.

Her self-admiration was interrupted by heels tapping in the corridor. Jasmine went to the door of the archives to see Bree in the corridor, her bright blonde ponytail swaying and sunglasses perched on her head like a crown.

'Well, look at this little hideaway,' Bree said, her voice upbeat. She entered the room, scanning the stacks of boxes with her eyes and observing the flickering light overhead; she raised her eyebrows. 'Very you, Jaz.'

Jasmine forced a smile. 'Bree, what are you doing here? I wasn't expecting you.'

'I was grabbing some stuff for the girls in town and thought I'd pop in. You know, check out where all the magic happens.'

Jasmine gestured vaguely at the shelves and cabinets, 'Not exactly magic.'

Bree grinned and leaned casually against the compactors. 'I'm glad you've found something you love. You've always been the 'old soul' of the family.'

Jasmine laughed despite herself. 'Thanks, I think.'

There was a brief pause, and Bree's expression became serious. 'Anyway, I came because I wanted to tell you something – thought it was better to do it in person.'

Jasmine's stomach knotted. Bree didn't usually "drop in" for serious conversations. 'Everything okay?'

'Yeah, yeah – don't worry.' Bree waved her hand dismissively. 'Actually, it's good news. Todd and I finally bought a house.'

'Oh! That's great!' Jasmine said, genuinely happy for her sister. 'Where is it?'

Bree hesitated as if choosing her words carefully. 'It's... across the river. In Chartwell.'

The words landed like a punch Jasmine hadn't braced for.

Across the river.

She nodded slowly, trying to keep her expression neutral. 'That's nice. Chartwell is a good area.'

Bree's tone softened further. 'It's not on purpose, Jaz. I know what you're thinking, and I promise we didn't do it to... challenge you.'

Jasmine's stomach sank.

Bree knew about the bridges, but she didn't understand.

The decision felt like an unspoken test.

'It's fine,' Jasmine said quickly, her voice light. 'I mean, you have to do what's best for the girls.'

Bree shifted her weight, studying Jasmine's face. 'You could see it as an opportunity,' she said gently. 'You've overcome so much, Jaz. You've beaten Medusa before – you could do it again. You used to live over that side, at uni.'

Jasmine forced herself to nod as her sister spoke. 'Maybe,' she murmured while a voice screamed, 'No, I can't'.

She imagined it all: her nieces, Morgan and Aria, loving the new home so much that they didn't notice her absence. Or if they asked, she would find polite excuses about work, being too busy, and needing to stay close to town.

There would be Christmas mornings she wouldn't attend, school concerts and birthday parties she'd miss.

All while she stayed safely on this side of the river.

Medusa wins again.

'Jaz?' Bree's voice brought her back to the room.

Jasmine cleared her throat and smiled faintly. 'Sorry, I was just thinking. It'll be nice for the girls. A fresh start.'

Bree observed her, trying to read behind Jasmine's mask. 'You'll love the house. It's modern, and I have a sewing room to put to good use. You'll come to visit, though, right?'

Jasmine nodded automatically. 'Of course.'

The words came out too quickly – a response she was used to giving. While she mouthed, 'Of course', her brain said, 'no, not ever'.

'Good,' Bree said, her smile returning, though Jasmine noticed it wore a touch of sympathy. 'We'll have to plan something soon – before it gets too crazy with the move.'

'I'd like that,' Jasmine lied.

Bree pulled her into a quick hug. 'I should go. Todd's waiting for me to grab the kids. But I'm glad I got to see your little cave.' She winked and headed for the door. 'Let's do dinner soon, okay?'

'Yeah, definitely,' Jasmine said, forcing another smile.

When Bree's footsteps finally faded, Jasmine slumped back into her chair, staring blankly at the half-organised box in front of her. The light flickered above her, and her heart still raced with the echo of Bree's words. Across the river.

She imagined the bridge, long beams stretching over the Waikato River. Her mind conjured the familiar terror.

What if I cross and someone I love gets hurt? What if, what if, what if?

She was spiralling.

She closed her eyes and pressed her palms to her temples. Bree's words replayed in her mind: 'You've beaten Medusa before.'

But right now, she didn't have it in her to fight.

She sat in the quiet of her little archive room, her anxiety rising. She spoke her compulsion to reassure herself.

Cobham, Victoria, Claudelands, Whitiora, Fairfield, Pukete.

Cobham, Victoria, Claudelands, Whitiora, Fairfield, Pukete.

Each utterance eased her anxiety.

Jasmine knew she had to join her colleagues upstairs for a meeting. The timing was awful.

But Medusa doesn't care about convenience.

When she felt calm enough, she dashed upstairs, putting Bree's conversation behind her, and grabbed her laptop. Glancing at Moana's office, Jasmine saw she had gone for the day.

'Where's Moana?' Jasmine asked Joel.

'One of her kids is sick, and she had to go,' Joel replied while looking at his screens. Jasmine was disappointed; she could do with some sunshine from Moana.

Composing herself, Jasmine strode purposefully into the meeting room. 'Kia ora, everyone,' she said, glancing around the table while faking happiness. The conference room was filled with a mix of local stakeholders, city councillors, business owners and Mana Whenua representatives.

She quickly connected her laptop to the screen at the front of the room, displaying her presentation on Von Tempsky Street. She turned to the group. 'I'll start with a brief overview of the street's history to provide some context before you move into the discussion.'

A nod from a councillor signalled for her to proceed. Jasmine launched into her summary, gesturing toward the projected slides featuring sepia-toned photographs and old maps.

'Von Tempsky Street was named in 1906, commemorating Gustavus von Tempsky, a soldier and artist who lived in New Zealand in the 1860s. He initially was here for gold mining but later became the leader of the Forest Rangers during the New Zealand Wars.'

The group listened as she continued. 'Von Tempsky's leadership was celebrated for its boldness but also criticised for the ruthless tactics employed against Māori communities. His death during a battle in 1868 marked the end of his career, but his legacy remains deeply contested. For many Māori, he symbolises the violence and dispossession of the colonial era.'

She noted one of the business owners from the street shifting uncomfortably in his seat; he was the first to ask a question. 'So, what's driving the push for a name change, after all these years?'

Jasmine was prepared for the question. 'The request came from a business owner from the street who feels uncomfortable about the name. You should know, our Council is not alone in needing to address these issues. There is a growing need to have place names that align with the values of the community.'

She noted the business owner shrugged his shoulders, dissatisfied with the answer.

'What are the alternatives being proposed?' asked a councillor.

'That's something for this group to discuss,' Jasmine replied.

Another participant, a young woman representing a community group, spoke up. 'This is about more than just a name change. It's an opportunity to educate people about our shared history and show respect for those who were here before colonisation.'

Another responded to her comment, 'Yes, but can you imagine the work involved in changing the name? We are speaking about maps, signage, history and even Google.'

Jasmine could see the discussion was about to turn into a debate. She glanced at the clock, aware her role was to provide the historical foundation, not steer the discussion. 'That concludes the historical overview. I'll leave the rest of the discussion to you all. Any other questions?'

A few hands went up, and Jasmine fielded enquiries about the historical research process and the accuracy of the details. As she stood to leave the room, the councillor stopped her. 'Jasmine, we will visit the street next week to take some up-to-date photographs and visit business owners. I would like you to come along.'

There it was again, an opportunity to avoid.

Jasmine smiled, 'Just let me know the time and date.' She knew her answer was loose enough not to commit or to lie.

Jasmine packed up her laptop, giving a small smile to the councillor as she left the room. She felt the weight of the topic while feeling her stomach tighten. It had been a confronting day. First, Bree's news. Then, the work meeting. And tomorrow, Joel's show.

It was the tennis-ball-machine effect: ball after ball, each thought slamming into her with relentless force. There was no dodging them, no chance to bat them away. She just stood there, taking the hits, feeling the bruises form in her mind.

As she drove home, she played music loudly to drown out her thoughts; then, at home, she chose to go for a run to exhaust her body to match her mind. But the thoughts of the show, Bree, and the bridges loomed large and gnawed at her until her stomach felt knotted, and dinner remained untouched.

***

Jasmine woke to Tui birds warbling outside her window, happy and carefree. She wondered if birds' brains ever became stuck like hers. Perhaps they ruminated about branches that were too thin or worms that were too fat to swallow.

Lying in her bed, staring at the ceiling, Jasmine dwelt on her dilemma.

Could she do it? Should she do it?

What if the bridge collapsed?

What if something happened because of her?

The thoughts were reasonable to her.

She threw off the blanket in frustration and swung her legs over the side of the bed. *Breakfast first, then I'll deal with Medusa.*

In the kitchen, Paige was already making coffee. 'Morning,' she said suspiciously, trying to gauge Jasmine's state of mind.

Jasmine appreciated Paige and her silent way of knowing how to help. She noticed food in the corner of Paige's mouth, evidence of a delicious breakfast already devoured. Jasmine gestured to her own mouth, brushing the corners, to point it out.

'Oh no,' Paige said, wiping at her face. 'Do I have something in my *mourners*?'

Jasmine laughed. 'I love that made-up word.'

Paige gasped in mock offence. 'Excuse me? *Made-up*? That is a proud piece of my language, thank you very much. When I was a kid, my mum called the corners of my mouth "mourners", which is short for mouth-corners. Apparently, I was a crumb hoarder. I used to store whole pieces of toast in there.'

Jasmine grinned as Paige continued.

'I was ten before I realised it wasn't a real word. Got absolutely roasted at school after confidently explaining to my friend group that "mourners" was a technical term.'

The morning's interaction was just the lightness Jasmine needed.

'Any plans for the day?' Paige asked while wiping her mouth properly this time. 'Because I was thinking of going to an escape room. A new one opened that is apparently next level.'

Jasmine loved the idea of a distraction from the evening's show. She also relished the challenge of using her problem-solving skills to escape a room. 'Yes! Let's go!' she said enthusiastically.

The pair headed into town, Paige filling the conversation as they went. At the escape room, they paid and waited for instructions from the worker. He bustled away at the counter, taking his job very seriously. Looking at his watch, he made his way to where they were waiting and started his instructions.

'Welcome to the escape room on steroids. It's the first of its kind in the southern hemisphere.' He stood with his tablet, reading instructions. 'Please don't pull anything off the wall with force. No clues are that hard to find. You will move through a series of rooms until you reach the last room, where I will let you out. You have one hour and no more.'

Jasmine smiled; she liked that he was a rule-keeper.

'The theme for your escape room is *Forest Fever*. That is all I have to say.'

The two were put inside the room with the door locked behind them. Jasmine wondered why she was so happy in this space. Many people found it confronting being locked in a room. But to her, it was nothing compared to the fears her brain could conjure up.

She scanned the room, getting her bearings and assessing every possible code or clue. Meanwhile, Paige started ripping displays apart, searching for loose objects and pressing every button in sight. Together, they made a good pair.

The friends soon decoded forest maps and identified key birds and their sounds. They moved to the second room, which had a theme of malaria. They used a thermometer, heating it with a lamp to reveal the number needed to unlock a first aid kit holding a map.

As the temperature on the thermometer rose, Jasmine wondered if it was real mercury moving.

Surely not; it must be a digitally generated device.

Mercury poisoning would be a horrible way to die.

She shook her head; she didn't have time to think about mercury poisoning.

But as she tried to work on the next clue, she couldn't shake the question about the thermometer. Was it digital, or was it mercury-driven? Her brain became foggy.

Medusa makes things foggy.

Paige, reading her thoughts, encouraged her, 'I'm sure glad they don't use mercury these days.'

Jasmine smiled and moved on.

The time ticked away, and Jasmine guessed they were nearing the hour mark – and the finish. They used the longitude and latitude to find the code to unlock the final door. Jasmine felt a thrill of excitement; they had solved the challenges.

The door slid open, and they hopped up and down, waiting for the big reveal.

But as the door fully opened, Paige froze. Her face swung toward Jasmine with concern.

On the other side of the door...was a small footbridge.

It had bubbling water underneath it in a small pool, and it looked like they had to stand on the bridge while touching each wall simultaneously.

'What the – !' Jasmine exclaimed and then burst into laughter.

Paige joined her. 'Can we cross it?'

Jasmine wiped tears from her eyes. 'I think I can manage this one.'

She skipped onto the tiny bridge and then crossed back over again, twice, for good measure.

'This is probably the only crossing I'll make today,' she joked while Paige nodded in agreement.

As they left the escape room, the worker eyed them suspiciously while they held onto each other, still doubled over with laughter.

He announced their final time. 'Fifty-eight minutes and forty-five seconds.'

Jasmine caught her breath, still grinning.

'You're just lucky I made it out, and you didn't have to carry me over that water,' she said to the confused employee. 'I could have been stuck on the other side forever.'

***

Jasmine kicked around the house, trying to be brave enough to go to the show, to cross the river. She flip-flopped between going and staying, between hope and reality, between anxiety and super-anxiety.

Joel sent her a message.

> See you soon. I'll give you a wink from the stage.

She stared at the message. She was such a lousy friend. Paige was ready to leave. Jasmine knew it was time to decline.

It was time to avoid.

She prepared a message to Joel and let her thumb hover over the send button.

No, she would go.

On an impulse, she grabbed her shoes to join Paige. Instantly, her mind spun up the usual horror reel. She bolted to the bathroom, barely making it in time before she hurled. Afterwards, she rinsed her face, staring at her reflection in the mirror. *I can't do this.*

She went to Paige's room.

Paige looked at Jasmine, who was shaking her head, 'Are you sure?'

Jasmine nodded, tears welling up. 'I thought I might. I wanted to, but...'

Paige didn't say anything for a moment. She just sat there, her expression kind. 'You've been making so much progress, Jaz. This doesn't erase that. It's one day – there'll be other times.'

Jasmine shook her head. 'Joel's going to hate me.'

'Joel could never hate you,' Paige said firmly. 'He might be disappointed, but he'll understand.'

Jasmine didn't believe her, but she didn't argue. She picked up her phone and typed.

> Sorry. Have a wicked migraine. Totally bummed to miss it.

When Paige left, Jasmine wandered the house, checking her phone compulsively, wanting Joel to text even though she knew he was on the stage. When Paige returned hours later, Jasmine was perched on the couch, waiting like a nervous child.

'How was it?' she asked, trying to sound casual.

Paige smiled as she kicked off her shoes. 'It was amazing. Joel was incredible. The whole show was.' She paused, then added, 'But, yeah. He did seem a little confused.'

Jasmine froze. 'What do you mean?'

'I told him you had a stomach bug, but he said you messaged, about a migraine. I think he was a bit... off. Not mad, just not sure what to think.'

Jasmine buried her face in her hands. 'Oh no.'

Paige rubbed Jasmine's back. 'Hey, just talk to him. He'll understand.'

Later, as Jasmine lay in bed, her thoughts turned to everything Medusa had stolen from her – graduation, the school ball, relationships. Tonight was another entry on a list that had grown far too long.

She knew nothing would change unless she found a way to loosen Medusa's grip. But the thought of making a change and facing the fear head-on felt impossible.

Chapter Five

What if my drink is spiked?

Jasmine went to work early on Monday, giving herself time to talk to Joel before others arrived. She hadn't heard from him since Saturday, and her last message was left on 'read'.

When she arrived, she saw Joel hunched over the screen of a colleague's computer. He looked tired, worn down from two weeks of late-night shows. A stab of guilt hit her when she saw him, a reminder that she had let her friend down.

Joel looked up, saw Jasmine, and gave a small wave, but there was no accompanying smile. She beckoned him to come over, and for a moment, he seemed to consider ignoring her. But eventually, he stood and walked to see her.

'Hi,' he started, his tone businesslike. 'I'm actually super busy today with a campaign to promote a new payment scheme, so I can't do lunch today.'

Jasmine could tell he'd been practising this line, and she noticed how his eyes avoided hers, looking over her shoulder instead.

'Joel, I'm really sorry I didn't make it on Saturday. I'm gutted – more than you know. Paige said it was amazing. She said you were as good as the original Seaweed Stubbs.'

Joel couldn't help but let a small smile creep through. 'I'd argue even better,' he said. But then his face sobered again. 'Jaz, I just don't get it. I didn't think you could lie, and why would you?'

'You're right. You're absolutely right,' Jasmine said, her voice trembling. 'I haven't been honest. But if you give me thirty minutes, I'll explain everything.'

Joel hesitated, looking around as though weighing his options. Finally, he sighed. 'Okay. Let's meet in the dungeons at lunchtime.'

Jasmine spent the morning working on a collection of old aerial photographs of local land, identifying traditional kūmara gardens from the region. The work was a welcome distraction from her anxiety about the upcoming conversation.

At 12 o'clock, Joel entered the room with an air of nonchalance.

'Would it be okay if we sat in here?' Jasmine asked, pointing around the room.

'Sure,' Joel muttered, sitting down, being sure to act aloof.

Jasmine took a deep breath. 'I'm going to give you a lot of information so that you can understand. Please don't ask questions until the end, and... please don't laugh.'

Joel raised an eyebrow. 'I'll try. But my default in tricky situations is to laugh, even at funerals, just so you know.'

Jasmine squirmed in her chair. 'Have you heard of OCD?'

Joel hesitated. 'Am I allowed to speak now?' Then, catching the tension in the room, he continued, 'Yeah, sure. It's Obsessive Compulsive something, like, when someone washes their hands all the time. Right?'

Jasmine sighed inwardly at the typical response. 'Well, kind of. Yes, for some people. But it's more than that.' She looked at him, trying to gauge his thoughts.

'An obsession is an intrusive thought on steroids. It's usually a fear about something... or many things. And the thought sort of gets stuck in a loop and is always there, in your mind.'

Joel nodded, giving her reason to continue.

'A compulsion, or an action, is something to reverse the thought, or break the loop.' She paused, 'It's hard to explain... but a compulsion might be a mantra or an action.'

Jasmine chose each word carefully to be factual, but on a fundamental level. Joel smiled and nodded, giving her confidence.

'After doing that action, there is a moment of relief from the anxiety. It is such a relief, that the next time the thought comes, the person would rather do the action than deal with the thought.' Jasmine keenly observed Joel's expression, looking for a grimace or a smirk. There was nothing. She continued.

'And, a thought can be as strange as you can imagine. For example, someone might be afraid of a certain word, colour, place or even a person.'

Jasmine saw Joel's eyebrows raise, perhaps wondering if *he* was an obsession. Rather than overload him with info, she brought the conversation to his own level.

'Joel, have you ever had a thought that caused you to worry, even just for a moment?'

Joel considered the question. 'Sometimes, I worry that someone might spike my drink when I'm at a bar,' he admitted a little sheepishly.

'That's a great example,' Jasmine positively confirmed. 'For someone without OCD, like you, that thought comes into your mind, when you are at a bar, and then it goes again. Your brain can figure out how important that thought is and how much value you should give it. To be careful, you probably keep your drink within sight.'

Joel nodded, 'I probably do that, without even thinking about it.'

Jasmine expanded on Joel's thought. 'If you had OCD, that thought might spiral. You might start worrying about drinks at supermarkets being spiked by workers or the city's water supply being poisoned. Maybe you'd start believing that you could just breathe in the fumes of somebody's spiked drink. The possibilities are actually endless.'

Joel nodded, 'Wow. That's a lot.' He stopped, realising he was supposed to just listen.

She continued, 'If you had OCD, you would do compulsions to help you cope. It might be that you avoid going to or driving past bars. Perhaps OCD tells you that if you tap the glass three times, it's safe to drink. Maybe you drink only boiled water. Or the worst case, you stop drinking altogether.'

'Eek, that's extreme,' said Joel, who quickly paused, looking eager to learn more.

'Well, Joel, it's extreme to you because your brain isn't built like that.'

'Right, the whole over-valuing-of-a-thought thing,' he said kindly.

'Exactly,' Jasmine said. 'But OCD thoughts aren't *my* thoughts. They arrive in my brain and stay there. If you x-rayed my brain, you would see OCD lives there uninvited.' She felt her emotions start to spill over.

Joel nodded, 'I think I understand.'

Jasmine regained control of her emotions. 'One of my favourite quotes that sums up OCD came from a man who spent his life getting weekly blood tests to see if he had HIV. He said that a "snowflake" of a single intrusive thought became a "blizzard" that blew the snow into every corner of his mind,' quoted Jasmine. As she spoke, she thought of the exhausting blizzard that blew through her mind during the weekend.

Joel nodded. He looked at her with kindness, almost pity. She paused, waiting for his reaction.

Joel leaned forward and, with kindness in his voice, stated. 'So, my friend has OCD.'

'Yes,' Jasmine whispered, happy to hear the word *friend* still applied. 'And *my* intrusive thoughts, which I call Medusa, tell me I can't cross the river. I believe something horrible will happen to someone I love – or to me – if I do.'

Jasmine bowed her head, tears slipping down her face.

Joel reached out and placed a large hand on her shoulder. 'Jaz, that's a lot to deal with. I had no idea.'

His kindness overwhelmed her, and she sobbed uncontrollably. 'I'm so embarrassed,' she managed through the tears.

'Don't be. I understand why you missed the show. I just wish I had known earlier.'

Jasmine nodded. 'Now that you know, do you have any questions?'

'Yes, I believe I have three,' he said, laughing. 'I mean, I sat and listened for a long time, so the questions accumulated.'

'Go,' she said, feeling lighter than she had felt in days.

'How could I not notice?' he asked. 'We are together *a lot,* and I haven't noticed anything about you other than a strange love of spreadsheets.' His comment lightened the mood.

'Well, I am the master of hiding it,' she answered truthfully. 'And, I think people are misinformed about what OCD looks like. If someone casually says, "I have to straighten the cushions to satisfy my OCD",' she said, making air quotes, 'I can promise you that person doesn't have OCD.'

She looked Joel straight in the eye, so that he knew it was important, 'No one with OCD announces it, and no one finds satisfaction in it.'

'Ah-ha. I still feel like I haven't been very observant, but I'll believe you. Question number two. Why didn't you tell me? We tell each other everything.'

Joel's question hurt a little. She knew she hadn't been the friend she should be.

'There's a one-word answer: embarrassment. I know my thoughts are irrational, why would I want my friends to know that too?'

Joel opened his mouth and closed it, obviously not knowing how to answer that question.

'My final question is, you speak about thoughts – plural. Do you have other fears that I should know about?'

Jasmine exhaled loudly. 'I don't know. Maybe. Probably. Sometimes.' Her answer not committing to the full truth.

'I wouldn't take risks that others take. I overanalyse conversations and look for the safest options for me and my friends. Right now, I have the river crossing one I'm dealing with. I've been through *a lot* of therapy and some medication to be where I am today.'

'It's great you've come so far,' Joel said with admiration. 'Sorry, it turns out I have another question. How did this particular obsession begin?'

'Hmm, that's a good question. A few years ago, I read the news about a bridge collapsing. Engineers hadn't picked up some cracks in it. I worried about the story and then a few days later, when I went to cross the river, I couldn't do it.'

Jasmine thought back to that time, and how the fear took her by surprise.

She continued with her story. 'I drove past the entry and around the block and back again and then just drove straight home. My brain just latched onto that idea and it morphed into the thought that by not crossing it, I would keep everyone safe.'

'Right. I guess I have never thought about it, but it sounds reasonable.'

Jasmine composed herself and finally felt relief.

She took deep breaths. 'Now, I have a request. Could you come to our house tonight? Paige illegally videoed parts of the show, and I'd like to watch it with you.'

Joel stood and took Jasmine into a big hug, squeezing her tightly. 'Deal, and can we check in on Evie and Ben? I've missed them.'

***

The afternoon crawled by. It was good to spend time in the dungeons; Jasmine needed a break from people. She tried to focus, but her mind drifted back to her conversation with Joel.

It felt good to share with him, but it also created some nervousness. What if he didn't mean what he said? No, she shook her head, trying to tip OCD out. Joel's reaction was genuinely soothing.

The hum of the scanner filled the quiet room. Jasmine paused over a photo of a bustling street, its sidewalks crowded with people in coats and hats, with horse-drawn carts. So much had changed. And yet, so much was the same. People worried and hoped.

She stared at the frozen moment and wondered: What did OCD look like a hundred years ago? There would be no ruminating thoughts about HIV, microwaves or car crashes. But she was sure OCD would have latched on to something.

It always did.

As she took the stairs to her office, she imagined what someone with OCD in the 1800s would have fixated on. Perhaps it was a fear of candles at home starting a fire, or of catching Malaria. Maybe someone worried about being beheaded. Jasmine shuddered; she could imagine that being something she would obsess about. Yes, the options were just as vast back then as the mind could imagine today.

She entered her office to see that it was just Joel and Moana, joined by Moana's three kids, who were wearing touch rugby gear, obviously about to go to a game.

'Hi, guys. How is everyone?' Caleb, Tama and Olivia all smiled back at her. 'Caleb, are you feeling better now?' Jasmine asked. She knew Caleb had been off school occasionally, causing Moana to be absent from work.

Caleb smiled in confirmation of his health. 'Good enough to play touch,' his mum said while holding up the sports bag.

'Your mum must be the best supporter of the year,' Jasmine said to the kids. They beamed, thoroughly proud of themselves for having such a clever mum.

Jasmine looked at Joel, 'See you soon?' she asked.

'Yep, see you soon.'

When Jasmine reached the flat, she heard Paige singing *Hairspray* songs in a cheerful but slightly off-key rendition. It made her smile.

'I bought bread,' Jasmine said, holding up the loaf like a trophy.

'I'm still hearing songs from Saturday's show,' Paige said as she stopped singing and leaned on the kitchen bench. 'Joel is going to love watching himself.'

Jasmine washed her hands and pulled out a chopping board to slice the bread. 'You know, I think he's missed Evie and Ben more than we have.'

'Yeah,' Paige replied thoughtfully, 'there's something about them. I know they're just names in a diary, but it feels like we're rooting for them, you know?'

Jasmine paused, her knife hovering over the loaf. 'Yeah. I feel that too.'

Joel entered the flat, making himself comfy immediately in front of the TV, holding a bag of chips and three cans of soda. 'I found chips in my car. Let's watch this great guy from the show,' he said, grinning.

Paige played the recording on the TV, and the three took great delight in reliving Joel's show. At times, Joel stood to join in with himself, adding exaggerated live actions. Paige rolled around the floor, laughing at distorted facial expressions as she paused frames. Jasmine soaked in every moment.

'It's going to be difficult to beat that,' Jasmine said when the video ended. Joel took a bow. Jasmine loved his confidence and that he so freely shared this moment with her without malice.

'Now, Evie and Ben,' Joel said, taking a seat and crossing his legs.

Jasmine pulled the familiar diary from the coffee table and set it on her lap. 'Ready?'

'Born ready,' Joel replied with a grin. 'Let's see what Evie has for us tonight.'

Jasmine opened the diary, smoothing the delicate pages under her fingers. 'Okay,' she said softly, 'let's find out where we left off.'

2 February 1935

Ben is working through his divorce, and until that is final, it wouldn't be proper for us to be together. We spend most of our time visiting with Mother or Maple. He has found a little home in Hamilton East that he hopes to purchase.

It's a modest house, but the lawn is large, and the veranda sweeps right around. The outhouse even has a laundry with a fire and copper to heat the machine, which is quite modern.

When the time comes, I should be very happy to make a home there. It will be good for Albert to have a place to settle and for Ben to put in his garden.

'Okay, so they're basically engaged,' Joel said, raising an eyebrow. 'That escalated quickly.'

'Quickly for us,' Paige reminded him. 'But back then, people didn't move in together before marriage. It's kind of sweet.'

'It's practically Married At First Sight without the lip fillers,' Joel said, laughing.

19 February 1935
I have been in quite a flux over life and my feelings for Ben. While recovering from a cold at Maple's, I had the most tremendous shock – I read in the paper that there had been an accident at a rail crossing. My heart nearly stopped when I saw that it was Ben who had crashed his work truck into the train.

Clive came and fetched me to check on Ben and Albert at their home. Ben didn't have a scratch on him. He's sore and resting for a few days but otherwise unharmed. What a blessing Albert wasn't with him. It was a miracle, indeed, to walk away from such a dreadful accident. The whole thing has left me shaken.

I realised how much I would have missed him if the worst had happened.

Jasmine paused, and the three of them looked at each other wide-eyed.

'That is ridiculous,' Paige said. 'I don't believe he was hit by a train and lived? Is this fake news?'

Jasmine focused on the research opportunity. 'I think we finally have something to go on. A crash like that must be in the newspaper archives on *PapersPast*. I'll look tomorrow.'

'Oh no, you're not leaving us out,' Joel said. 'We're not ending on a cliffhanger like that – let's look now.'

Jasmine grabbed her laptop, navigating to the *PapersPast* website. 'Okay, let's do it together. I just thought you weren't into all this research stuff,' she said, suppressing a grin.

Paige leaned in, clutching her knees in excitement. 'I feel like we're detectives in a show.'

They huddled around the screen as Jasmine opened the 1935 Waikato papers. She entered keywords and waited as the search wheel spun, taunting them.

'Come on, come on,' Joel muttered, tapping the table like he could hurry it along.

Finally, the page refreshed. Jasmine scrolled past a few dead ends until a headline caught her eye:

Truck Damaged in Train Accident

'Here it is!' Jasmine announced, clicking into the New Zealand Herald article from 1935.

The three of them read aloud in unison, stumbling over each other in their excitement:

> *A collision occurred late this afternoon at the Grey Street level crossing, between the Frankton-Cambridge train and a motor-truck, the property of the Farmers' Co-operative Auctioneering Company, Limited. The driver of the lorry, Mr B. Budekin, was greatly shaken and was removed to his home in a condition of shock. The rear axle was found to be badly damaged.*

Joel leaned back, crossing his arms. 'We've found him.'

'It's him,' Jasmine agreed, her brow furrowing. 'But 'Budekin'? That doesn't sound like a name I've ever heard.'

'True,' Joel said, squinting at the article. 'Maybe the reporter scribbled the name down wrong. People spell my name wrong all the time.'

Paige looked at Joel with her you-are-so-ridiculous face. 'Your surname is Williams. No one spells that wrong!'

'Yes, sometimes they miss the second i, or they add an a. I'm sure the *Britain's Got Talent* guy, David Walliams, is one of my cousins.' Joel said, muttering to himself.

'Maybe Ben didn't want his full name plastered everywhere, so he gave a dodgy version,' Paige added.

Jasmine started typing name variations into the government records search bar. 'I'll try 'Budikin' and 'Buddekin'; maybe we'll find something.'

'What about 'Budweiser?' Joel laughed in hysterics. The other two couldn't help but giggle at the pun.

The search turned up nothing new. Joel drummed his fingers against the table while Paige scrolled aimlessly on her phone.

'It's like looking for a ghost,' Paige said with a dramatic groan. 'And there's no social media to search. It's much easier to be a stalker today.'

'We'll have to keep digging.' Jasmine said, closing her laptop.

'And reading,' Joel added, always quick to lighten the mood. He leaned in conspiratorially, 'Or we could just accept that Ben went undercover as a secret agent.'

Paige laughed as Jasmine stared at the name on the screen – *B. Budekin.* Something about it felt familiar and nagged at the edge of her mind like a loose thread waiting to be pulled.

'Well,' she said finally, closing the laptop, 'we're closer than yesterday. We'll figure it out.'

'Do you think we just missed the bigger story?' asked Joel, 'I mean, Ben was hit by a train, literally! And he survived. It is a miracle.' He gasped, holding his mouth. 'Oh no, I sound like Evie.'

'It's true, that's big news. Imagine if it were a different story – this diary could take quite a dark turn,' said Paige.

'Well, they live another day, and that's enough for me tonight. I have to go to sleep – I still have a show hangover,' Joel said, getting out of his seat.

He hugged the girls as he left the house.

Paige went to the bathroom to get ready for bed, but Jasmine sat for a while, thinking about how much her brain had been through over the past few days.

It had been exhausting.

She loved the time with her friends and having a project; it was such a good distraction, and tonight seemed to have mended her friendship with Joel.

She ran her hand over the diary, whispered, 'Goodnight, and thank you' to Evie, as she blew her a kiss.

Chapter Six

What if we drown?

The weekend rolled around, and summer was in full swing as Christmas approached. The trio took advantage of the long, warm nights to escape the city for the beach. As they headed towards the West Coast, leaving the city behind, they used the 30-minute drive to sing along to the radio and relax. Jasmine enjoyed being a passenger, resting her head against the door as she watched the trees and sheep whizzing by.

Her gaze moved to the towering windmills on the hilltops, their great blades turning steadily, harnessing the wind's force to generate power. Their motion was involuntary and repetitive. Jasmine considered how Medusa's endless cycle of thoughts drained her while the turbines' repetition generated something useful. She wished she could channel her thoughts into energy.

The first stop at the beach was at the wharf to collect fish and chips before heading to the estuary, where Jasmine threw down a blanket on the black sand.

Joel unwrapped the dinner: hot chips, fish, and a pineapple fritter. 'Yes! Best fritter ever,' he said, admiring the food, 'made with actual pineapple. None of that canned nonsense.'

Jasmine smiled at her friends. 'I wonder if Evie and Ben ever came here?' Jasmine asked as they settled into dinner. 'I guess it would have been a bus trip over a gravel road back then.'

'Or a sneaky trip with the work truck once it was back from the panel beaters,' Paige joked.

'Ah, there's the archivist, thinking about the diary' Joel teased, pointing at Jasmine. 'She managed to switch off for what... two hours?'

'Well... what would you say if I told you I brought it with me?' Jasmine replied coyly, holding back a grin.

'I would say that we should have seen it coming,' Paige laughed.

'Swim first, though,' Joel said, pointing at the estuary while devouring his dinner like a man who had lived on toast for a while.

'Okay, but be careful. No one drown,' Jasmine added.

The friends dipped in the ocean, which was cooler than expected. They quickly returned to the warm sand. Feeling they had accomplished all the key aspects of the journey, they stretched out on their towels, letting the warm sand beneath them relax their bodies. Jasmine, as always, took the role of reader and began to read the next portion of the diary.

26 August 1935

I helped Albert prepare for the Fairfield School fancy dress ball. He looked so smart. I went with him and Ben to the Alexandra Hall which was beautifully decorated with multicoloured streamers hung across the ceiling, and the stage was filled with mimosa, fernery, and bowls of pussy willow and spring bulbs.

Joel snickered, and Jasmine paused. 'Sorry,' he said in between giggles. 'I'm pretty sure the primary schools don't promote a bowl of pussy willow these days. How did Evie write that without making a joke!'

'She doesn't have a childish mind – that's how,' said Paige, throwing sand his way. 'Pussy willows are very pretty plants,' she added, making Joel giggle even more.

'Shall I continue?' Jasmine asked. Joel nodded, trying to hold it together.

I helped in the supper room. It was a real credit to the work of the ladies' committee that I volunteered to join. Everyone welcomed me.

Paige interrupted, 'I love how she is so on board with being a mother for Albert. Step-parents get a bad rap, but in my experience, there are some pretty amazing examples'.

'Well, that's true. Just look at Jesus; his stepdad was Joseph,' Jasmine added sincerely.

'Huh.' Joel looked at Jasmine, confused. 'Are you adopting all of Evie's traits now?'

Jasmine shrugged. 'Just trying to bring balance to the conversation.'

30 August 1935
It's been a long winter, and I am looking forward to being through the worst of it. Ben's divorce was finalised in court this week. We are preparing to marry in December. I feel it is a blessing that he is older than I am, it's proper.

Joel scoffed. 'Proper? That's such a different time. Imagine saying – "It's good for me to marry an older man because it's proper".'

Paige quipped. 'Tell that to Leonardo DiCaprio's girlfriends.'

Joel snorted as he laughed at her joke.

Jasmine enjoyed the banter they were having and smiled.

I've faced a few unexpected battles. Mother is concerned that Ben has already been married and has a son to care for. While she does care about Ben, she doesn't think it's wise for me to marry him.

However, her concern is one of my reasons for affirming the decision. It's because Ben is so good at looking after Albert that I feel drawn to him. For so long, I have yearned to be a mother and I will have that with Ben and Albert.

The other upsetting thing is that the pastor at the Baptist Church, where I have been a patron for years, refused to marry us because Ben is a divorcee.

'Argh! How many ways can people discriminate?' Joel said with frustration, stabbing the sand with a stick. 'It feels like we always have to find something to hold against people.'

'It does seem like we never learn,' Jasmine answered sympathetically before continuing.

It saddens me. I always imagined standing at that altar with my friends in attendance. He is trying to help, making an effort with Mother and he found a Methodist minister willing to perform the ceremony. It feels like an answer to prayer. As I so often say, 'More things are wrought by prayer than this world dreams of.'

The wedding will be small with just a few of my cousins. Mother's friend is making a wedding cake, which we'll share with guests in the church hall.

'Can you imagine anyone today getting away with serving just cake in the hall?' laughed Joel, then added while screwing up his nose. 'And, it was probably a fruit one with marzipan.'

'My cousin's wedding cake alone cost $2,000, I'm not sure what the whole day cost but it must have been close to $50K. It was epic but it crippled them financially,' Paige shared.

'What would you rather have, a small wedding with discrimination or an OTT wedding wherever you liked?' Joel asked.

'Hmm, neither. Just give me world peace, please,' Paige joked.

13 December 1935

Tomorrow, I move from spinster to wife, and Miss to Mrs. I can't wait to build a home with Ben – a place filled with children and friends. Ben is a kind and good man, a true gentleman.

I had my final day of work last week and received a thoughtful letter of thanks from my employers. Now, I look forward to tending to our little family in our home.

'Wow,' Paige said softly, 'that's so... pre-women's liberation. I'm not sure if I'm even cheering for her. It sounds like she's about to lose her identity.'

'She sounds happy, though,' Joel countered. 'And she writes about politics and voting. She hasn't gone full *Real Housewives* on us.'

'That's easy to say coming from a man,' Paige scoffed.

Joel snorted. 'It's not often I'm accused of being too macho.'

Jasmine flipped the page, 'The next entry isn't until February, two months later. That's disappointing not to have wedding details.'

'Honeymooners, probably too busy to write,' Paige said, with a wink.

'Eww Paige, that's like joking about your grandparents' sex life,' Joel said with disgust.

2 February 1936

It's been six weeks since the wedding, and it has been quite busy. Our first Christmas as husband and wife was simple but lovely. I knitted Ben gloves for work, and he bought me a grapevine for the garden. It won't bear any fruit this year, but hopefully, it will next year. We plan to grow it up the fence by the clotheslines, and eventually, it can grow over the beams by the outhouse.

Albert has kept busy these school holidays, helping Ben in the garden and carrying wood for the copper.

18 March 1936

I have been terribly ill and unable to keep up with my housework, but Ben and Albert have taken over many of my chores.

Though the sickness is dreadful, I don't mind – I am so pleased to carry a child for Ben and fulfil my dream of motherhood. The baby will arrive in October, near my birthday.

They say the first three months are the worst in how you feel, and the last three months are the worst in how you look.

'Who says that?' Paige scoffed. 'I never saw a pregnant woman look her worst.'

'Well, they didn't muck around,' Joel added. 'Married and a honeymoon baby.'

'I'm sure they felt the pressure to start a family, both being older, for their time. It sounds like Evie wants a few,' Jasmine suggested.

As she went to continue, she glanced up and was surprised to see Joel had tears in his eyes. Without a word, she slid closer and rested her head on his shoulder. Paige stayed quiet, letting Joel share if and when he felt ready.

Eventually, Joel broke the silence. 'It's kind of perfect – marriage, kids, it's simple. It's just... I'll never have that. Not naturally. But I am happy for her. She deserves it.'

The friends sat quietly until Joel broke the silence again, this time his voice was curious. 'I'm sorry to bring up Medusa, but I have a genuine question.'

Jasmine, surprised, answered, 'So long as Paige goes next with sharing something vulnerable.'

Paige laughed, 'You know I don't have anything; I'm an emotional rock.'

Joel continued, 'We've been sitting here on this beach for more than an hour, watching kids jump off the footbridge into the estuary. I've been watching you, Jasmine, and you seem completely unfazed by the scene right in front of you. What's the difference?'

Jasmine looked at the simple walking bridge spanning the estuary. 'It's a fair question,' she admitted. 'The only thing I can say is that OCD isn't reasonable. It picks random things to fixate on and ignores others. Like, someone with Contamination OCD might leave dirty tissues on the floor without concern. It makes no sense.'

She glanced at the bridge, 'It doesn't set off danger vibes. It's just for walking – no cars. If I fell off, I'd be able to swim to shore safely. But I don't have a desire to try.'

Joel nodded, processing her words. 'Right. So, if you were to walk over it, you'd feel okay?'

Jasmine shrugged. 'I *think* so.'

Joel ventured carefully, 'Could we walk over a Hamilton bridge with you?'

The suggestion hit her like a punch, and she felt the familiar rattle of her snake, coiling and rising in protest. Her internal voice answered immediately, *No.*

'I don't think I could,' she said. 'If I fell in the river, I wouldn't survive.'

'So, would it be fair to say,' Joel asked, his tone thoughtful, 'that you're more afraid of the water underneath than the bridge itself?'

The question caused Jasmine to think. *What was her real fear?*

She attempted to answer. 'Maybe. But it's not as simple as that. Remember, OCD is not logical. The fear is just fear itself.'

Joel nodded. 'Okay. I have one more question, and it's genuine. If you walked across the bridge wearing a life jacket, could you do it?'

The absurdity of the question caught Jasmine off guard. Paige and Joel exchanged glances, both apprehensive about her reaction. Then Jasmine started to laugh. It was a deep laugh that had her curled into a ball on the towel. A family playing cricket in the sand glanced over, checking that all was well.

Joel and Paige couldn't hold back and joined her in laughter until the three of them were wiping tears from their eyes. The image of Jasmine, wrapped in a life jacket, marching across a Hamilton bridge was too much to bear.

Once she had composed herself, Jasmine finally replied, ‘You know what? OCD hates being laughed at. So, maybe, just maybe, if it was dark and no one could see me, it might be a solution.’

Joel grinned, satisfied. ‘If you ever decide to try, I know a guy with a life jacket.’

Joel gathered his things and carefully shook the sand away from the girls’ faces. ‘As much as I have loved this, I think it’s time to go.’

The girls followed, peeling themselves from the comfort of the sand and collecting the rubbish.

The sun was starting to set, and the glow on the horizon cast beautiful shades across the beach.

Jasmine thought about Joel’s question. She liked that he was trying to help, and maybe his ‘ridiculous’ idea had some merit.

Maybe it could be a way to loosen Medusa’s grip.

Maybe.

Chapter Seven

What if the Christmas tree catches on fire?

It was the final week of work for the year, and there was one more thing Jasmine had to avoid before relaxing for the summer.

Avoidance. Distractions. Compulsions. All tools to survive obsessions.

The trip to Von Tempsky Street over the river was scheduled; Jasmine waited for a magic excuse not to attend. She sifted through ideas and decided to run an excuse past her trusty HR friend, Moana. Jasmine made her way to the work cubicle, giving an imaginary knock on the open doorway.

Moana laughed and pretended to open it. 'Come into my office,' she said, smiling.

Jasmine sat on the spare chair and took a moment to look at the children's art on the wall. There were drawings of hearts, dogs, and flowers, giving the space a lift. Jasmine didn't want to make the reason for her visit a big deal, so she started by asking after Moana's kids and whether they were excited about the end of the school year.

'To be honest, Jazz-a-dazz, we really need the break. Caleb has suffered a lot with anxiety during the past few months, and he's just hanging in there. I have to force him to school.'

Moana's news surprised Jasmine, who wondered how she had been so unaware of her friend's struggles.

Moana continued, 'We just don't know how to give him the help he needs; the teachers are trying to support him in class, but they have thirty other kids to help. It's all a bit of a mess.'

Jasmine considered her following words. She wanted to be helpful without revealing her own struggles. 'He has a great mum, which is huge,' she managed, acknowledging how helpful family could be.

'I guess so, but it's all new ground. I'm a bit lost. Doing a fundraiser for the kids' sport is definitely where my strengths lie,' Moana said, half laughing. 'Anyway, how can I help you?'

Jasmine now felt silly bringing a 'problem' to Moana. 'Oh, nothing really. I just wanted to know if I can decline a meeting that falls outside my job description.'

'Oh,' Moana said, surprised. 'Do you not want to be involved?'

'The truth is, I think I add no value to further discussions. I have helped the team with the historical information they need, and I'm pressed for time with other projects.' The sentence had been well rehearsed.

Moana smiled. 'Of course, you can decline to go. I mean, you don't need HR permission. Is there something more to it?' she asked.

Jasmine realised how odd the conversation must sound; she had made it a bigger deal in her head than it needed to be. 'No, it's always nice to sound out my ideas before I act on them,' Jasmine said.

'I wish other people could think like that,' Moana replied. 'Now, I have to meet with someone about why they can't take coffee beans home. There's always one who likes to break the rules,' she looked at Jasmine and winked, knowing she had probably said too much.

Jasmine returned to her desk, clutching a folder as if it were armour against the small white lies she'd told. Missing the Von Tempsky Street meeting made sense – she *had* completed her part of the project, and her schedule *was* packed with other priorities. There was no reason to be there.

And yet, she knew the decision was influenced by Medusa, who had slithered into her work. She shook her head, determined to focus on the tasks that mattered. There was no point wasting energy on guilt – it wasn't like anyone would miss her at the meeting. But as she typed up notes for another project, she couldn't ignore the unease tugging at her.

Medusa had made her lie, and it didn't sit right.

***

The Council office was set to close for two weeks, giving the trio time to indulge in holiday fun. As Christmas Day drew nearer, the three friends spent an evening at the house, discussing their plans.

'Paige and I will head to Te Awamutu for the day to be with our families,' Jasmine said. She would usually be at Bree's house in the morning, sharing in the girls' excitement as they discovered half-eaten carrots and bulging Santa sacks. She wondered if they would notice her absence or if this would be the beginning of her fading from their lives.

'Let's have Christmas dinner together on Christmas Eve,' suggested Joel. 'With all the trimmings, as Evie would say.'

Jasmine smiled at Joel. She wondered who would be at his Mum's house this year or if he would celebrate with her. It seemed they were in contact less and less. 'Do you want to join us in Te Awamutu?' Jasmine asked.

'Nah, I'll visit Nan and Mum and see what's happening. Let's celebrate the night before,' he said. 'Let's eat together and see where the night takes us.'

Christmas Eve arrived with the tree modestly decorated but glowing with fairy lights. The three friends gathered around the table at Jasmine and Paige's home laden with KFC, salads, retro brandy snaps, ambrosia and a cheap bottle of wine – an impressive effort for Millennials. They shared funny stories from past Christmases: failed gifts, awkward family moments and their evolving beliefs about Father Christmas.

'I was ten when my mum sat me down to tell me the truth,' Joel laughed. 'Apparently, I was the only kid in my class still arguing for Santa's existence. Deep down, I knew I was lying to myself, but I was pretty good at it, even back then,' he joked while scooping ambrosia into a bowl.

'I never believed,' Jasmine said. 'Bree made sure to cast doubt early on, and I just couldn't make the math work, even at five.'

'Oh, that's so sad,' Paige said. 'I was a true believer and did the whole reindeer and cookies for Santa routine – and I still do.'

They spent the evening playing board games and singing karaoke. Joel wasted them on the mic, but the girls outdid him in charades, with the simplicity of their acting trumping his over-acting.

Joel glanced at the clock. 'I have ten minutes before I need to head off. Can we have an update from Ben and Evie, just to join them in with the festivities?'

Jasmine quickly retrieved the diary and perched in the big armchair they'd bought for the house. She adjusted her Santa hat, cleared her throat, and began.

6 June 1936
It's bitterly cold. I can feel the snowy weather from the south. I must be very brave to go to the outhouse. Once the copper is heated, it becomes bearable. Even with the extra warmth from carrying the baby, I struggle. The frequent trips to the lavatory make it harder still.

Jasmine read about the challenges of Ben and Evie's first winter in their home with broken pipes and the contrasting joy of family life. They hosted neighbours for cups of tea and had family stay.

'They really knew how to socialise back then,' Joel remarked. 'Sounds like a real community where no one was left alone, or dead, for weeks, unnoticed.'

'Ew, morbid,' Paige interjected.

'I'm just saying,' Joel continued, 'we have a loneliness epidemic now despite all our technology. But in the 1930s, they connected so much better.'

'Well, look at us,' Paige said, gesturing around. 'We're reading together and chatting. That counts for something.'

Jasmine continued.

12 June 1936
Ben brought me a lovely surprise last week: a Singer sewing machine he was given by a workmate moving to Palmerston North. It fits perfectly in our hallway.

I've sewn sheets for the baby and added them to my trousseau chest, which is filling nicely. I've knitted cardigans and a hat. Mother is making the booties. It's just three months to go.

Whenever I think about the baby, I imagine a real bonny baby with beautiful red hair. Time will tell.

Jasmine paused, giving time for Joel to leave. He smiled as he stood. 'Alright, I'd better get going. Have a wonderful Christmas. I can't wait to hear about your day.'

They hugged goodbye, and followed him out to the car, giving Paige a chance to place her carrots for Santa's reindeer. They giggled about how childish it was and were soon singing *Last Christmas* at the top of their voices as Joel drove away. He honked his horn in time to the music, drawing curious looks from the neighbours.

Inside, they began tidying up the kitchen, leaving it spotless for Christmas morning. As they worked, Paige casually worked the conversation around to Christmas morning. 'Jaz, I just want to check – would you like me to take you to Bree's tomorrow? We could even try the life-jacket idea.'

Jasmine's stomach clenched, 'It just isn't worth it,' she said quietly. 'I'd like to go, but I can't.'

Paige nodded. 'Okay, but I just don't want you to miss out on things all the time.'

'Thanks, Paige. One day.'

Probably never if Medusa gets her way.

Paige shuffled off to bed, sneaking one of Santa's cookies as she left. Jasmine ensured the doors were locked. It was the kind of night that burglars liked. Next, she flicked off the twinkling lights of the tree to ensure they didn't cause a fire. With everything in place, she headed to bed.

***

Jasmine woke early with the sun streaming in her window. The country had just marked the longest day of the year, and the mornings were light at 5:30am. She imagined her nieces on the other side of the river, tearing into packages. Aria would be meticulous, keeping paper and cards, while Morgan would lose gifts in the pile of paper that her mum would need to sort through.

Jasmine wondered why the girls hadn't asked her about her lack of visits. She wasn't sure what was worse – telling them the truth or letting them think she wasn't interested in them.

Unaccustomed to having a free morning on Christmas Day, Jasmine wondered what new tradition she should start for herself and decided that lying in bed with a book sounded perfect. It was 8am when she rolled out of bed and headed to the kitchen to make pancakes.

Jasmine busied herself in the kitchen, preparing chopped strawberries from her small patch, noting how proud Evie would be for using home-grown produce. Paige appeared mid-morning with her hair tangled, resembling a 1980s rocker with a perm. She dragged a large, wrapped package.

'Ho ho ho,' she said, giggling and patting her non-existent large belly. 'Merry Christmas, Jasmine. You've been such a good girl this year.'

The friends hugged and decided breakfast could wait until after gifts.

'Biggest gift goes first,' said an excited Paige, making the rules as she went.

She handed over the large gift wrapped in pink paper with glitter dots. Jasmine carefully opened the gift and started to laugh. Inside was a woman's life jacket with 'Team Jasmine' screen-printed on the back.

'It's from me and Joel, and it's kind of a joke gift – but seriously, it's also for real.'

'It's actually one of the most thoughtful gifts I have ever received. I'm not sure if I'll use it for the purpose you intended, but I will definitely use it for any water situation. Safety first,' admitted Jasmine.

She handed her gift to Paige, who squealed like a child. She tore open the paper and looked a little confused at first. Inside was an A5 spiral-bound book with a cover that read, *Paige's Journal.* Inside were photos of Paige through the years, dispersed through lined pages for recording memories.

'I bought one for Joel too, seeing as you both enjoy reading Evie's diary. I guess it's an archivist's kind of gift,' Jasmine explained, feeling a little unsure if the gift would be popular.

'I *love* it, and it's so personalised. I'm totally going to write in it, starting today!' Paige exclaimed.

The two enjoyed the slower pace of the morning before making their way to Te Awamutu and their family homes. Jasmine spent the afternoon laughing with the family and exchanging gifts. The nieces didn't question her absence that morning, and no one mentioned Medusa's control.

The day was perfect BBQ weather and the family spent most of the time outside, playing a newly unwrapped game of cornhole over and over again. Jasmine smiled at the girls' enthusiasm to play for hours, noting that some repetitions are *positive.*

It was almost midnight when Paige and Jasmine pulled into the driveway. Jasmine pulled out her phone and read a text from Joel.

Epic gifts, thanks. See you tomorrow? I'm keen for a lake walk.

Yep, need to walk off Christmas food.

As she turned off the light, Jasmine thought of the jacket with her name on it and the endless hours of cornhole she had played. She had great friends and family. *Who needs the east side anyway?*

And with that, she closed her eyes on another Christmas Day – one with all the trimmings.

Chapter Eight

What if I got arrested?

The following afternoon, the friends met to walk around the lake in the middle of the city. The walk was filled with chatter about celebrities and upcoming movie awards. Joel raved about Dunkirk and explained in great detail why it deserved Best Picture in 2018.

'This is much better than fighting the crowds at the mall,' said Paige, who was never much of a shopper, even on a good day.

'I never know how anyone has money left to spend after Christmas, but they do,' said Joel.

'They probably don't, but they just spend anyway. And we all know what Evie would say about that,' laughed Jasmine.

In unison, the three responded, 'A penny saved is a penny earned.'

Evie had favourite idioms she regularly quoted, and the three friends were slowly adopting them.

During their walk, they discussed the possible baby names that would likely be announced in today's diary reading. They predicted the classics: George, William or Elizabeth.

At the end of the walk, they sat on their chequered picnic rug in the shade and turned to the diary. A breeze off the lake rustled the pages; Jasmine held it close to keep it safe. She opened to where they had last finished and prepared to continue. Instead of a page of writing, she found a yellowed envelope glued in. On the front was Evie's name and the address of the hospital's Elizabeth Rothwell Building – the birthing centre. She showed it to the others carefully.

'Oh, wow, Ben must have written a letter to Evie while she was at the birthing centre recuperating. Mothers used to stay for two weeks after having a baby,' said Jasmine.

'The hospitals would never cope now if they kept patients that long,' Joel commented, a little cynically.

'So, we assume we have a baby,' squealed Paige. 'Open it!'

Jasmine carefully opened the envelope. It felt like a gender reveal, and she was about to announce the much-anticipated baby of Evie and Ben.

Clearing her throat, she began.

My darling,
I have been thinking about you, my darling

'Good strong start with two "darlings",' Joel interjected.

'Shh,' hissed Paige.

I have been thinking of your tender heart all day, knowing God will heal it.

Jasmine paused. Something about the tone of the letter unsettled her. Her heart began to race. She scanned her eyes further down the page, trying to make sense of the words, and then she saw it. Her stomach tightened as she realised what she was about to share. 'Oh no,' she said, pausing. 'It's not good news.' She continued as her friends looked worried.

I spent the evening at home, unsure of how to occupy myself, but writing to you seemed the best thing I could do.

We said farewell to our wee baby this afternoon. It was a quiet but lovely service; the minister spoke with such kindness. I carried the little casket, holding our dear soul from the car to the graveside.

Many friends have sent flowers and wreaths, with words that brought comfort. Shall I share them with you, my darling?

'Who plucked this bud?' said the gardener,
'I,' said the Master,
And the gardener held his peace.

I can picture our little one at the centre of heaven.

The letter stopped abruptly. Jasmine's voice broke as she lowered the letter, and they sat in silence.

'Is there anything written from Evie?' Joel finally asked, his voice subdued.

'Um,' Jasmine murmured, flipping through the diary pages to distract herself from the lump in her throat. 'There is no next entry, the diary ends.'

'Well, this totally sucks,' Joel said, exhaling sharply. 'I thought we were in a rom-com, and now we're in a tragedy. It's like *The Lion King* when Mufasa died – I never got over that. And now I feel bad for crying when she got pregnant,' Joel said, letting his emotions spill over.

'And she's staying in the maternity unit with all the other mums and their babies while receiving a *letter* explaining the funeral,' Paige said, her frustration evident.

'And poor Albert, he's only ten – it must be a lot for him to process,' Joel ranted. 'I don't think I want to read anymore. This is not the happily-ever-after I was looking for.'

Jasmine, usually the first to find a way to keep their spirits up, simply folded the letter back into the envelope. 'Unfortunately, life isn't always happily ever after,' she said quietly. 'Hopefully, there is good news in the next diary that I can collect from work next week.'

The trip home was quiet. Jasmine was surprised by how the news had impacted them all. It was Evie's good heart that had kept them all on an even keel, and their lives weren't supposed to be difficult – that was what their own lives were for. Evie and Ben's story was the trio's reality show, one that was supposed to inspire.

Jasmine knew that now, with a birth and death date for the baby, she should be able to find the registration, and from there, she could uncover a surname. Jasmine explained to her friends that the bad news meant she could possibly find a descendant.

'Can we look when we arrive home?' asked Joel.

'Sure, if that's the kind of thing you want to do on your holiday,' said Jasmine.

'Strangely, it is. Evie's been a mystery long enough, and it's time to know who our inspiration is.'

***

The trio arrived home feeling sweaty from the outing; each of them showered and made toasties for dinner. Jasmine pulled out her laptop and opened the tabs for all the sites she would use to research Ben and Evie. She explained that the New Zealand Department of Internal Affairs made public the birth details of people who died more than fifty years ago.

'So, we might just be in luck and find the last names of our friends,' she said, referring to Evie and Ben. She filled in the known details in the search fields and immediately received the alert: *You must include a surname.*

'Urghh, we need a surname! We are back to the start,' said Joel.

'It's okay,' Jasmine said, pulling up the Hamilton Cemetery records. 'We might be able to find it through the cemetery.'

'Oh,' Joel exclaimed. 'The Council runs this site? How did I not know that?' He giggled in embarrassment.

Again, the search field asked for the surname of the deceased person.

'We don't know the baby's name either,' Paige pointed out.

'Let's try 'Baby,' Jasmine suggested, typing it in. Her stomach sank as the screen filled with more than two thousand entries.

'That's way too many to scroll through,' Paige sighed, already giving up.

'The results are alphabetical by surname,' Joel noted. 'Why don't you look in the Bs, like from the train crash story?'

Jasmine skipped ahead through to the B surnames, half-expecting to find nothing. Still, she liked the hunt and that her friends were just as invested. She scrolled quickly, eyes scanning for anything close to Budekin.

'Keep going to the end,' Paige urged, suddenly more engaged.

Then, the name appeared: Faith Burdekin.

'Burdekin!' Paige and Joel said at the same time.

'I know that name,' Paige added, sitting up straighter. 'There's a reserve by the university – I used to park there when I was running late and couldn't be bothered walking.'

'Yes, I knew it was familiar!' Jasmine said.

'Okay, now what?' asked Joel, excited.

'Now we can really learn some details,' said Jasmine. 'But be warned, you might find some spoilers, like death dates.'

'No, we're not doing that,' said Joel firmly. 'You already said we can't skip forward, and I've accepted that. So no, we just find out names and addresses – no death dates.'

The friends navigated through electoral rolls and marriage records. Piece by piece, the puzzle came together. By the end of the night, Evie and Ben were no longer just names – they had histories. The friends discovered birthdates, parents' names, Evie's maiden name and where each of them grew up.

Evie was from Auckland and Ben was from a farm in the Far North. Jasmine jotted everything down, mapping out the past of Evie and Ben.

The electoral roll listed a Nixon Street address for their first home. A quick search on Google Maps pulled up an image of a 1930s villa, its sloping porch wrapping around the house. Large windows framed every room, and delicate lace curtains hung in the window panes. The house had been lovingly preserved.

Joel leaned in, studying the screen. 'So that's where Ben came home every night... and where Evie heated the copper.' He tilted his head. 'It's good to have a visual – it's not what I pictured.'

'It probably didn't look as grand back then, and I'm pretty sure it's had an extension when you look at the roofline. It's cute.'

'Let's go for a visit,' suggested Joel. 'While we're on holiday. We can visit the baby at the cemetery.'

Jasmine hesitated, and then Joel clasped his mouth. 'Sorry, Jaz. I forget about the east side thing.'

'It's okay. I think you guys should go, it's a great idea. Take photos, or I'll video call in.' She offered a small smile. 'It's a good filler until we get the next diary.'

As they packed up for the night, Joel leaned back in his chair, arms folded behind his head, gazing at the ceiling. 'So, do you think they ever had more children?' he asked thoughtfully. 'I mean, losing their first baby like that – it must've been devastating. But I feel like they'd try again.'

Jasmine closed her laptop, nodding slowly. 'I've been wondering the same thing. Evie's such a nurturer.'

'I just want to know if they had their happily-ever-after,' Paige added.

'Maybe the next diary will have answers.' Jasmine kept her tone neutral, though deep down, she had a feeling that Ben and Evie's lives would continue to be a mix of joy and hardship.

Joel sat up suddenly, grinning. 'Well, on other topics – I have a date tomorrow night.'

Paige raised an eyebrow. 'With?'

'Lucca,' Joel said, beaming. 'A sparky "who enjoys conversation and fun," according to his profile.'

'What prompted this decision?' Paige asked, amused.

Joel shrugged. 'I'm free in the evenings with the show finishing, and I decided life's too short to sit around waiting for things to happen.'

Jasmine quipped. 'That's a lot. I hope that wasn't on your profile – "Seeking companion to share short life".'

'Exactly, and it worked,' Joel laughed. 'I'm sifting out the shallow ones.'

***

Jasmine was in a deep slumber the following evening when she heard soft knocking at her window. She lay in bed, choosing which option was most likely. It could be a branch rubbing the window, or more likely, an intruder luring her out?

Her heart skipped a beat as she picked up her phone, ready to call the police. She carefully pulled back the curtain, and in the soft moonlight, she could see the figure of a man, and she let out a scream.

She sighed in relief when she recognised Joel's prominent stature, and as her eyes quickly adjusted, she could see he was pointing to the front of the house.

Jasmine grabbed her dressing gown and rushed to the door, glancing at her phone she saw it was after 2am.

She opened the door and, seeing her neighbour also looking out his window, she gave him a reassuring wave.

Joel flew inside like a whirlwind. 'What's going on?' Jasmine asked, rubbing her eyes.

'Wake Paige up. I've got such a story for you.'

Paige stumbled out of her room, grumbling and squinting at the light. 'Did someone scream?'

Wide awake and in complete "Joel mode", he launched into his tale.

'So, the date was going well. Lucca – good looking! Into movies, easy conversation. Anyway, we were eating outside the restaurant, seated on the footpath, right by the road and traffic lights. And this ute pulls up with three guys in it, and they yelled hateful comments at us.'

'What the,' Paige interjected, horrified and fully awake.

'I was pretty embarrassed,' Joel continued, 'but Lucca? Oh no, he was *mad*. He starts yelling back at them, full-on swearing and everything. So the manager comes out and tells *us* to leave! Like we were the problem! Apparently, *we* were "creating conflict".'

'What idiots,' Jasmine said sympathetically.

'I'd have given them a piece of my mind if I'd been there,' Paige said, fired up. 'And the manager too!'

Joel raised a hand. 'Wait, there's more. So, we're walking along the street, trying to change the subject, but Lucca's still all broody – and I do love a broody man, haha.'

He paused for impact, and then went on, like he was on stage. 'Then we spot the ute parked on the side of the road.'

'Oh no,' Jasmine whispered, sensing the escalation.

'Oh yes,' Joel said dramatically. 'Lucca goes to the boot of his car and pulls out some kind of tyre tool. You know, one of those gadgets for checking and adjusting tyre pressure. And he tells me he's going to let the air out of their tyres.'

Paige gasped. 'Did he really?'

'Yes! I was like, "No, don't do it!" on the outside, but inside I was totally cheering for him. Anyway, within minutes, two tyres were completely flat.'

'Joel!' Jasmine exclaimed, her snakes rattling. 'What if you'd been arrested?'

Joel continued, ignoring the question. 'After that, we went across the road to a bar and sat by the window to watch the show. You should've seen those guys when they came out! They were cursing and stomping around like toddlers. It was exhilarating.'

'It's brilliant,' Paige said, laughing at the saga.

'And, are you seeing him again?' Jasmine asked nervously.

'No way,' Joel said firmly. 'I can't condone that kind of reckless behaviour.'

'But it *was* kind of satisfying, wasn't it?' Paige pressed.

Joel hesitated, a sheepish grin spreading across his face. 'Okay, I'm not gonna lie, it felt amazing.'

Paige nodded, adding, 'Unless people stand up to bullies, they'll keep getting away with it.'

Joel sighed. 'I don't know if deflating tyres fixes anything, but... yeah, it felt good.'

'So, how did you leave it?' Paige asked.

'I had such an adrenaline rush that I did some of the best dancing of my life at a club, and then I came here. I told him that I would message him sometime, but I think I'll just leave it for now. Too much drama for me.'

'Oh, the irony,' said Paige, referring to Joel's love of the stage.

'Well,' Jasmine said, suppressing a yawn, 'next time you need a vigilante crew, count me out. But also, let me know that you're safe.'

'Next time,' Joel said, 'I'll take you with me, then I know I'll be safe.'

Jasmine smiled. 'Safety is one thing I do really well.'

Chapter Nine

What if my friends fall off the bridge?

New Year's Eve approached, and the three friends made plans for Joel to stay over at Paige and Jasmine's house to celebrate. The diaries were paused until Jasmine collected the next one from work, which gave an excuse to take a break and live in 2018.

As the clock ticked toward midnight, the trio settled into the couches, with the earlier celebrations fading into a reflective calm. Jasmine reached for the notebook she had been scribbling in throughout the day and then flipped it open.

'In my official role as "archivist" in this friendship, I thought it might be fun to look back at some highlights of the year before we dive into resolutions.'

Joel groaned, 'I hate resolutions. *But*, if this is an official list, I assume my appearance in *Hairspray* is on your page.'

'Sure,' said Jasmine as she exaggerated adding his news to the list. 'Okay, here's what made headlines this year, soon to be last year.'

'The #MeToo Movement,' Jasmine gave a little clap before continuing.

'A USA report on climate change, which was then totally ignored.'

Joel looked surprised as if it was news to him.

'We had a royal wedding with Meghan Markle and Prince Harry,' Jasmine added.

'And we lost her in *Suits*,' Paige groaned.

'Closer to home, Rocket Lab launched a rocket into orbit from New Zealand.'

'Finally, something cool!' Joel said.

'Our own Prime Minister, Jacinda Ardern, had a baby, ran the country, and banned plastic bags. While Mark Zuckerberg lost $119 billion in a single day over data privacy fallout,' Jasmine summarised.

'Ouch,' Joel winced.

'And sadly we lost Stephen Hawking, Stan Lee, Aretha Franklin, and Mac Miller.' Jasmine said, closing the book.

Paige nodded. 'I'd forgotten how much happened. It's been such a mix of highs and lows.'

Joel asked. 'What do you think Ben and Evie would've thought of that list? The world's changed so much since their time.'

Jasmine looked at her list, trying to identify which areas were of most interest. 'I hope Evie would've celebrated a woman prime minister. And Ben would've admired Rocket Lab. They probably knew who Stan Lee was. I'm assuming in a few years, they will be buying comic books for Albert.'

Paige chimed in. 'But they'd probably be confused by some things too. Climate change and Facebook scandals, how do you even explain those?'

As the first fireworks burst outside, Jasmine grinned and closed her notebook. 'Alright, resolutions, people!'

The three shared outlandish hopes, like winning a lottery and using the fortune to rename the city while owning a superyacht.

Joel entertained the idea of hitching a ride on one of Rocket Lab's rockets until he learned they were primarily uncrewed.

Eventually, they narrowed their goals to more realistic aspirations, like making advancements at work and getting fitter.

Jasmine stayed quiet about her own goal. She didn't want to raise expectations, but a thought lingered in the back of her mind: could 2019 be the year she finally crossed the river? The mere idea sent a ripple of anxiety through her stomach.

***

In the morning, Jasmine waited for her sleepyhead friends to wake. She had plans for the day and wanted to share them. By the time they stumbled out, blurry-eyed and ready for breakfast, she had already baked muffins.

'So, we have two more days of holiday,' Jasmine began, laying out the plan. 'I think you two should go ahead with the visit to the cemetery and house, and if you go early, we'll have time to go to the movies this evening. I heard *Spider-Man: Into the Spider-Verse* is amazing.'

'Ata mārie to you too,' Joel teased, mimicking Jasmine's tendency to skip morning greetings.

Jasmine ignored the comment and continued, 'I'll join you on Messenger video once you're... there.' She hesitated as she thought about her friends travelling over the river.

'Okie dokie,' said Paige, sounding like a ten-year-old as she munched on a muffin. Jasmine marvelled at Paige's ability to leave the house with such ease, without checking locks or even without showering.

Joel looked less thrilled about the early start. 'I should've stayed at my own house,' he muttered as he grabbed a muffin to go.

'I'll call when we're there,' Paige promised through a mouthful, shutting the door behind her.

Jasmine needed a distraction.

Knowing her friends were crossing the river rattled the snakes in her head. She put in her earphones and used noise to drown out her thoughts until her phone buzzed with a video call from Paige.

Jasmine answered quickly, resting the phone on the counter. She could hear Joel and Paige arguing about which direction to go.

'Jaz, this cemetery is *huge*!' Paige exclaimed. 'It will be like looking for a needle in a haystack.'

'It's okay,' Jasmine said. 'I have the plot number.' She gave directions, sending them to the section of the cemetery where children were buried.

Jasmine listened to the crunch of gravel under their feet and the occasional puff of exertion as they argued about who was right. A few minutes later, Paige's voice came through excitedly. 'We've found it!'

The camera flipped to show a row of headstones before zooming in on one that stood out with a metal cot around it, made from what looked like iron. Now seeing the cemetery, she could visualise Ben carrying a tiny casket to that place and Evie carefully choosing the perfect resting place, a cot.

Inside the cot was a simple headstone: *In remembrance of our baby. Faith Burdekin, 1936.*

Paige and Joel fell silent. Paige gently laid hydrangeas she had plucked from a hedge onto the grave. 'I'm sorry, baby,' she said softly. 'I wish you had made it.'

Joel cleared his throat. 'I hope you don't mind, but I have prepared something to read.'

Jasmine saw Paige nod as Joel pulled out his phone. 'It's just here in my notes. It's a poem written by someone I follow – she also lives in Hamilton. She lost a baby too and, well, I thought it would be appropriate to read it.'

'Aww, Joel, I didn't know you cared so much,' Paige said, with adoration.

'Just don't tell anyone, okay?' He cleared his throat again, ready to read in his best drama voice. 'It's written by Payton Cowley and it's called *Little Hands*. And Faith Burdekin, we dedicate this to you.'

Your little hands, so delicate
stole my heart and flew away with it
How I wish I could've seen what those little hands could do
how I wish I could've held them as they grew.

To hold them close as time uncurled
guiding them as they take on the world
What I wouldn't give to spend a day
doing nothing but watching you play.

Years have passed, with others now here
yet your tiny hands remain so near

In quiet moments, I still see
your little hands reaching out for me.

Among the laughter and the play
your presence near fades away
And though you had to quickly depart
your little hands still hold my heart.

'*Whoa,*' Jasmine breathed. 'It's like it was written for Evie.'

'Yeah, that's what I thought when I read it. There's more to the poem, but that's the part I wanted to read,' Joel said, obviously emotional.

Paige took his arm, and together they walked Jasmine down the row.

'This is the saddest place,' Paige said quietly. 'So many children.'

The two showed Jasmine the rows of headstones, all dedicated to children. They each felt a reverence.

Ready to move on to the house, they disconnected the call. Jasmine kept busy waiting for them to make it to the next historical site. This time, she didn't need to distract herself but had to manage her impatience. It would be only a short time before they reached the house, just a walk from the cemetery. She thought how comforting it must have been for Evie to live so close to her baby's grave.

Thirty minutes passed, and Jasmine wondered if her friends were lost. When her phone buzzed, she answered quickly; this time, three faces filled the screen.

'Hi, Jaz,' Joel began. 'Good news and bad news. The bad news is we couldn't photograph the house for you.'

Jasmine was confused; where had they gone? Joel was clearly holding back the good news, bursting to share it.

'The good news is... we're inside the house.'

Jasmine's heart sank. She was thrilled for her friends but couldn't help feeling the sting of being left out.

OCD had robbed her of another experience.

She clapped her hands, even as disappointment stung her.

'There's more,' Paige teased. 'Actually, much more.'

Jasmine squinted at the screen, her curiosity growing at who the extra in their video call was. Paige introduced him.

'Meet Noah, the homeowner of Evie and Ben's house,' she said while giving a thumbs up and a wink.

Noah gave a half-hearted wave, looking awkward but kind.

'Hi,' Jasmine said, feeling out of place. 'I'm Jasmine. I've been working with these two on a project to...'

Joel interrupted, unable to contain himself. 'We told him everything, Jaz! He's very interested in the diaries.'

'Okay,' Jasmine replied cautiously, worried the diaries might be up for discussion with a stranger.

'There's more,' Paige said dramatically.

Jasmine laughed, wondering what could be added to their story. Maybe he was selling the house, and Paige wanted to buy it.

Paige continued with big eyes, 'His name is – Noah Ben Burdekin.'

The cogs in Jasmine's mind turned. She opened her mouth but closed it again, twice.

Noah stepped in. 'Hi. So... Ben and Evie are my grandparents. I bought this house about five years ago.'

Jasmine stared and then managed to ask, 'Grandparents? Not great-grandparents?'

Noah laughed. 'No, I'm the youngest of the grandkids. Bit of an afterthought, really.'

As Noah spoke, Jasmine realised the spoilers she'd been avoiding were about to unravel. So, Evie and Ben did have children *and* grandchildren.

Joel and Paige handed the phone over for Noah to hold. Jasmine couldn't help but notice how handsome he was. He was tanned despite summer not yet being in full swing. He had a well-trimmed beard that nearly matched the buzz cut of his hair. Jasmine found herself thinking that Ben and Evie had passed down some good genes.

Noah launched into conversation.

'I'm so interested in these books. Where did you find them?'

Jasmine explained they had been donated to the archives sometime during the past ten years and that she had started reading them to identify the owners.

'I'm actually blown away,' he said.

Jasmine enthusiastically spoke about what she had learned about the house and where the two had lived in Hamilton.

Noah looked impressed as he listened. 'Your friends suggested I stop by the council to meet you and collect the diaries.'

Jasmine's heart raced. She wasn't ready to lose the diaries, but as if reading her thoughts, Noah added, 'I'm happy for you to finish your research first.'

She smiled, noticing his features mirrored the couple in the wedding photo: Evie's slender frame and Ben's look of determination.

She replied, 'Your grandparents have kind of been adopted by us, so we'd love to finish the diaries, but can I give you the ones we have already read?'

'Great,' Noah said. 'I'll drop by next week, I often go to the Council for work anyway.'

Jasmine saw the irony. Noah was a frequent visitor to the Council building. He had been right under their noses, and his grandparents' memoirs had been right under his.

As the call ended, Jasmine resolved to look her best every day until Noah visited. There was something about him – a connection she couldn't quite place. Maybe it was his grandparents' influence. Or perhaps it was something more.

***

Jasmine paced the house, waiting for Joel and Paige to return. She wasn't just curious about what they had found; she also wanted to know more about Noah. When she heard their car pull into the driveway, she opened the door to greet them eagerly.

They burst into the room, filling it with chatter as they recounted their visit, one fact tumbling out after another. Jasmine soaked it all in, living the experience vicariously through them.

The pair explained that they had parked outside the house, debating whether it was too cheeky to take a photo when the garage door opened and Noah walked out. Feeling guilty for loitering, they quickly explained their historical interest in the house. Noah pressed for more details, and soon, they spilled the beans about their fascination with his grandparents.

'Jaz, it was so fun walking inside the house. The guy, I mean Noah, even has the Singer sewing machine on display in the hall that was hers. And the veranda where Ben and Evie sat is still there.'

'What did Noah think of us and our addiction to his family?' Jasmine asked, though what she really wanted to say was, *What was Noah like?*

Joel shrugged. 'I think he was a little overwhelmed at first, but then he got really into it. Ben died before he was born, so I think he was intrigued to know more about him.'

'He'll love reading the diaries. I look forward to meeting him,' Jasmine admitted.

Paige chuckled, noticing Jasmine's enthusiasm. 'He's very nice, Jasmine. And, he's divorced, with two daughters.'

'Aha,' Jasmine replied casually. 'And how old would you say he is?'

'About 35, I reckon.'

'Good work, guys,' Jasmine said, steering the conversation back to their progress. 'Look how far we've come during these holidays. We've gone from not knowing a surname to having a whole family tree, addresses, and even finding the family.'

'I know, right? I'm not sure I was ready for all that information. But it does feel like a bit of closure before we go back to work.' Joel said, resting his feet on the footstool.

Jasmine agreed. She hadn't been ready to learn so much of the story's ending in one afternoon, but she liked the turn it had taken.

Chapter Ten

What if I had an allergic reaction?

The first day back at work always hits the hardest, Jasmine thought as she pulled the door of her house shut, not quite ready to face the routine of having a job. Murphy's Law – it was the hottest day of the summer, just calling for an excursion. Paige was still at home, sleeping, almost teasing Jasmine to abandon the archives and enjoy the perks of a teacher.

Despite her sluggish start, Jasmine felt a familiar sense of satisfaction as she began her tasks. With a new year ahead, she assessed how far she'd come and set fresh goals. There were exciting projects she wanted to propose, like using the Council's social media to share historical content and a timeline about the city's mayors. She planned to collaborate with the library and museum to ensure all collections were digitised.

Heading down to the dungeons, she found the next diary while packaging up the others for their new reader. She was fully immersed in her work when Joel arrived, slumping into a chair with an exaggerated sigh.

'Work is so lame,' he groaned. 'Why do we have jobs?'

Jasmine suppressed a smile. She didn't want to admit that, despite her earlier reluctance, she was actually enjoying her time in the dungeon.

'Come on. Some fresh air will help.' She locked up, and they headed out for lunch, leaving the diary behind until Paige could be with them.

They were halfway up the stairs when Paige bounded down toward them, her curls bouncing with her energy.

'Surprise! And you two thought I would still be in bed, hah!' she yelled at the top of her voice.

Jasmine quickly hurried back to grab the diary while Joel immediately perked up at the sight of donuts in Paige's hands. 'Let's go!'

'You are so easily bought, Joel Williams,' Paige said as they made their way out into the sun.

The three found a spot on the grass in Garden Place, where Jasmine opened the diary. It was bigger than the previous ones and had a hard, black cover, almost like a child's exercise book. She noticed immediately that the handwriting was not what she was used to, and the entries looked shorter.

'It looks like we have a change in author. It must be Ben.' She felt a little sad that Evie hadn't continued with her story. But Jasmine understood.

Grief can do that.

'Oh, and it's 1939. Almost three years have passed,' she explained.

'What! Are you sure you got the right book?' Joel protested.

'Absolutely.' Jasmine confirmed.

'Gutted,' Joel said, 'it's like missing two seasons of your favourite show.'

Jasmine read Ben's words out loud.

July 17, 1939
This diary is being commenced on a suitable day. It is my thirty-eighth birthday. The birthday feast was really celebrated at tea yesterday, with Sunday being a more suitable day. Gran came over and had tea with us.

I have received some lovely presents. Firstly, there was a beautiful long-sleeved pullover which Evie knitted in secret for me. I have had the use of the pullover for some weeks because the weather is so cold, but all the same, it is for my birthday. Then there is a luffa, which is a thing I have wanted for some time, also from Evie.

From Gran, I received a nice tie. From Albert, this book. The cake, which was baked by Evie, was a great success, and I took a slice each for my two workmates, which they enjoyed very much.

'Oh, it's quite a change in style,' said Paige, instantly noting Ben's entries were more like a list of events.

'Also, funny that his wish list included a luffa. Oh, to live in such a simple time,' Joel added.

July 19, 1939
Beautiful day after a sharp frost of 18.5 degrees at Ruakura. Work as usual.

'Um, was it that cold here in the 1930s?' asked Joel seriously. 'Is that a typo?'

Paige laughed, 'I think it's Fahrenheit, not Celsius. That changed sometime in the 1970s, I think.'

'Rigghhtt makes sense,' Joel said, a little embarrassed, while quickly Googling the Celsius equivalent. 'FYI, it's -7 degrees, which is definitely cold,' he added, redeeming himself.

Evie had quite a day at home. The callers were Gran, Maple and Mrs. Fran. We received a letter from Mary in Paeroa; she has been very ill with kidney trouble.

'Are we supposed to know these people?' Joel asked, concerned he was behind the rest of the class.

'I guess Gran is Evie's mum and Maple, we know, but the rest are all new.'

'Oh well, sorry to hear about your kidney, Mary,' Joel joked.

Jasmine continued.

Albert attended the pictures to see The Wizard of Oz, compliments of Gran.

At this last line, Joel sat up straight. 'Oh, that's exciting. Imagine going to the cinema to see what would become one of the most famous movies of all time.' His eyes gleamed. 'Shall I tell you some facts about that movie?'

Jasmine smirked, sensing Joel's attempt to redeem himself for his earlier misstep about temperatures.

'Go for it,' Paige sighed, turning a daisy in her hand, preparing it for a daisy chain.

Joel launched into his list. 'Okay, first: Judy Garland was just sixteen when she played Dorothy, and *Over the Rainbow* almost got cut from the film! Also, the ruby slippers. In the original book, they were silver. They changed them to red to take advantage of Technicolor. And, the Tin Man's costume was so uncomfortable that the actor had to be hospitalised due to a reaction to the aluminium dust.'

Jasmine thought about her idea to switch the word dust for glitter. Aluminium glitter sounded less harmful than aluminium dust. Either way, she didn't want a part of it.

'Sounds like a fun time to be an actor,' Paige quipped.

'Still,' Joel said, 'it's amazing to think that Albert saw it when it was brand new. It must have been magical.'

Jasmine smiled, picturing Albert in a cinema, wide-eyed as Dorothy and Toto stepped onto the Yellow Brick Road. She smiled at her friend; the little lesson seemed to have taken him out of his back-to-work slump.

World matters continue much the same. Considerable tension still exists over the city of Danzig, and hostility remains between Britain and Japan. There is no post today. Evie has had a slight upset stomach. We suspect the pork from dinner last night, but it could just be a passing illness. It has just struck seven o'clock, and Albert is off to bed. We believe it best to keep him to a regular bedtime. Evie now oversees his homework and checks it over each night. His teacher is assigning work more regularly, and we hope keeping Albert diligent will help him progress in school.

Jasmine stopped. 'What do you think about Ben's diary compared with Evie's?'

'A few things stand out already,' said Paige, who looked like she hadn't been listening. 'He has a pattern: he talks about the weather, what Evie did, what work was like, who visited, and what mail they got. Those must be the most important things of the day for him.'

'Yeah, they are very social. I can't believe the steady stream of visitors. I'm jealous,' stated Joel, 'but why a daily report about the mail?'

Jasmine knew why Ben paid so much attention to it.

'All the family and world news happened at the mailbox. Also, the bills arrived, magazine subscriptions and the newspaper,' she explained. 'It was a daily lifeline to the world that we unfortunately don't have, with phones and email. There is such a morale boost from receiving a letter.'

As she spoke the words, the facts gave her an idea. 'Oooh, I'm going to write letters to my nieces and post them. How exciting would it be for them to receive a letter out of the mailbox? It could make up for me not visiting.'

'I love it. We will try it in class, too. I bet the kids don't even know what snail mail is,' Paige said encouragingly.

'I don't even know how to post a letter,' Joel confessed, laughing. 'Like, where do you buy those stamps, and where do you put them on the envelope?'

Satisfied with her idea, Jasmine resolved to find some of these 'rare' stamps and envelopes.

'Read on, Jaz,' prompted Paige, 'but perhaps just read the bits of interest – leave out the weather and the mail.'

Jasmine read on.

9 August 1939

Evie managed to get a lot of washing done, which will lighten Monday's workload.

'That's what I'm talking about. Let those facts stay in the book,' Paige pointed out.

Jasmine nodded. 'Got it.'

Over the past few days, she has received gifts and loans of baby clothing for the baby boarder we hope will arrive next week for a short stay of two or three weeks. Maple's contributions were especially generous, and Mrs. Nairn also added some.

'Um, did we miss something?' Joel asked. 'Why is Ben so relaxed about this news?'

Jasmine shrugged, 'I'm not sure; he didn't know we would be reading it 80 years later with no context. It sounds more like they are going to have a visitor.'

It is natural that Evie does not wish to dip into her own beautiful trousseau, which has been lying in readiness for so long. Who knows? Perhaps it may still be needed someday.

'Spoiler alert, she *will* need it one day,' Paige said.

12 August 1939

Evie had a busy day. This morning, she took charge of our temporary boarder, Molly Taylor, aged seven months.

She brought the baby to town and Plunket this afternoon for feeding advice and check-ups while also managing numerous other tasks. As for me – work as usual. Today marked the first day of the August holidays for Albert, who spent the entire day with Evie, helping as much as he could.

'So, I guess they are fostering a child?' Paige said, asking more than stating.

'Maybe. I wonder if it's the first time.'

Jasmine started to flick through the pages, looking for more information.

'Hey, no more spoilers,' said Joel. 'I'm already a bit disappointed we know about Noah.'

Jasmine smiled. He was good at holding her to her own rules.

'Okay, just seeing where we were heading,' she said, defending herself.

'AKA spoilers!'

Jasmine felt that it was a good place to stop, and the three reluctantly left the sunlight to return to the reality of the day.

'Four hours to go,' Joel said, sighing.

'And then about 350 days until the next summer holiday,' Jasmine added.

'Not for me,' Paige said, unable to avoid the reminder of her teacher's holidays. Her two friends hissed at her and she shuffled away, leaving them to return to their office.

***

Jasmine was proud of herself for arriving on time at work for a second day. There were still empty desks due to the holidays, and she was glad she still didn't need to have mundane how-was-your-holiday conversations.

In her bag were two letters, including $5 each for her nieces, which she was excited to post during lunch.

She and Joel were at her desk, laughing at videos of Christmas gifts that had gone wrong, when Joel gave a little gasp and made eyes at the door.

Jasmine turned to see the man from the video, standing there, taller than she had imagined, holding a folder and wearing a casual work uniform that spoke to a profession as a builder. Her stomach fluttered.

'Hi, Joel and is it Jasmine?' he said with an easy smile. 'I hope I'm not interrupting.'

'Um, no, we were just looking at, well, nothing really,' Jasmine offered weakly.

Noah offered an outstretched hand to Jasmine, and she took it. It was firm, official. 'I really want to thank you for looking after those diaries,' he expressed sincerely.

'Not at all,' she replied, gesturing to one of the seats in the room. 'I've been looking forward to sharing them with you.' She handed them to Noah with a mix of pride and trepidation.

'These are the ones we've read so far,' she explained. 'They cover Evie and Ben's courtship, early marriage and their life together. It's a glimpse into another time, and I hope you'll find it as fascinating as we have.'

Noah ran his fingers over the worn covers, his expression reverent. 'Thank you for sharing these. It's incredible to think these have survived.'

'They've been keeping us company for weeks now,' Jasmine said, pointing to Joel, who was trying to blend into the background. 'I feel like they're part of the group.'

Noah smiled.

As they continued to talk, Jasmine was struck by his genuine interest. He asked thoughtful questions about the diaries – about Evie's stories, Ben's experiences, and the moments that had surprised her. He had an attentiveness that Jasmine admired, and she found herself speaking more freely than she usually did with new acquaintances.

As he got up from his chair to leave, he said, 'I'll read these carefully and take good care of them. I promise to check in and share what I find.'

Jasmine quickly added, 'If you have any questions or just want to talk about them, feel free to call or text me.'

Noah nodded. 'Perfect. Let's exchange numbers,' he said, holding the stack of diaries carefully.

Jasmine, trying to delay his departure, added, 'I'll let you know when we are through with the next diary.'

As he walked out, Jasmine could feel Joel's eyes on her. He came and stood beside her, and in a high-pitched voice, supposedly intimidating hers, he said, 'If you need me, call me.'

She punched his arm as he tried to dodge her reaction.

He continued, in his voice now, 'Is it just me, or is he wonderful? He can call me if he needs help,' Joel said while fluttering his eyelids.

Jasmine looked at Joel, wondering whether to expose her thoughts or not. She smiled, adding, 'And Bree said I couldn't meet anyone in the archives.'

That night, as she ate dinner with Paige, she thought about Noah and what he might learn about his grandparents. She wished she could read with him. It's a story she could do a second time.

She contemplated sending him a message, but doubted herself. *What if she said the wrong thing? What if she offended him? What if he thought she was coming on too strong.*

Even with that decision, she kept checking her phone, drafting texts, and then deleting them. Relief came as she climbed into bed, and her phone buzzed with a message from him.

It's taking me a bit to understand the handwriting. I might need a lesson. I didn't know about that train crash!

Jasmine smiled, her heart doing a little leap. She quickly replied, carefully choosing every word.

Oh yeah, crazy. I'm glad you like the diary.

I cross that railway line often. I'll pay more attention :)

If you want some help deciphering the writing, let me know.

Thanks. I might just do that. I'll pop in again when I'm in the building.

That will be great.

And with that, Jasmine felt like all her "useless" skills of library work and family history research paid dividends. She might just have met *her* crush through it.

She put her phone down, her grin lingering as she turned off the light. Maybe 2019 was going to be better than she had dared to hope.

Chapter Eleven

What if there's a gas leak?

Jasmine was in her dungeon, cataloguing a new donation of city photographs. The cool room was perfect for her to take time on this task. As she worked through the afternoon, she sorted a stack of images of central city buildings, suburban developments, and the opening of schools.

As she turned to a photo in the pile, she saw it was an aerial shot of the city's bridges. The unexpected sight hit her like a jolt, her pulse quickening as her chest tightened. Without thinking, she shoved the offending photo back into the box.

Jasmine stood abruptly, pacing the room in tight circles. It was usually in a controlled environment of her therapy sessions where she was shown a photo like that. The mere sight of them put her mind in overdrive, with all her fears tumbling through. What if just holding the photo triggered disaster?

After a moment of hesitation, she decided she couldn't delay a countermeasure. Quietly, while gripping her jaw to provide some form of control, she whispered the names of the bridges, her compulsion easing the knot in her chest with each word.

Cobham, Victoria, Claudelands, Whitiora, Fairfield, Pukete.

She repeated the names of the bridges, each set helping relieve her anxiety.

She continued until the feeling subsided, her breathing slower now, the tension retreating like a tide. Jasmine glanced at the boxes, thinking they might still hold some power over her. She shoved the problematic box back on a shelf.

She was about to leave when she heard footsteps in the hallway. Looking up, she saw Moana.

'Hello, Jaz-a-dazz,' Moana greeted her. 'How was your break?' It was Moana's first day back, and the two of them exchanged the customary post-holiday updates.

Jasmine was still in flight mode from the exposure to the bridges and struggled to make small talk. However, she could see that Moana wasn't her usual self. Jasmine paused and looked at Moana questioningly.

Sensing the need to explain herself, Moana began, 'I was speaking with Joel about Caleb. And Joel said you might know how to help. You see, Caleb just got diagnosed with OCD.'

Jasmine didn't see that conversation coming; how had she missed OCD right under her nose?

Her initial reaction was anger with Joel for referring Moana without asking, but that feeling soon left as Jasmine looked at Moana's worried face.

Jasmine took a breath, the words tumbling out like ripping off a bandage. 'He suggested you should speak to me because *I have* OCD.'

Jasmine was shocked to hear the words that came out of her mouth. Perhaps the openness with Joel and Paige had made it easier to discuss.

Moana's eyes welled up. Tears began to spill down her cheeks, surprising Jasmine, who awkwardly grabbed a tissue and handed it over.

Moana dabbed her eyes, composing herself. 'I think... I think that's the most relief I've felt in days. If someone like you – so put-together and cool – has OCD and is still *happy*, then maybe it's not as bad as I've been imagining.'

Jasmine offered a kind smile. She wanted to say, *You should have seen me five minutes ago. It's tough. It's constant. It's silent.*

But instead, she looked sympathetically at her friend and asked, 'What can I do to help?'

'Please tell me anything that will help him. I'll try everything,' Moana said earnestly.

'First, you need a good therapist,' Jasmine began. 'I can give you some names. I also have books you can borrow and I listen to a few excellent podcasts. But, what he needs most at the moment is love and acceptance. He will be frightened, wondering what has taken over some of his brain space.'

'What about medication? Does it help?' Moana asked while nodding and taking notes on her phone.

'It's a good conversation to have with your doctor. I have used it at times alongside exposure therapy. I found the best progress came when I fought back against OCD.'

Jasmine could hear the voice of her therapist as she spoke the words that had been so often spoken to her.

Moana looked confused. 'I've read about exposure therapy, but I don't understand how it works.'

'Tell me what's going on with Caleb,' Jasmine asked.

Moana recounted how it all began with Caleb's resistance to doing things he had done before. Finally, it all came to a head with an incident in the science lab at school. A video on lab safety, with examples of accidents and gas explosions, had left Caleb shaken. He'd refused to set foot in the lab since. At home, his worries had spiralled, finding dangers everywhere.

Jasmine nodded, recognising the patterns: imagined dangers and ruminating thoughts that churn over and over.

'Those are classic OCD moves,' she said softly. 'I know them well.' She paused, choosing how best to explain things. 'Moana, what's something that *terrifies* you?'

Moana thought quickly and replied, 'Snakes. 100 per cent.'

Jasmine laughed inside. She understood adverse feelings towards snakes.

'Okay. Imagine I asked you to enter a room with snakes on the floor. What would you feel?' she asked, obviously knowing the answer.

'Don't even suggest it. I have goosebumps just thinking about it,' said Moana, shuddering.

'Just keep that in mind because when you ask Caleb to step into the science lab, he feels the same level of fear that you would have entering a room of snakes.'

Moana nodded. 'That's a lot of fear.' She looked crestfallen. 'How will we help him?'

'You will help Caleb feel safe through small steps. Start with something easy, like drawing a science beaker. Sit with him while he feels the fear, let it come in. Distract him, play a game, even make the beaker funny – add googly eyes or a silly face. Once he can handle that, move to the next step. For example, have him hold a real beaker. Let his brain learn it's okay.'

'And then?' Moana asked.

'Build on it. Maybe you'll drive past the science lab and look at it from the car. Then you might stand at the door. Eventually, you'll walk inside, and it will terrify him, but he will be prepared. Every time Caleb faces the fear and realises nothing bad happened, he shrinks OCD's power.'

Moana exhaled, overwhelmed but determined. 'That sounds like so much work, but we'll do it.'

'It's worth it,' Jasmine said gently. 'Remember to celebrate his victories, have rewards ready, like his favourite snacks.'

Moana continued taking notes on her phone. 'Any other hot tips that we can do now?'

'Yes, let him give OCD a name, a really good villainous name. It will help you talk about it in the third person. Oh, and come up with some code words or emojis that he can text you when the words are too hard to say. The poo emoji is a good one,' she added laughing.

Moana smiled faintly. 'Do you think this will work?'

'I know it can,' Jasmine said firmly. 'I've done it myself. It's hard – painful even – but it's worth it. Some of my thoughts are in remission because I fought back.'

Moana's shoulders seemed to relax for the first time since they started the conversation. 'You've given me hope, Jasmine. I mean it. Who knew we employed an archivist *and* a counsellor?'

Jasmine grinned as Moana stood to leave. The familiar light-heartedness had returned to her colleague's voice.

'Anytime, Moana. If Caleb wants to talk, I'd be happy to share what I know. OCD can be a lonely and consuming place to be.'

'I do have a favour to ask,' Moana said. 'I have joined a support group. It's mainly online, where people ask questions and give support. It's for parents of children with OCD in New Zealand. There is a monthly meeting in Auckland that I'm going to next week. Would you come with me? It will be my first meeting.'

The snakes rattled. Jasmine knew how they could feed off other people's OCD and create opportunities for new thoughts.

'Can I think about that? I do want to help, but that would be confronting for me. There are fewer than ten people who know about me and OCD, and to go to a room where I admit to it would be, well, confronting.' Jasmine explained

'Of course. I shouldn't have asked; it's just all so new to me.'

'I *will* think about it, and thank you for asking,' replied Jasmine.

They hugged before Moana left the room, leaving Jasmine alone with her thoughts. She sat for a moment, turning the conversation over in her mind, knowing she couldn't offer advice and not take it herself.

If she could tell Moana that Caleb could beat OCD, then she would have to face Medusa.

She would *cross that bridge*.

Literally.

***

On the way home from work that day, Jasmine phoned her mum from the car. They spoke about the summer break and going back to work. Then, Jasmine shared the reason for the call.

'I want your advice,' she began. 'I have a friend who has a ten-year-old son, who has been diagnosed with OCD.'

'Oh, so young,' said her mum with pure sympathy.

Jasmine continued, 'She has asked me to accompany her to a support group in Auckland for one of their meetings. It's with other parents of children with OCD. I wondered what you thought of the idea and whether you would have gone to something like that as a mum?'

Jasmine could imagine her mum thinking and weighing up the best words to use.

'I would've loved to meet other parents who were in the same situation. To be honest, I still would like to meet them. When we were in the thick of it, I thought I was the only mother in New Zealand who had a child with OCD. I didn't know what I was doing, I don't know if we really ever helped.'

Jasmine felt awkward with the admission of guilt. It was possibly true, but 15 years ago, OCD was far less understood than it is now. She continued, 'So, you're saying that it would be helpful for my friend to go,' she said, summarising her Mum's thoughts, then asking, 'What about me? Do you think it would be risky for me t o go?'

'Jasmine, only you can know if it is risky, but from what I have seen over the past few years, you have much more control of things. Helping your friend would be another dent in OCD.'

Her mum's words confirmed what Jasmine already knew. She should help anyone with OCD.

By not helping, she would give OCD more power.

'Thanks, that's what I thought you'd say. I just needed to be sure.'

***

When Jasmine arrived home, Joel's car was already in her driveway. She laughed; he had really taken the first week back with difficulty and already needed time with his friends.

She remembered that she was supposed to be angry with Joel for telling Moana about the connection to OCD, but that had passed now.

As she entered the house, stifling hot from the summer's day, she saw the two sitting outside, swinging on a deck chair together with icy drinks. They were giggling together, scrolling through their phones. She saw Ben's diary waiting beside them.

When they saw her, they sat up and pointed at a drink for her.

'Welcome home,' said Paige, 'And how was your day? Oooh, did Noah visit?' she squealed, already a bit tipsy.

'Haha, no,' Jasmine said, snatching the diary. How did Paige already know Jasmine's thoughts?

'Let's read,' said Jasmine quickly, moving the topic away from Noah.

15 August 1939

The international situation is still very tense. The Anglo-Japanese position is still unsettled. Still uneasy about Danzig.

We trust that peaceful settlements will be reached in both cases. Evie visited the cemetery today and put some nice flowers on the little grave. Today marks the anniversary of three years.

26 August 1939

Albert and I attended Knox Church this morning for a beautiful memorial service for little Barry Clarke and also a prayer for Divine intervention on behalf of the international situation.

Evie is a bit tied at home just now on account of our baby boarder. Mrs Taylor, the baby's mother, paid us a brief visit this afternoon. I expect that she was pining for a sight of her baby.

Evie takes it all well with the extra work and finds it all natural. Tomorrow I go in for an operation for my goitre but she doesn't seem concerned that it will be too much to manage with me away.

'Quick, someone find out what a goitre is; I'm hoping it's something on the foot, not the brain,' Paige said, trying to reach her phone.

Joel put her out of her misery and read from his phone. 'Goitre is a condition where your thyroid gland grows larger,' he said, trying to sound like a professional. 'Hmm, is it okay that I don't know what a thyroid is either?' he asked.

'It's a gland in your neck that produces hormones which regulate metabolism, heart rate, and other bodily functions,' Paige answered effortlessly. Then, looking at Joel's surprised face, she defended herself, 'What, I'm a school teacher, we teach these things!'

'Not to first-year students,' Joel stated.

Jasmine laughed at her friends, then kept reading. She was excited that the following entry was in Evie's handwriting, keeping the diary for Ben while he was in the hospital.

'Ooh, we haven't heard her voice in a few years, I've missed her,' Joel said as if he were speaking of his mother.

4 September 1939
Ben's operation for Goitre took place at 8am and we were thankful he is over it alright. I saw him for about two minutes this afternoon. Albert and I took Molly to Plunket. She has gained 1lb this week. Mum came over to sleep while Ben is away. I took Albert to Waikato Hospital to be X-rayed.

'Dang, all this while she has no car and a baby to look after. She's a supermum,' Paige marvelled.

6 September 1939
Weather little better, but equinoctial gales blowing hard. Did a big wash. Albert went to school, but came home not well, temp 101.

Joel interrupted, 'Just FYI, I know that is Fahrenheit.'

Paige nodded, 'What about equinoctial - that's a word we've left in the last century.'

'Says you,' laughed Joel, 'I use it all the time.'

Jasmine continued.

7 September 1939
Received the result of Albert's x-ray. He has to stay home from school for a month and in bed for two weeks. His condition is not serious, I am glad to say.

I visited Ben at Cassell Hospital and was pleased to see him much better. Of course, the news abroad has us all much disturbed, making it difficult for us to be happy about any of it. Our Prime Minister, Mr Savage has declared we are to stand with England in the war. 'We range ourselves without fear beside Britain, where she goes, we go!'

Jasmine paused and stretched. 'That's the end of Evie's writing. Ben must be back out of the hospital. Shall we stop here?' she asked.

Joel sighed. 'Just read a little longer – I don't want to get off this chair.'

14 September 1939
Evie had a very successful trip to town. I took Molly to see the nurse. Mrs Taylor called this evening and collected her baby. So Molly has left us after being here nearly a month. Evie has worked wonders with that baby, and it is hoped that Molly's mother will be able, to some extent, at any rate, to continue the good work. Indeed, very great credit is due to Evie for the general care and improved health of Molly.

'He's so supportive of Evie, so proud of her. It's really nice they could help the baby until mum was well,' Paige said fondly.

18 September 1939
Evie called Mrs. Taylor and found her far from well, so she brought baby Molly back to stay with us for a few days. Albert's prescribed fortnight in bed is almost completed. There still seems to be a little cough left yet, but there is no doubt that it will clear up with the summer weather coming shortly.

'Eek, I spoke too soon. That sounds like she was in a bad way,' Paige said with concern. 'Lucky Evie called on her. Do you think she had postpartum depression? Probably undiagnosed back then.'

Jasmine scanned through and looked for more information on Molly. 'I'm not sure. Maybe? It's strange she is sick for so long.'

22 September 1939
Albert and I made our first trip to town after both being laid up. We each had our hair cut and did a little shopping as well. Evie bought a hundred onion plants today and planted them very nicely indeed.

'One hundred onion plants! That's a decent supply. What will they do with the onions? Start a pickle farm?' joked Joel.

The grapevine looks ready to give us a fruitful crop. It's grown steadily over the past few years and now provides shade. The grapes are the sweetest I've tasted, and Evie loves them. I make sure the grapevine is kept healthy for her.

'Aww, so sweet and simple. He tends to the grapevine just for her,' Paige said sentimentally.

Molly is doing very nicely, and Nurse Lowe, on passing this afternoon, remarked on that fact. Evie rang the Hospital today and inquired about Molly's mother, Mrs Taylor. They said that she was feeling a lot better, but would be there for a few days.

'It all seems a bit loose, doesn't it?' questioned Paige, 'I mean, just collecting the baby from the house, having to call the hospital for an update. Where's all the red tape and child protection stuff?'

29 September 1939
Baby Elizabeth arrived. Mrs. Brook took Evie in her car and fetched Elizabeth from Campbell-Johnstone Ward.

'Wow, that little villa will be bulging with Albert and two babies. How exciting for them. She's really all-in to mothering,' Paige said with admiration.

5 October 1939
The government has announced the formation of a Maori battalion.

Everything is happening so quickly, and I worry about all the young men who are quick to enlist. Mr. and Mrs. Taylor came around just before tea and took little Molly home. We will miss dear little Molly very much indeed and we hope that the parents will be able to take good care of her.

Elizabeth is a dear wee soul, and we feel almost sure that she can smile even at nearly three weeks old. Today, Evie took her to the fair at Nixon St Hall, where Elizabeth won first prize for a baby of her age. We are all very pleased.

'Eww. A baby show!' Paige stated more than she asked. 'What was the criteria to win?'

Jasmine shrugged, 'Yeah, that's weird.'

Joel gave a little laugh. 'Here we are, thinking it's weird to hold a baby show, but we're all judging each other on Instagram.'

Jasmine nodded, 'Fair point.'

She continued reading until the entries ended in March 1940. It was comfort food for the three friends, but again, there was frustration in it ending so abruptly.

'Didn't they realise how annoying that would be for a reader? I might have to leave a review,' said Paige, laughing.

'Yeah, it's hard jumping years at a time, just saying,' Joel added. 'But, they're in a good place, they have some babies, and Benjamin has his goitre fixed. Hopefully, the 100 onion plants will get them through winter.'

'I'll collect the next book tomorrow, and this one can go to Noah,' Jasmine said.

Paige gave Joel a wink, 'How convenient.'

Chapter Twelve

What if the fireworks start a fire?

It was a few days later when the three friends had another lunch date. They hadn't read together since the final entry from Ben's diary about the 100 onion plants. Jasmine opened the next diary and recognised Evie's writing.

'We're back to Evie,' said Jasmine.

'Phew, kind of,' laughed Paige. 'No offence, but I'm more of an Evie-reader,' Paige added, creating a whole new genre of reading.

4 November 1940

Today is my 32nd birthday, and I find myself spending it in bed.

Ben gave me this beautiful diary, thinking it might help occupy my time. I must admit, it's been a long time since I've put pen to paper. The loss of four babies has brought Ben and me tremendous grief, too hard to write about.

'That's rough, no wonder neither of them wrote anything for a while,' Paige said sympathetically.

But through it all, we've held onto faith, and now, here we are, just weeks away from welcoming a baby into our lives.

The doctor ordered complete bed rest for the entire pregnancy. It's not been easy, but Mum has been such a blessing, taking care of the housework, and Ben has been wonderful, looking after Albert.

Today marks 36 weeks.

With each passing day, we become closer to meeting our baby.

Joel and Paige listened as Jasmine shared Evie's words about pregnancy issues. Heartburn and cramps, heat and a rash. But through it all, Evie testified to the blessing of making it this far. The ailments and bed rest were willingly endured by Evie as she hoped and prayed that this baby would arrive.

Jasmine paused at the end of an entry in December, where the diary held a letter, glued in. She felt a little nervous, remembering the previous letter that held such sad news. She opened it with trepidation, scanned the page and smiled as she saw the good news.

'We have a letter from Evie to Ben,' she announced.

Dearest Ben

As the quiet of the evening settles in, I am full of gratitude that our little girl is with us. What a gift she is.

I cannot describe the joy I feel seeing her beside us at last.

She is such a precious gift to us, worth the wait and all the whispered prayers. We will continue to pray for her and Albert. I think of William Blake's poem:

'Sweet babe, in thy face

Holy image I can trace;
Sweet babe, once like thee
Thy Maker lay, and wept for me'

Sleep well my dear
Love, Evie

'Aww, they speak to each other with such affection. Where are people like that today?' asked Paige.

Joel tried to hug her, 'I'll start using those terms for you. Or, you could date a 90-year-old.'

Paige shoved him and then moved quickly to the celebration. 'Yay, though, they have a baby!' squealed Paige.

Joel picked up a blade of grass and flicked it in the air. 'Eight months is a long time to be in bed. She must have really wanted those kids.'

'We don't know the baby's name. I guess we can ask Noah for that information,' Jasmine said, flipping through the pages.

'I guess you will,' Joel teased, raising an eyebrow, enjoying his jab at Jasmine.

Jasmine ignored him, focusing on the diary. 'Wait, it looks like the baby is called Rose.

'Rose. That's such a classic name,' Paige said thoughtfully. 'Does it say much about her?'

'Only that she had red hair like her father,' Jasmine replied.

She read more entries about Evie and Ben's joy in parenting. Rose was always referred to as their wee baby. Every milestone was mentioned, smiling, burping and sleeping. Rose was taken in the pram daily to the shops where Evie proudly presented her to anyone passing by.

The trio followed Evie's story for three more years, quickly jumping through time, until 1943 when they read about another need for bed rest for a pregnancy.

They read through eight months of Evie's worries and anxiety about keeping the baby until full term. The three friends felt anxious too, uncertain if this baby would survive.

In October 1943, Evie made a heartfelt entry, giving thanks for the safe arrival of a son, Thomas.

Jasmine read the entry about the arrival.

My heart is always full and overflowing with thanks to God.

Thomas is just six weeks old now, and I still can't quite believe that I am a mother, let alone with two little ones. There were many days when I doubted this day would ever come. After the losses, I had almost resigned myself to the idea that motherhood might not be my path.

Ben has been wonderful, though I know he worries about me. He tries to lighten the load where he can, but his work keeps him busy. However, we are all happy. The grapes have ripened at just the right time. Ben makes sure there is always a full bowl beside the chair I feed in. It's a treat in the middle of the night.

'Yay, I could finish reading there,' said Joel, 'she has her happily ever after.'

'They are only in their thirties and forties, there's heaps of time for drama,' Paige said. 'I know from teaching little kids that anything could happen yet. Thomas might become one of New Zealand's most wanted.'

'Why?! Why would you say that?' Joel said with shock. 'You probably just jinxed their story.'

'It's already happened,' Paige scoffed, 'I can't change the past.'

'Have you seen *Back to the Future*?' Joel argued.

Jasmine interrupted. 'I'll quickly read to the end of 1945, we are almost there.' She speed-read entries of trouble with Albert at school and the first steps for Thomas. They finished on an entry from 1945 that left them feeling a little uncertain.

9 April 1945

Ben continues to worry me. Ever since his last operation, he hasn't been himself.

He's anxious about his health and takes regular trips to the doctors looking for answers, but so far, no one can give him a solution.

They say it is all imagined. He hasn't been able to work with the worry, and I can see how much this weighs on him. It's a burden for all of us, but especially for him, and it breaks my heart to see him this way. I don't know what we will do.

'Oh man, don't tell me they have a new trial,' said Joel passionately.

Jasmine shrugged, 'We have to go, but let's hope things improve in our next reading.' Although she had a suspicion that things were going to become worse. Evie wouldn't have mentioned it if it weren't already bad.

The friends stood up, stretching, trying to drag out the inevitable as long as possible. Jasmine carefully packaged the diary into its envelope, ensuring its preservation. It wouldn't be long before she handed over the final diary. She knew she would miss Evie and Ben's accounts. They all would.

Joel turned to look at them both. 'I have some fireworks left over from New Year's parties. Shall we go let them off at the park tonight, to celebrate the new babies?' he asked.

'Maybe,' said Jasmine cautiously, 'it's pretty dry right now – are there fire restrictions?'

'No, it's nothing like that. It's just some sparklers and little fountain thingies,' Joel insisted, giving reassurance.

'Sounds like fun, especially if we have a drink or two,' suggested Paige, who was still entirely in holiday mode.

'Okay, I'll bring them over after dinner,' Joel added, happy with his contribution to their fun.

***

True to his word, Joel arrived with a party box of fireworks. 'There's something about setting things on fire that just excites me,' he said, laying out the options on the table.

Jasmine eyed up the weaponry cautiously. She saw more than sparklers.

'I'm not sure if we can let these off tonight, Joel. We'll scare the neighbourhood pets.'

'These are all good, they are all silent ones. Fireworks are very clever these days, you can burn yourself in silence.' He looked at Jasmine's concerned face and quickly added, 'Jokes.'

Jasmine, Paige and Joel waited until it was dark and made their way to the local park with the fireworks and a torch. Jasmine felt uneasy about the plan; she was there more for safety than for fun. Joel took the role of chief lighter and runner.

They all watched with "oohs and aahs" as fountains of colour erupted like a geyser. With each finished firework, Joel placed the empty canister into a bucket, ready to return to the house.

'Just one to go,' he said. 'This one is called Apollo.' He did his usual ritual of lighting and running as Paige and Jasmine sat, waiting to be amazed.

To their surprise, instead of spouting forth colour like the previous works, the object flew into the air like a rocket, screeching as it went. The sound ricocheted and bounced across the park while the rocket disappeared into a grove of trees at the fence line.

Jasmine and Paige leapt to their feet. 'Joel! What the hell?!' Jasmine yelled, 'Not so quiet! And where did it go?'

Joel and Paige laughed, holding each other's arms. 'Let's get out of here,' Joel yelled, picking up his bucket and sprinting across the park.

Jasmine followed, checking over her shoulder for any sign of the rocket.

The three of them arrived at the driveway, breathless after running from the scene of the crime.

Joel dumped the bucket around the edge of the house to hide the evidence.

'See you tomorrow!' he said as he jumped in his car to leave.

Paige, now wiping tears from her eyes from laughter, blew him a kiss. She turned to look at Jasmine, 'You okay?' she asked.

'Yeah, I just always worry about the pets.'

She lied.

The whole time they were at the park, Jasmine saw all the dangerous possibilities: to themselves, the environment, and the animals. A small part of her enjoyed the display of colour, but most of her didn't enjoy it at all.

OCD hijacked a fun moment.

'Well, goodnight. See you in the morning,' Paige said, carefree and unaware.

Jasmine prepared for bed. She knew she was close to being in an OCD spiral. She quickly went into prevention mode.

It's just OCD.

It's just Medusa being a bully.

Everything is fine.

She needed a distraction. She tried to occupy her brain by counting backwards and then switched, focusing on the room. What could she smell? What could she see? What could she hear?

But Medusa kicked in. She could smell smoke, see flames and hear sirens.

Perhaps sleep would help. She hopped into bed and closed her eyes, but the thoughts flooded in.

What if the rocket set fire to the trees?

What if the rocket set fire to the house?

What if people were inside?

What if they die?

What if the police arrest us?

Medusa was strong and unleashed. Jasmine threw back the covers in anger.

She *would* give in to Medusa.

Tiptoeing past Paige's room, she grabbed her jacket and shoes and went outside. Using her phone torch, she first checked the bucket, touching each exhausted firework to ensure it had no flame. Satisfied it was safe, she then went to the park.

The logical part of her brain knew that the most significant danger she was in was walking alone, late at night.

But the Medusa part of her brain convinced her that there was a greater danger of a possible slow-growing fire.

She hoped Medusa would be satisfied with confirmation that there was no fire.

Medusa was not satisfied.

Jasmine needed to find the rocket and ensure it was not a fire risk. She made her way to the corner of the park where the rocket had landed. Now that she was in the bush, she realised she had no idea where the rocket had gone. It could be high in a tree or even over a fence.

It was hopeless.

She walked out of the shrub and stood in the middle of the field. She looked around, scanning the sky for any glow and sniffing for the smell of smoke.

How long do I have to wait?

And then she shouted. 'How long do I have to wait until you are satisfied?'

She sat on the ground and cried.

And waited.

Jasmine wasn't sure *how* she had gone to sleep, but she knew what woke her.

The soft rain on her face startled her. She sat upright, looking at her phone. It was 1:13am.

She slowly stretched her sore limbs, shifting her body on the hard ground.

There was no sign of fire, and now that the rain had arrived, Jasmine felt satisfied there would be no fire – and no arrest.

She quickly made her way home, slipping past Paige's room and into her own bed, which felt softer than usual.

As she drifted off to sleep, she told herself, *Next year, don't go to the fireworks.*

But she heard Medusa's voice reply.

Yes, you should go, or how will you know if it's safe?

Chapter Thirteen

What if I overmedicate?

The following day was rough. The bags under Jasmine's eyes were obvious, and her constant yawning gave a bad-sleep vibe. She had a headache and longed for the day to finish.

'You look hammered,' Joel said as he leaned on his friend's cubicle. 'Can't you handle a late-night fireworks party?'

Jasmine yawned as she nodded, 'More than you know,' she replied.

'Can I get you a coffee?' Joel offered.

'No, it's okay. I'll take some paracetamol if I need to,' she replied.

Joel moved to his own desk as Jasmine rummaged in her bag to find some pain relief pills. She held the box in her hand as she looked for her drink bottle. Moana came by the desk for her usual morning chat and to check in on everyone. Jasmine kept the conversation upbeat and didn't admit to her pounding headache and fatigue.

As Moana moved on to her own cubicle, Jasmine returned to the issue of her headache. She looked at the box in her hand and instantly had doubts.

What if I already took the medication?

She took the pills out of the box and saw that several had been taken previously. There was no way of knowing if she had taken any today.

Medusa hissed doubts into every corner of her mind.

She looked around the room, trying to remember if she had taken the pills, wishing she could replay the moment on a hidden camera. If she took some now, she'd live in fear of having overmedicated.

It was safer to take none.

She threw the box in the bin and jotted the current time on a Post-it. At lunchtime, she'd buy a new pack – then she'd know exactly how many had been taken, and how long it had been since she possibly took some.

Deep down, she knew she hadn't taken them.

Letting Medusa off the leash last night had been a mistake. She'd given too much rein.

'I'm off to the dungeons. See you at lunch,' she called out to the room. With that, she took herself away from the office, enjoying the moment to massage her head privately.

She sat there preparing documents to digitise as she leaned on the wall beside the scanner. The library staff had asked her to help organise a display on the history of local high schools, and she enjoyed the humming sound of the scanner as she sat in peace.

There was a knock at the door of the dungeon. Looking up, Jasmine was surprised to see Noah. She quickly smoothed her hair back into her ponytail and glanced down at her outfit. She hadn't made much effort that day, but figured she looked okay and he couldn't see her headache, although she had no control over the bags under her eyes.

'Noah, hi,' Jasmine said, smiling. 'Come in.'

'I'm sorry to interrupt you so soon after my last visit, but I just wanted to drop off some chocolates to thank you, properly.' He handed her a box of Roses chocolates with a card attached.

'Oh, that's so kind,' she said with genuine surprise.

'A simple thank you didn't feel like enough,' he said, offering a smile. It made her heart lift and she felt happy.

'How is it going with the diaries?' she asked.

'I'm a little addicted,' he confessed, 'Last night I stayed up until 2am because I couldn't stop. I'm learning so much.'

Jasmine smiled. She could have added that she stayed up until the same time, but it would be hard to explain why.

Jasmine felt her fatigue flee away; the joy of seeing Noah seemed to be a healing balm.

'I can imagine how meaningful it is for you to read them. We loved them, and we're not even related to the writers,' she said as she opened the chocolates.

'Do you have a favourite flavour?' she asked, pushing the box towards him.

'I'll always go for the Peppermint Crème,' he replied without hesitation.

Jasmine also loved the Peppermint Crème but didn't want to agree with everything he said. While handing him one, she added, 'Great choice. I'll take the Turkish Delight.'

'Eww,' he said, feigning disgust. 'I always wondered what kind of person ate those.'

She laughed. 'It's great. Everyone leaves them in the box for me.'

Noah stalled, 'Before I go, could I ask for your help in interpreting a few words? I took photos on my phone.'

'Absolutely,' Jasmine said, gesturing to a chair.

Noah pulled his chair right up beside Jasmine. She found herself glancing at his arms and hands, noting how he held his phone and moved.

'Where are they?' he muttered, scrolling in the wrong direction.

Jasmine waited, not minding that he was taking time to find the pictures as she sat next to him.

'Ah, here it is. What is this word?' he asked, zooming in on a photo of the diary's text.

Jasmine laughed. 'That word is "slag," and the word before it is "basic". Apparently, it was used in the garden to add minerals. We had to Google it.'

'I thought that's what it said, but couldn't imagine it was right. What about this word?' He swiped to the next photo. 'It looks like 'growl.'

'Oh, that's 'Government,' shortened to Govt. You'll find Ben does that a lot too.

Noah showed a few more photos, and Jasmine was able to help him with all of them. Satisfied with her answers, he stood to leave.

'Shall we go upstairs and get the next diary?' Jasmine asked, hoping to prolong the visit a little longer.

He agreed and they took the stairs, chatting easily along the way.

Jasmine felt her colleagues' eyes on her when they entered the office. Trying to keep him from meeting people, she quickly handed over the finished diary.

'Excellent. I'll hear from you then?' She nodded, and he offered an awkward wave, his lips curving into a fleeting smile before he turned and left the room.

Jasmine noticed that her headache and fatigue had vanished. Noah's visit had special powers. She sat back in her chair, exhaling slowly. There it was again, that fluttering feeling she'd been trying to ignore.

She had no doubt now: she had a crush. Her mind whirled with questions she didn't have the answers to.

Should she say something? What if OCD made her unlovable?

For now, she would focus on finishing the diary, so she could contact him again. She flicked her friends a message.

Need to read the diary tonight, so we can give it to Noah

Paige responded.

Good excuse to deliver it with dinner :)

Joel was quick to reply

LOL. Probably my turn to cook. Pizza?

Jasmine gave the thumbs up. She loved how few words were needed to orchestrate evening plans, even if it did resemble caveman-level communication.

As Jasmine finished for the day, she chatted with Moana, who lit up when she arrived at the work cubicle.

'There's my favourite archivist,' she said, offering Jasmine a bowl of jet plane candy. Jasmine picked a purple one.

'Interesting choice,' said Moana, as if the colour revealed Jasmine's personality. Jasmine wondered if there was a world of food-based personality types she didn't know about.

The two chatted about their day, and Moana showed Jasmine her latest online purchases, which she had delivered to the office to keep them hidden from her husband.

Finally, Jasmine moved to the reason for her visit. 'Moana, I've decided to come to the support group with you. But I won't be able to disclose that I have OCD. It would be too much for me to share.'

Moana hugged Jasmine. 'Yes, please. I'll drive, and you can choose the music,' she joked. But Jasmine knew the lightheartedness was masking the nerves they both felt about the outing.

'It's next week, on Wednesday. We'll leave work a little early if that's okay. I'll get it approved with HR,' Moana added with an exaggerated wink, her grin conspiratorial.

Jasmine couldn't help but laugh.

With their plan set, Jasmine gathered her things and went home. She felt a strange mix of nervousness and resolve about the upcoming meeting. She hoped she wasn't stepping into a tinderbox of other people's obsessions just waiting to ignite hers.

OCD thrives on heightened anxiety, and unpredictability is its favourite fuel.

But Jasmine reminded herself why she needed to do this. If she didn't push back, her world would remain small, confined by the limits her OCD tried to impose.

It was time to stretch those boundaries.

Even if only a little.

***

The three friends gathered around the coffee table in the lounge, plates of leftover pizza and wedges in front of them. Joel leaned back on the beanbag.

'So, Jasmine, how's Mr Handsome Builder doing? Did he enjoy the diaries, or were they too "basic slag" for him?' He laughed, clearly proud of his teasing.

Jasmine couldn't help but smile a little. 'He thought they were fascinating, *actually*.' She casually reached for a wedge, but Paige wasn't about to let her off the hook.

Leaning forward with a grin, Paige said. 'This is a Hallmark movie waiting to happen!'

Jasmine played it cool. 'I just think he's... alright. Fine, more than alright. I mean, he's thoughtful and interested in the diaries, and he brought chocolates.'

'He brought chocolates!' exclaimed Paige, 'Oh, that's serious.'

'Just keep calm,' said Jasmine protesting, 'I don't need you two planning my life with him.'

Joel dramatically clasped his hands together. 'You heard her, Paige. Let's skip the reading and pick out wedding venues.'

Jasmine groaned in protest, but her flushed cheeks betrayed her. Her friends erupted into laughter as she opened the next diary, eager to shift the attention.

26 April 1945

Ben took Rose to the ANZAC Parade yesterday to see returned servicemen and women. It was a proud moment for him. With the war's end so near, there is hope in the air again.

The parade set off from Knox Street church, weaving through town. Rose was captivated, and I'm sure the sight will leave a lasting impression. I stayed home with Thomas and reflected on how many mothers sacrificed their sons for war.

I cannot imagine my heart bearing such a decision. I hope it's one Thomas will never have to make.

I was pleased Ben left the house. It was the first time in a while he had felt like going anywhere, but the excuse to take Rose out won him over.

'That's sounding positive,' said Joel. 'Ben's out and about again.'

'I guess so, but he isn't working. What income are they living on?' expressed Paige with concern.

Jasmine continued.

5 August 1945

It's been a lovely Sabbath today. I attended church with Rose and Thomas, who joined Sunday School. I helped teach the little ones – they're delightful.

At dinner, I was too tired to light the coal range stove, so we had salads and cold meat from a tin. Everyone seemed full afterwards, and we finished with an apple pie I baked from the Muellers' apples.

We miss Ben terribly. Rose cries at the dinner table every night. It seems to be when his absence is noticed most. Thomas is too young to understand, which, in some ways, is a blessing.

Joel sat up straight. 'Ben's dead?!' His voice cracked with disbelief.

Jasmine flipped back a page, scanning for something she had missed. 'I don't think so. That can't be right.' She frowned, trying to recall her research. Ben had been on the latter electoral rolls – he had to be alive.

'So, he left them?' Paige gasped.

'No way,' Joel argued. 'Evie is his lobster.' He mimicked Phoebe from *Friends*, pinching his fingers together.

'Read on, Jaz!' demanded Paige.

25 October 1945

It's been quite a week. Rose has been home sick with chicken pox, and now Thomas is showing symptoms.

I am utterly exhausted, caring for them both day and night. I just need to pour out my thoughts here, where no one can hear them. Apart from prayer, this book is the only place to turn. I never saw myself in this situation. Alone, bringing up the children.

Albert has left home too, at just 16. It's probably for the best, as he was getting into some trouble. I couldn't cope with it on top of everything else. Having two babies in the house hasn't been easy for him.

With so much change and with Ben gone, I guess he felt the need to find his own place in the world.

'Come on, Evie, tell us what happened to Ben,' Joel said with surprising exasperation.

I felt an ache watching him go. It seems like only yesterday he was at my desk, asking for a peppermint. I pray this new chapter will bring him the stability and purpose he seeks. His leaving also means I am without the help I so desperately need. And Ben is still away, for I don't know how long.

'Ahh, he's *away*. Maybe he has a job that requires travelling.' Paige pointed at the ceiling. 'Sorry for doubting you, Ben.'

Joel sighed. 'But Albert leaving at 16? It seems like yesterday to her that he was a child, but it was only a few weeks ago for us, too.'

Jasmine turned the page. 'We're eighteen months ahead, to 1947.'

'Geez, Evie, we could use some consistency here,' Joel grumbled.

2 February 1947
Another wonderful day at church. It is a relief each week to gather with friends and hear the sermons.

After church, we went to the Lilburns' house for lunch. They insisted I rest in their spare room while they minded the children.

I protested at first, but soon succumbed. I slept for three hours. It was much needed. In fact, the entire day was a Balm of Gilead to me.

'A balm of what?' Joel interrupted.

'I'm on it,' Paige said, Googling. 'It's a biblical term meaning relief from suffering or spiritual healing.'

'So, like food for the soul?' Jasmine asked.

'I guess you'd say that – if you were 60,' Joel joked. She threw a cushion at him.

Yesterday was a huge day. The children and I took the early bus to Tokanui for their annual sports day.

The children had a wonderful time chasing balls and cheering on Ben, who reluctantly joined in the egg-and-spoon race. It was all a bit of nonsense, really. Later, he showed us around the gardens he tends. They are vast, but he's done a splendid job.

Joel frowned. 'Sorry to interrupt, but does anyone know what she's talking about?'

'Yeah, I'm confused too,' Paige admitted. 'Why is he working at Tokanui, so far from home?'

'Wait, where is Tokanui?' Joel asked, feeling left out.

Paige slipped into her teacher's voice. 'Tokanui is an old hospital near Te Awamutu. It used to be called a mental hospital, though we wouldn't say that now.'

'Before we called it a mental hospital, it was called a lunatic asylum,' Jasmine added apologetically. 'When I was a kid, people would joke about it, "You must be from Tokanui" – like it was an insult.'

Joel made a face. 'Is it still open?'

'No,' Paige answered. 'It closed in the late 1990s. Thousands of New Zealanders had lived there, some for their entire life. Many died there. There's even a cemetery with about 500 graves, some unmarked.'

'Eww, it sounds a bit morbid. How come you know so much?' Joel asked them both.

'I used to work in a library, and people often came searching for family records.' Jasmine explained. Then she added, 'Honestly, I always feared I might end up there. People were committed for the most benign reasons, including having OCD, being gay, or simply not fitting societal expectations. I even read about a girl who ended up in an asylum because there was no foster care placement for he r.'

'So, this place – Tokanui – Ben's working there as a gardener?'

Jasmine glanced at Joel. 'I'm not sure. I think maybe he has been admitted there. Remember when Evie said he was struggling?'

Joel shot up from the beanbag. 'No, no, no! This news is the second unhappily ever after they've dished me, and I don't want to hear more.'

Jasmine closed the diary. She understood.

Some truths are hard to confront.

'It's okay. We don't have to read more,' Jasmine said. She would never force uncomfortable thoughts on someone.

Paige shook her head. 'Sorry, I need to know what happens. Maybe he comes home next month.'

Joel sighed, covering his ears. 'Fine. But I'm only half-listening.'

Jasmine turned the page.

Ben seems happy where he is, though he does ask if he can come home. I believe it's better for him to stay there. The doctors can help him, and the garden keeps him busy. Still, I miss him terribly, and every time he asks, I doubt myself.

I had a lovely visit from Maple, Clive, and the boys, along with Mum. They came down from Auckland on the train and stayed the night. It reminded me just how nice it would be for Rose and Thomas to have their cousins nearby.

Thomas and Rose are growing so well, though they fight a lot. I don't have the energy to discipline them. Next weekend, the three of us will visit Ben at Tokanui. I know he'll be so pleased to see the children, and hopefully, that will settle them.

'I doubt that,' scoffed Paige, 'not many seven-year-olds are settled by going to a mental hospital.'

8 November 1947
The evenings are getting longer, though it never feels like enough hours in the day.

No matter how early I rise, there's always more to be done than hours to do it in. My sewing machine and knitting needles have sat untouched all year.

The children are still too young to be much help, but they certainly create plenty of work. I make sure they're always clean and well-dressed when we leave the house.

To help ends meet, I've taken on caring for children, and we have another little soul living with us at the moment. It's been an adjustment to waking in the night again, but I've developed a good routine.

'Wow, she sounds exhausted. And she's taking on more children,' Joel interjected, sounding sad. 'No wonder my mum took losers into our home. She probably hoped they would be helpful.'

Jasmine stalled and glanced at Paige. Joel's mum wasn't spoken about often. The conversation was uncharted territory for their friendship.

He looked at them both and laughed, 'What? Do you think I can't talk about my childhood?'

Jasmine shrugged, 'You do seem to avoid it.'

'It's all good. There's not much worth talking about. I felt loved most of the time, and I was fed. I survived.'

Jasmine didn't know what to say. She paused, looking for the right words, wondering if Joel was too confronted by the diary's content.

'Read on,' he said, smiling, 'I don't need to be Doctor Phil-er-ised.'

2 December 1947

Today, something upset me deeply. When Rose fetched the post from the mailbox, she found a note making fun of her and her 'strange' father.

Rose was distraught and didn't understand what was so strange. She tried to guess who had written it, but I told her there was no point. People are entitled to their opinions.

Later, when she was in bed, I burned the note in the coal range and had a quiet cry. Some things are better left unseen by little eyes.

I'm not sure why it bothered me so much. I just imagined that everyone was supportive, not unkind.

The three sat in silence. Joel was the first one to break it with a surprising statement. 'I'm going to message Lucca. I think we should have that second date.'

And with that, he stood up and left the room.

'He's taking it hard,' Paige said, 'It's not as fun when he isn't in Joel mode. So, tell me more about meeting Noah. Joel totally seems to have a crush on him,' Paige said with her teenage voice.

'It's probably just silly, like a fantasy. But he's pretty nice, and I like that he's interested in his past.' Jasmine paused, then added, 'I think the word I would use to describe my feelings is *intrigued.*'

'Hmm, like curious or fascinated. That's a high compliment in my book,' Paige affirmed. 'I see one fault and that is that he doesn't have a best friend or brother to introduce me to.'

'True. Perhaps I'd better find a new diary series to bring home,' Jasmine joked. She then turned serious, 'But what do I do about Medusa? When do I confess.'

Paige made a thoughtful sound, 'You'll know when. But I wouldn't lead with it.'

'I guess so. I first need to convince Noah that I'm cool before I drop that info on him,' Jasmine said, chewing her cheek while she thought about how to portray "cool".

Paige laughed, 'Well, that's going to be tough to convince him of.'

Jasmine reached for a cushion to throw at her friend but she was out of ammunition. Instead, she stuck out her tongue.

'Well, that's mature,' Paige said, flipping the bird as she left the room.

Chapter Fourteen

What if I ended up in an asylum?

It was a lazy Thursday afternoon, with summer rain and sunshine, forcing the friends to lie around the house after work. They played Boggle and Bananagrams, proving Joel's theory that they were prematurely ageing into boring university lecturers. The late afternoon sun streamed through the flat's slightly grubby windows.

Joel was sprawled in his favourite place – the beanbag in the corner, scrolling through his phone, while Paige reclined on the couch, her feet propped up on the armrest, also on her phone. Jasmine was perched cross-legged on the floor, sipping a juice and twirling her hair.

'So,' Paige said, breaking the silence. 'Joel, what's the latest with Lucca? Did you book a second date?'

Joel grinned, setting his phone down. 'I thought you would never ask. We're meeting tomorrow night, and I've strategically chosen a quiet, tucked-away bar. The fewer utes, the better.'

Jasmine nodded. 'Smart.'

'I just want one drama-free date,' Joel said dramatically. 'Is that too much to ask?'

'I mean, you do have a flair for the theatrical,' Paige teased.

'Ha, ha,' Joel said sarcastically. 'What would *you* do if someone yelled at *you* from a car?'

'Depends,' Paige said, tapping her chin thoughtfully. 'Am I holding a smoothie or a brick?'

Jasmine nearly choked on her drink, laughing.

Joel continued with his news. 'I'm glad I messaged him. I know that it's silly that a note in the mailbox 80 years ago pushed me to do it. But really, have people always been so mean?' Joel asked rhetorically.

Jasmine wanted to answer the question, whether he expected an answer or not.

'I've always told myself that the world needs people on the fringes to keep it balanced. Once they make it through the hard years, they become amazing people who change the world.'

'If they survive childhood first,' Joel said. 'I was just so bummed about that note, I couldn't sleep that night, actuals!'

Jasmine nodded. 'You just want everyone to be happy.'

'And I can't even tell myself, "it's not real" like I tell myself when I watch MAFS,' he joked.

'Come on!' Paige interjected. 'We all know you think MAFS is real.'

Joel giggled infectiously. 'Yeah, I do.'

Jasmine asked, 'Do you want to keep reading? It's the last diary, so we'll find out the ending soon.'

'Yep. I need to support Ben. Even if it's 80 years too late,' Joel said.

Jasmine smiled as they settled in, the diary lying open between them.

She began where they had last ended.

21 December 1947

We visited Ben today to wish him a Merry Christmas. He seems to have deteriorated.

I don't know if it's his condition worsening or if he's simply pining for home. He misses the children terribly and has taken to writing poems and drawing pictures for them. It breaks my heart to think of him alone at Christmas.

This will be our third Christmas apart, and though you'd think I'd be used to it by now, it remains the most challenging day of the year. This year, we'll spend it at Maple's in Auckland for a little distraction.

Jasmine paused, waiting for comment, but none came. She turned the page, announcing, 'The next entry is June 1948'.

'Oh, no Christmas news? She always gives us a Christmas recap,' Joel said, showing his listening skills had caught every detail.

It's been so long between entries that I wonder what the point is of writing in these diaries. I will keep trying, just in case Rose or Thomas wants to know more about their childhood.

'Or if Joel, Jasmine and Paige treat you as an influencer,' Joel added, speaking of himself and the others in the third person.

But, at the rate I am writing, they won't gain much insight. Ben is still away from us. I hoped we would see some progress from the electric shock treatments, but they don't seem to have made a difference. I can't help but wonder if it's doing more harm than good.

Joel gasped. 'Electric shock therapy! Do you know that gay people *literally* used to receive EST as part of 'gay conversion'? And back then, they didn't put them under general anaesthetic.'

The three looked at each other, no one knowing what to say or how to console.

'Drink, anyone?' asked Paige, and they all started laughing to relieve the tension.

'Yes, please. I deserve it,' said Joel. Then he added quietly, 'Actually, *I've* never been sent away to a mental institution so I shouldn't complain.'

'Let's change the topic,' said Paige, standing up to grab the drinks.

'No, I'm invested now; let's keep reading. Drinks can wait,' said Joel in an uncharacteristic tone.

12 September 1948
After three years at Tokanui, Ben has been moved to Kingseat Hospital in Pukekohe.

'Oh, I know that place,' offered Joel. 'It's an old asylum that has been turned into Spookers, the scream park. I've been on a scary date there, although the scariest part was that the guy showed up in Crocs and socks.'

Jasmine laughed, grateful to see Joel's commentary was back on track.

The shift from Tokanui feels like progress. Perhaps a change in environment might give him confidence that things are improving. He told me about the flowers he's helping to plant in the hospital garden and how much he enjoys being outside; although he is very suspicious of the doctors and thinks they are trying to poison him.

'I wonder if he lost their trust with the EST,' Joel said. 'It would be hard to trust people after that.'

The three friends read through the next few years. Evie wrote about school progress for the children and moments with her sister and mother. She mentioned Ben less; her new normal being accepted. Jasmine read quickly, desperate to reach a spot where the news would reverse. She noticed the diary was nearing the end, with the dates now in 1950. Five years had passed since he had gone, and it looked like Ben was being removed from their lives.

20 November 1950
Ben has moved out of the hospital and is in the care of his sister in Auckland. I don't know how to feel about it.

I am pleased for him, but little has changed during the past five years. But I must not dwell on that. We are resigned to our lot in life.

I must consider that eventually, he might come home. I am quite nervous about the idea. We are so used to having him gone now. Unfortunately, the children will never know the father he was to be, although he is still kind and gentle.

'She's torn,' Paige said softly, wiping a tear from her eye. 'She wants him back but is scared of what that actually means for their family.'

'Sometimes, it is better on your own,' Joel added. 'I mean, I'm in Ben's court and want to see him happy, but he's not the man she married. I couldn't blame her for choosing herself and the kids.'

Jasmine continued. The end of the diary was just pages away.

30 December 1950

I must write about our Christmas Day. It was one of the best ones we have had in a while.

Rose, Thomas, and I travelled to Auckland to spend the day with Maple and Clive, and Ben joined us at their house. I was so worried. It would be the first time in years that the children had seen him outside the hospital. I didn't know how they would respond. Maple and Clive were terrific hosts, providing all the Christmas trimmings. But more than anything, I was relieved that Ben could experience Christmas in a home instead of a hospital.

His sister helped him choose gifts for the children. He gave them a pair of plastic toy chickens that lay eggs. They spent hours playing, laughing uncontrollably.

I don't know if it was because the toy was so amusing or because it was the first gift they had received from their father. Ben seemed comforted by their laughter, though I could tell it overwhelmed him at times. I am uncertain if we could cope with him at home.

'Ouch, that doesn't sound good,' Paige said, inhaling. 'Joel, just prepare yourself for your not-perfect ending.'

'Mental health struggles can do that to you; it can squash love and hope,' Jasmine said with genuine sadness.

3 March 1951
Ben has returned home.

'Gasp,' Joel said, 'I didn't think I would live to see the day.' He jumped up and clapped his hands. 'Read on!'

He prefers to keep to himself, living in his room. It's a relief to have him here, just to have security around.

However, I find myself caring for him much like I do for the children. I make sure he eats properly, rests, and takes care of himself.

I have realised that when I married, I promised to stay beside him, "for richer or poorer, in sickness and in health and for better or for worse." I fear I was dealt the poorer, the sickness and the worst. But it's a promise I will keep.

Jasmine stopped. 'I'm sorry to say, that's the end of the diary. It's just copies of Ben's poems and the pictures remaining.'

'What, no more Ben and Evie, but what happens next? I need my happily ever after.' Joel said firmly. 'And how am I going to make important decisions like when to go on a second date with a loose canon?' he asked.

'I'm not sure the diaries ever gave you that message,' Paige pointed out.

'You know what I mean.' Joel said, adding, 'I feel like I did after watching La La Land – distraught after such a long emotional investment.'

'I wonder if we can find out more from Noah about what happened next?' Jasmine suggested.

Paige giggled, 'Start making a list of all the reasons to contact him.'

'Do you think he knows about Tokanui and stuff? I'm guessing he did but didn't mention it.' Joel said.

Jasmine also wondered if Noah knew about his grandfather's mental health. Surely. But she thought it was strange that he hadn't referenced it.

Later, as the night wound down and the house grew quiet, Jasmine slipped into bed with the diary. It was time to read Ben's poems and examine the pictures he had drawn. She hoped for some final insight they might give her.

She carefully turned the pages, each one holding precious content. Jasmine felt as though she were handling something sacred, something profoundly unique.

These were the writings of a man confined to an institution, separated from his beloved family. Each page revealed the thoughts and emotions of a father who adored his children and longed to be with them.

The drawings were simple yet heartfelt, including boats, horses, dogs, ducks, and flowers, all coloured in with paint or coloured pencil. Each picture was inscribed with Ben's handwriting: "Love to my little son Thomas. From Daddy" or "Love to Rose, from Daddy".

One particular drawing showed a grey and unwelcoming hospital building with a clock tower and a flag. Jasmine snapped a photo to enlarge the image on her phone. This art was Ben's perception of his surroundings, a place of confinement. Another drawing depicted a duck with a nurse's hat holding a tag in its beak that read "Mental Nurse". Jasmine wondered about his intent. Was he calling them 'quacks', or did he simply enjoy drawing ducks?

Then, she began reading the poems.

Thomas's horse's name is Ned
He's better when he's fed
Gallops smartly every day
Taking Thomas on his way
He likes a box of nice bright
chaff
And almost seems to laugh
When he finds some extra juicy

oats
And through the air he floats
Then he gallops freely on
O'er the journey long
And swings along from mile to
mile
You can almost see him smile
He likes to run along the track
With Thomas on his back

Love to Thomas, from Daddy
X

The poem oozed love for his son. Jasmine felt sad that Ben was in that place.

She continued reading his poems.

To my wife
Heart of purest, richest, gold
Self forgotten in deeds untold
Stayed by that consistent love
Goal reached at last for which
you strove

Jasmine's frustration bubbled up as she read. Ben's eloquence poured from the pages, his intelligence and devotion to Evie undeniable.

How could someone like him have been sent away, locked up?

The thought crept into her mind: what if that had been her fate? Left alone to ruminate, subjected to electric shock therapy for her obsessions? The idea made her stomach churn, but she kept reading to honour Ben.

Life, like an ever-rolling
stream
Moves onward to the sea
And looking backwards
it would seem
That it was meant to be...
Sometimes it's tears
One moment's time we cannot
know
Destiny's next move
Her whims and forays

With ours her fingers inter-
wove and sidelong, glances of
her majestic head
Prelude? We know not what
perhaps its blossoms red
Perhaps a cold full stop

The words struck her: *Looking backwards, it would seem that it was meant to be.* Ben's acceptance of life's cruel whims carried a kind of dignity that she couldn't help but admire.

But she didn't like the sound of *destiny's next move*, as if "she" was playing a strategic game that only destiny could win. Her *whims and forays* taking unexpected paths, *her majestic head* taking control, like Medusa.

She shivered at the mention of *a cold full stop*. Was that death? Or was it Tokanui?

She continued, finding each verse giving her more insight into the mind of a clever man. The same man they had grown to love in the diaries.

His next poem was undeniably for Evie. Jasmine's heart ached as she read lines that radiated devotion.

To womanhood, next to the Di-
vine
Your love would follow to the
gallows tree
Knows no boundary, no dis-
tance line

No thought paltry mean or
wee

I've cursed the fate which
brought me here
And bitter have been my exile
vows
But through it all I hold still
dear
Soft memories which invade
me now

Ben, the exile, cursing the fate that brought him to this place. He felt her love even from a distance, through *vibrations floating there.*

She closed her eyes for a moment, the weight of his longing for home and Evie moving her. Overwhelmed, Jasmine wiped a tear from her cheek. Was she crying for Ben, for Evie, or herself?

One thing was sure: it gave her renewed determination to beat OCD. If Ben could endure years in a mental institution, she could face the soft couch in her psychologist's office.

Grabbing her phone, she emailed Dr Kris: *I'm ready to progress.*

Chapter Fifteen

What if I said something offensive?

Jasmine slept in the next day, waking to her second backup alarm. The night's readings had exhausted her, and she felt uninspired to go to work.

She picked up her phone to check the weather, not that she needed confirmation of the heat she could already feel, but to see just *how* hot it would be. To her surprise, there was a message from Noah on her phone.

> Thanks for the addresses of the places Ben lived. I drove by them yesterday. Surprised to find I did a renovation on one of them a few years ago. Classic.

Jasmine grinned and replied.

> That's cool! Hey, we finished the final diary last night, so you're welcome to collect it next time you're passing.

She tried to make it sound casual. She lay in bed, watching the three dots moving on her screen. She knew she should be moving too, off the bed and into the shower, but couldn't pull herself away.

> Cool. How about we go to dinner tonight? I'll get it from you then.

Jasmine's stomach flipped. Was this her come-to-church moment? She was excited but instantly faced with a dilemma. What if she agreed to dinner, and he suggested eating on the east side?

Medusa wasted no time inserting herself into plans.

Jasmine quickly outsmarted her.

Sounds good. Let's meet in town and find something there. I can come from work.

She thought it sounded reasonable, nothing suspicious or overly planned.

Great. See you at 5.30? Hood Street?

See you there.

Her initial reluctance about the day vanished, and she leapt out of bed and into the shower. She carefully chose an outfit that would work for both a date and the office. She packed a small makeup kit with a toothbrush and toothpaste, ready to refresh herself at the end of the workday.

As she passed Paige's room, she saw her still in bed, clearly making the most of her dwindling holiday break.

'Hi ya, I'm off to work, but FYI, I won't be home for dinner,' Jasmine told her.

Paige raised her head slightly. 'Cool. Have you got that support group thing?'

'No, that's next week,' Jasmine replied, drawing out her response and teasing Paige into further questioning.

'Right. Do you have counselling?'

'No, but I'll do that next week too,' Jasmine said, suddenly realising how full her next week was becoming.

'Okay, so are you on a secret spy mission or something?' Paige asked, her curiosity piqued.

Jasmine hesitated momentarily before finally confessing, 'I think I might have a date. I'm meeting Noah after work to give him the last diary.'

Paige's face lit up. She gave a thumbs up, smiling knowingly. 'Cool. You better tell Joel at work, or he'll be dark about missing this news.'

Jasmine laughed and headed out the door, suddenly feeling like her day held endless possibilities.

Her day at work passed swiftly. She had a couple of large projects that helped occupy her time. She noticed she glanced at her phone more often than usual, checking the time or reliving the conversation thread with Noah.

Jasmine and Joel were just about to step outside at lunchtime when rain appeared for a tropical-like downpour.

'Damn, we'll have to be social in the staffroom,' Joel said, holding his packed lunch, which he had uncharacteristically managed to prepare.

'It's all good,' Jasmine said positively, 'Moana might be there, and we can have some fun conversations, like why we should ban the letters G and K from the alphabet,' reflecting on the previous lunch convo the three had.

The pair went to the staffroom and spotted a vacant table in the corner. They smiled politely at the others in the room before sitting by themselves. Joel darted his eyes toward the neighbouring table, hoping Jasmine would follow his gaze and mouthed, 'There's Mastercard'.

Jasmine remembered Joel's codename for Felicity, who was so busy talking that she overlooked the two of them there. The friends sat and listened to the neighbouring conversation, entertained by in-house gossip and work insights.

Brian from accounts entered the room with his lunch bag filled to the brim. Brian was always good for lunchtime chats; he loved movies, and he and Joel could spend an hour together easily.

Jasmine smiled at Brian to invite him to their table. He nodded and pointed to the sink, where he stopped to fill his water bottle. While waiting for Brian to join their table, Jasmine and Joel overheard Felicity's conversation.

'Oh, there's Brian,' she said with a slight scoffing tone, 'what's he wearing?'

Jasmine peered past Felicity to see Brian wearing nothing significant, just a suit pants and a light-pink shirt.

'It's a bit gay,' Felicity said, laughing and looking for a response from the others at her table.

Jasmine saw Joel's face redden and his teeth clench. She shook her head at him as a warning not to react.

Brian made his way to their table, and Jasmine warmly welcomed him, chatting about his family and the holidays. Felicity's voice groaned in the background, and Jasmine tried to block it out.

Finally, Felicity stood, preparing to leave. She stretched and then announced, 'Look at the crooked painting,' pointing at the framed art on the wall. 'My OCD can't cope with that.'

Jasmine rolled her eyes as Felicity walked over and straightened the frame. From the corner of her eye, Jasmine saw Joel leap out of his chair, making a loud noise on the linoleum as he did, causing her to jump.

'Felicity,' he said calmly but firmly, 'did straightening that picture make you feel good?'

'Yes,' she answered proudly.

'Well, just so you know, *that* isn't OCD. So, don't go throwing that label around. OCD would never make you feel good.'

Jasmine felt her face go red. No one would know he was defending her, but she felt like she was in the spotlight.

Felicity feigned a laugh. 'Well, it's good to have everything straight,' she said.

'I bet you would like *everyone* straight,' Joel said, moving on to the other insult he had heard.

Felicity looked confused.

Joel picked up his lunchbox as dramatically as he could and announced loudly to the room.

'Nice seeing you, Brian. I love that shirt, by the way. It really suits you.'

Looking confused but proud, Brian answered, 'Thanks, my wife chose it. Initially, I wasn't sure about it, but it has grown on me.'

'Well, tell your wife that she has style.' And then Joel stormed out of the room.

Jasmine smiled awkwardly, muttering something about needing to be at her desk. She farewelled Brian and exited the room.

Outside in the corridor, Joel was waiting with his fist in his mouth.

'That felt so good,' he said, 'what shall we do next? Shall we let the air out of Felicity's tyres?' he asked.

'Um, no. I think you deflated her with your words.' Jasmine replied, glancing back into the staff room where Felicity still looked confused.

'Good. I hope she learned something.'

'I think she's unsure what she learned,' Jasmine laughed. 'But thanks for defending me. I loved it.'

Joel beamed. 'I loved it, too. I think I'm unleashing a new me.'

***

By mid-afternoon, Jasmine had completed more than she'd planned, leaving her a small window of time to freshen up before leaving the dungeon. She ducked into the staff bathroom with her bag, quickly reapplying makeup and tidying her hair. She studied her reflection, second-guessing her outfit for a moment before reminding herself that it wasn't a full-fledged date but dinner and a diary handover. That's all.

She grabbed her things and the final diary and headed out. The warm air hit her as she emerged from the Council building, making her thankful for her light top while hoping her make-up didn't melt. Hood Street wasn't far, and as she walked, she rehearsed casual conversation starters in her head.

Her nerves simmered beneath the surface, but she reminded herself to breathe. It's just dinner. Nothing more.

She felt a little steadier when she reached the meeting spot. She spotted Noah waiting near a bar. He waved when he saw her, and she felt the tiniest flutter in her chest. Was it her imagination, or did Noah look a bit nervous? She noticed him wipe his hand on his jeans and briefly worried he might be planning to shake her hand again. Thankfully, he didn't.

'You look nice,' he said.

Strong start, Jasmine thought, suppressing a smile. She could practically hear Joel chiming in her head with approval.

Not wanting to fall into a clichéd conversation about the weather or her walk from work, she launched straight into a solid, open question. 'How was your day?'

'Pretty good, thanks. It's kind of quiet at the moment. Many contractors are still on holiday. Once they're in, work will ramp up as we catch up and make the most of the good weather.'

'Where are you working at the moment?' she asked, genuinely curious.

'I'm right here in town, working on a commercial building. Which is why it's been easy to pop in,' he said, gesturing casually.

Jasmine thought about his response. Was he saying the only reason he'd been stopping by was because he was working nearby? Reading too much into a situation was a Medusa trick. She mentally reined herself in. For now, it was just a pleasant dinner with someone who seemed genuinely kind, and that was enough.

The conversation over dinner flowed easily. Noah wanted to know about Jasmine – where she went to school, how she got into archival work and what her family was like. She discovered he grew up in Hamilton, attended Hamilton Boys' High School, and became an apprentice builder. He openly shared about his marriage ending.

'Yeah, it was pretty tough when my wife left. It turned out I liked her more than she liked me – or rather, she liked my workmate more than she liked me. So, when it all ended, I had to leave my job too. It ended up being for the best, though, because I started my own company. The girls, though – they're great.'

Jasmine was impressed by how easily he spoke at length. There was no awkwardness, no stunted personality. He could connect. She felt comfortable asking questions, and when he mentioned his daughters, she asked about their interests and school.

'You'll have to meet them,' he added. 'Then you can see the house at the same time.'

Jasmine had about five thoughts at once: Is that a second date? How will I ever visit the house? Would his girls like me? I should pull the pin now. What would he think of Medusa? She managed an awkward, 'That would be great.' She noticed he observed her hesitation.

'No pressure. If you want to see the house, I think you'd like it. But yeah, no pressure,' he said, fumbling a bit.

Jasmine reached out and touched his hand. 'Thanks, I really would like that.'

She knew it was genuine. She would like to visit his home, meet his kids, and see him again. For now, the other questions could wait. Medusa could take a backseat for this dinner; Jasmine would deal with her later.

Noah seemed encouraged by her response. 'Shall we walk?' he asked. 'Back to your car?' Then he added, 'I'll just pay the bill.'

'I'll join you,' Jasmine said, pushing out her chair.

'No, I want to pay for this. It's *my* thank you,' Noah insisted.

As he walked to the bar to pay, Jasmine allowed herself to watch him. *It really is a date if he's paying*, she thought.

Don't get ahead of yourself, Jasmine, Medusa said.

As they strolled the street, Jasmine noticed Noah wasn't in a hurry, perhaps even taking his time. Her mind raced: *What will he do when we arrive at the car? Hug? High-five? Shake hands? Fist-pump?*

She smiled at the ridiculous thought of a fist pump.

'I'm surprised we didn't talk about Ben and Evie much. I thought we would,' Noah said.

'Well, I'm trying not to give any spoilers, although you probably know most of what's going to happen,' she replied.

'I don't know much about my Grandad. My dad never talked about him. But reading these diaries is making me question that. I should have asked more.'

Jasmine felt a sinking sensation. Noah didn't know about Tokanui. Should she tell him?

'The diary I gave you tonight is quite insightful. I think you'll learn a lot from that,' she said carefully.

'Once I finish it, we'll have a debrief?' he asked.

There it was – a definite let's do this again.

'Yes, that would be great. Well, this is me,' she said, pointing to her car.

'Oh, that was fast,' he said, clearly disappointed.

'So, you'll let me know when you're ready for the debrief?' she asked.

'Yes. Soon, hopefully.'

'Thanks for tonight,' she said, trying to convey her sincerity. 'I enjoyed your company.'

'Thank you. This surprise meeting has been a great start to the year,' he said, leaning in for a hug.

Jasmine's mind went into overdrive. He's going for the hug. Wait, he's going left – no, right. Jasmine awkwardly adjusted her arms to meet his, but as they closed the gap, she realised he was moving in for a kiss on the cheek. She quickly adjusted her head, but in the shuffle, their mouths brushed awkwardly.

'Oh,' she said, embarrassed. 'That was strange.'

'I hope that doesn't count as a first kiss,' he laughed. 'It was pretty amateur.'

Jasmine smiled, liking the sound of where he was heading. 'I don't think it counts. More of a hug-kiss,' she joked.

'Would you like to try again?' he asked sheepishly.

'I would,' she replied, stepping onto her tiptoes to meet him. As their lips met, a wave of disbelief swept through her. Here she was, kissing the very handsome grandson of Evie and Ben.

The kiss was soft, warm, and unhurried. As far as first kisses go, it felt perfect, though she kept that thought to herself.

'I wasn't expecting that,' she said, slightly breathless.

'I wasn't planning that... well, maybe I was. But not tonight,' he admitted sheepishly.

'Well, this time I'm going – and I'll hear from you soon,' Jasmine rushed in response.

Without thinking, she raised her hand for a high-five.

He paused, amused, then gave her one back.

'Honestly, I thought this night might end with a fist pump or a high-five,' she said with a grin. 'Just wanted to see it through.'

He laughed – clearly, she'd won him over.

As she drove home, she shook her head at portions of her conversation and the high-five.

It was a speciality of people with OCD to overanalyse conversations. The 'what ifs' could be applied to any situation, literally, as Joel would say.

As she came into her house, she was surprised to see Paige standing there at the door, smiling with her hands behind her back.

'Guess what I'm holding?' Paige asked.

'Um, a knife?' she said, joking while realising it was the first thing that came to her mind.

'Haha, no. A letter.' Paige presented Jasmine with an envelope with a child's handwriting on it and colourful love hearts on the back. 'From your nieces!' Paige added, just in case Jasmine hadn't guessed.

'Ooh, I'm so excited,' Jasmine said, dumping her bag and sitting down to savour the moment.

She carefully opened the envelope and brought out the pieces of paper. There were two notes from the girls telling her about their holiday and a hand-drawn picture of themselves eating real fruit ice cream at the strawberry farm.

'So that's how they spent their $5,' Jasmine said, 'I approve!'

She turned the pages around, looking for a hint of any extra information. 'This is so fun. I'm going to reply tonight,' she added, kicking off her shoes.

'So, the date?' Paige asked.

Jasmine smiled, 'Let me tell you all about it,' she said with a grin.

The two friends got comfy while Jasmine happily shared the tea – every last detail.

Chapter Sixteen

What if I need to keep my urine?

The rest of the week slipped by with the usual rhythm. Her date with Noah played on her mind, and they were now regularly texting. Jasmine noticed Noah hadn't mentioned starting the new diary. She resisted the urge to press him on it, knowing the entry about Tokanui loomed like a shadow in the pages, and she didn't know if she wanted to be present when he read it.

The day of the support group visit arrived. Jasmine told Noah she had a work 'thing' in Auckland and would be out of contact for the night. She closed the dungeon early and made her way up to Moana's cubicle. Moana enthusiastically greeted her, 'Here's my rock, Jazz-a-dazz.'

Jasmine smiled back, hoping her nerves weren't too noticeable. 'Of course. It'll be good for both of us.'

Moana nodded, 'I'm glad you're coming. I already feel better knowing I won't be walking in alone.'

As they left the city, they soon found themselves in the green expanses of Waikato farmland, with its neatly divided paddocks. Jasmine watched the scenery blur by as Moana skillfully navigated the expressway.

The smell of coffee hung in the air of the car, from their travel mugs that Moana had tucked in the cup holders. She had also packed a little food bag of goodies to snack on during the ninety-minute car trip.

'So,' Moana began, 'tell me everything you know about OCD. I've read lots, but coming from you, it makes so much more sense. You don't speak in all the medical jargon.'

'That's a hard one. There are layers of things I don't understand. Whenever I read about someone else, I am amazed at how OCD can impact people differently. It seems that no two obsessions are exactly the same.'

'Hmm, start with the obsessions; tell me more about them.'

'Okay, but stop me if it's too much or too hard.' Jasmine went into teacher mode.

'When I was first diagnosed, I was told there were four types of OCD: Checking, Contamination, Symmetry, and Ruminations. But now, just thirteen years later, we know so much more. It's recognised that Relationship OCD, Religious OCD, and Mental Contamination are all categories.'

Moana made the right noises of someone who was paying attention and learning, giving Jasmine confidence to continue.

'People have intrusive thoughts around Harm OCD, Paedophilia OCD, or Hoarding. There's research now that eating disorders can be linked with OCD.'

'A-ha, a-ha,' said Moana, nodding. 'And someone with OCD has one of those areas, like Caleb, who probably falls under contamination?'

'Well, most people who have OCD can adopt obsessions in multiple areas. It kind of leeches onto as many areas as it can,' Jasmine said, fiddling with the corner of her top.

'I used to have Moral OCD and Contamination OCD. Both are in remission at the moment. But if they start to creep back, I'll need to take control quickly.'

Moana nodded, her expression softening. 'Oh, that's disappointing. But you said you're in remission, so... does that mean it can go away?'

'The intrusive thoughts can diminish,' Jasmine said. 'I guess it kind of lives there, hard-wired into the brain. But yeah, sometimes the symptoms lessen or go away. Usually with a lot of effort.'

She paused and then added honestly, 'Sometimes, the effort is too great and it's easier to live with the compulsions.'

She could see that Moana was disheartened, which hadn't been Jasmine's intention.

'Yeah, I get that,' Moana said, thoughtfully. 'And you already explained treatment, so can I know more about some of these categories? Maybe Caleb has more than one, and I don't even realise it.'

Jasmine smiled. 'That's an observant thought. *He* might not realise it either because it'll just feel like that is how his brain works. There have been a lot of decisions in my life that I didn't realise were driven by OCD.'

As they made their way along the expressway, Jasmine shifted in her seat, adjusting the air vent to blow directly onto her face. The brief pause in conversation was welcome. The discussion was more confronting than she'd expected.

She stole a glance at Moana. Her hands were firm on the wheel, eyes locked on the road ahead, but her jaw was tight. The conversation weighed on her, too.

Outside, clusters of sheep grazed lazily near the roadside, their woolly bodies dotted across expansive, uneven paddocks. Jasmine watched them in silence. They looked peaceful, chewing methodically, unmoved by the cars speeding past.

'So,' Moana said, her voice soft but steady, 'tell me about Moral OCD, the one you used to have? I've never heard of it.'

Jasmine dug deep. That time was a part of her life she had happily left behind. She hoped Medusa's snakes were asleep. She didn't want to give them airtime.

'Moral OCD, or Scrupulosity,' she began, 'is like living with a courtroom in your head 24/7, and you're both the judge and the defendant. Every action, every thought, gets scrutinised to the extreme. I'd worry endlessly about things like whether I'd told a lie or if I'd offended someone unintentionally.'

Moana nodded, her expression a mixture of sympathy and curiosity. 'That would be exhausting. How did you deal with that? I mean, it sounds impossible to escape.'

'It wasn't easy,' Jasmine admitted. 'It took therapy, understanding, and lots of time away from school.'

Moana fidgeted in her seat, perhaps uncomfortably with the conversation, thinking about her son. 'Did I hear you say the word 'paedophile'?' Moana asked with trepidation.

Jasmine softly continued, 'Paedophilia OCD, or POCD, is one of the most misunderstood and heartbreaking types of OCD. It's not about someone wanting to harm children – it's the exact opposite. It's when intrusive thoughts pop into someone's head telling them that they *might* be a paedophile. These thoughts go against everything the person values. It is very upsetting.'

Jasmine looked at Moana and could see tears rolling down her face. 'Oh, how would I ever know if Caleb had those thoughts, and what would I think?'

Jasmine reached out and touched Moana's arm to offer comfort. 'Just remember, OCD can take things that someone values and turn them upside down. If Caleb ever had those thoughts, you know that he must have very high values. OCD messes with what is important.'

'I guess I'll carefully cross that bridge if I need to,' resolved Moana.

Jasmine laughed internally at the irony. If only Moana knew that crossing a bridge was the last idiom Jasmine would use.

Jasmine offered reassurance. 'Just remember, OCD preys on what someone cares about most, and it's not a reflection of their true intentions or character.'

'So are you saying that because you had Moral OCD, you find cheating or lying bad?'

'I do. I never want to be associated with those things,' Jasmine admitted earnestly.

Moana took a deep breath as they approached Auckland, the crisscrossing lanes of the spaghetti junction weaving before them.

'Okay, final lesson. Tell me about hoarding. Am I bad for actually finding that one interesting?' Moana asked, lightening the mood.

Jasmine smiled, grateful for the shift in tone.

'Some people with OCD hoard compulsively as part of their anxiety. It's not just collecting or refusing to throw things away; it's often driven by a deep fear or emotional attachment to those items.'

'Right, I can see that would be reasonable,' Moana said, showing that she was listening.

'Someone might believe they have a moral obligation to keep something, or worry that discarding it could cause harm,' Jasmine carefully explained.

'I once read about someone who kept jars of urine because the idea of throwing them away caused unbearable distress. Now, researchers have also identified Hoarding Disorder as a separate diagnosis. It overlaps in some ways but is distinct from OCD.'

Moana nodded slowly. 'So, it's not just being oblivious to messiness?'

'No' Jasmine confirmed. 'It's driven by fear. Most hoarders are fully aware of the chaos. It's incredibly hard for them to let go of things without feeling intense distress.'

'It's so much more complicated than I ever knew, I have a lot to learn,' Moana said.

The car slowed as she took the off-ramp and navigated toward the building where the support group meeting was held. Jasmine glanced out the window at the small community building. It was just as she imagined: out of the way and needing some TLC.

Moana parked and turned to Jasmine with a shaky but determined smile. 'Well, here we go,' she said, gripping the steering wheel momentarily before releasing it.

Jasmine patted her arm. 'Thanks for bringing me,' she said – and she genuinely meant it.

***

The room was bright but unassuming, with neutral walls and worn carpet. Stackable chairs were arranged in a semicircle, the kind of seating that encouraged interaction but left just enough space for personal boundaries. Jasmine quickly scanned the room. A few parents were already seated, their expressions a mix of friendliness and uncertainty.

Jasmine felt a sudden pang of self-awareness. She hadn't been in a group setting like this before, especially where she needed to blend in. What if they asked her parenting questions? She smiled at those in the room, trying to project calm confidence. Moana, by contrast, had an air of determination like she belonged.

'I guess we're the new couple,' Moana whispered, leaning into Jasmine with a wink. 'Do we look the part?'

Jasmine stifled a laugh, whispering back, 'If I were to have a wife, you would be my first choice.'

Moana giggled, 'I always love a fun comment from Jazz-a-dazz.'

The humour settled Jasmine slightly. As they chose seats near the middle of the semicircle, she tried not to overthink the reasons she was there. Everyone had their reason for coming, and no one seemed poised to interrogate them. For now, she was just one of them: another face in the semi-circle, ready to listen, learn, and quietly support.

The coordinator, Anita, had a calming presence and a voice that struck just the right balance of authority and compassion. She welcomed everyone warmly, outlined the evening's format, and gently broke the ice before handing over to Dr Carter, a psychologist specialising in OCD.

Dr Carter looked young, and Jasmine marvelled at how confidently and clearly she addressed the group.

She began with an analogy that she had read.

'Imagine two boys at a lake, skimming rocks. One picks up a rock, glances at it, and tosses it across the water. The other picks up a rock, examines it closely, and decides it might be gold. He pockets it, convinced it has value. He repeats this over and over – sometimes skimming, sometimes saving.

'By the end of the day, one boy has spent carefree hours skimming stones, while the other is weighed down by a pocket full of worthless rocks.'

She paused, letting the image settle. 'These are the daily decisions your children face when a thought enters their mind. Do they toss it away? Or do they hold onto it, examine it too closely, assign it value, and carry it with them – allowing it to weigh them down?'

The room was silent as people nodded.

Dr Carter continued, outlining treatment options with an encouraging and realistic tone. Jasmine nodded along, the concepts familiar to her.

Dr Carter emphasised the value of information, urging parents to learn all they could about OCD to support their children better.

As she spoke, Jasmine noticed Moana glancing her way as if reassured by the validation of Jasmine's earlier explanations.

When Anita invited the group to share, the stories began cautiously but soon flowed more freely as the room warmed with solidarity.

One mother described her daughter's debilitating contamination fears, changing clothes endlessly, washing them repeatedly, and refusing visitors in their home. Another parent recounted a son's nightly checking of the doors and windows to ensure their safety. A couple shared their struggles with their teenager's need for constant reassurance about catastrophic scenarios that played endlessly in her mind.

Jasmine knew that 'what if' game all too well.

Jasmine's heart felt torn as she heard about a boy whose hoarding tendencies had rendered his room inaccessible and a child who suffered from Scrupulosity so badly that he had to be home-schooled.

Others offered glimmers of hope, parents celebrating small victories like a child going to school after being absent and another family who made a well-planned skating outing where their child used the hired boots.

Jasmine recognised pieces of herself in their stories, but more than that, she saw the quiet heroism of these parents and their children. Despite the worry, they were here, searching for answers.

Jasmine felt like a fraud, sitting in the room, keeping her own stories and successes to herself. The more she listened, the more she wanted to help. As the evening was about to close, she stood abruptly while raising her hand.

'I just want to say how impressed I am with all of you and how dedicated you are to helping your children.' Beside her, she felt Moana shift in her seat, likely wondering where this was going. Jasmine hesitated but pressed on.

'This is hard for me to share, but since I probably won't see any of you again, and what is said in this room stays in this room, I want you to know that I have OCD.'

A ripple of nods and quiet smiles met her words. Encouraged, she continued.

'When I was 15, my parents bought me a kitten. I had wanted one for so long, and OCD had just started to take hold of my life. I think they thought it would be a good distraction.' She looked around the room, trying not to stare at any one person for too long. 'The day they brought that kitten home was incredible. I had never felt so happy.'

She smiled and continued. 'But then, OCD hijacked the situation. It seems that the bigger the emotion, the bigger the OCD response. By the end of that day, I was convinced it was a mistake. I worried it would be run over and devastate us all.' Her voice dipped. 'So I asked my parents to take it away.'

A few people made understanding noises, encouraging her to continue.

Jasmine continued, 'But they didn't. Instead, they got advice. They refused to return the cat and reminded me, over and over, that those thoughts weren't my thoughts. They were OCD's thoughts.'

She saw people jotting notes and prompting her to continue. 'From then on, we learned that whenever we had a day filled with big emotions, we had to prepare for it and anticipate an OCD spike.' Jasmine glanced around the room, meeting the gaze of parents who had spent so many sleepless nights worrying over their children. She offered them a small, reassuring smile.

'And I'm sharing, well, I don't know why I'm sharing,' she giggled nervously, 'but I know your kids will be some of the most resourceful, creative, strong, and determined problem-solvers you'll ever meet. They overcome challenges that most people can't even imagine. And they should be celebrated.'

She exhaled and sat back down. 'Thank you.' Her voice faltered as she finished, wondering if any of it had made sense.

A member of the group raised her hand to comment. 'Thanks, I needed to hear that. Can I ask, how did you feel about the cat?'

'Oh,' Jasmine said, realising she had missed a key part of the story. 'After a few months, I moved on to a new obsession, with my cat,' she said, laughing at herself. 'The cat slept on my bed every night until I left home. We loved each other.'

As the meeting ended, parents surrounded Jasmine with questions. They wanted to know what had worked for her, how old she had been when she first noticed symptoms, if she had a good counsellor, and how long it would take for their children to improve. Jasmine answered as best she could, sharing snippets of her journey. Before she knew it, she had shared her contact details with several people and even agreed to return to the next meeting to speak again.

When Jasmine and Moana finally escaped to the car, Moana burst into laughter, mimicking Jasmine: 'No, Moana, I don't think I could come. Okay, Moana, I'll come, but no one can know about my OCD. Oh, hi, I'm Jasmine, and I have OCD, here's my phone nu mber!'

Jasmine laughed at herself. 'Who knew that it feels good to confess your secrets to a bunch of strangers?'

Moana glanced at her as she pulled out onto the main road. 'I was so proud of you. That took guts.'

As Moana navigated the traffic, she launched into conversation, 'I learned a lot and also realised I have so much more to learn.'

'Yes, it's a very complicated beast,' Jasmine agreed, 'I'm still learning and researchers are too.'

'One thing I wanted to ask, but didn't have the time, was, how often does someone have an obsessive thought?' Moana asked.

'It is as varied as the number of people who have OCD. But, I once read that those who have OCD can spend up to 15 minutes in every hour managing OCD.'

'Wow, that's got to take a toll,' Moana said, sounding a little dejected. 'How can it take so long, can you give me an example?'

'Okay, let me think,' Jasmine paused, trying to find an idea that wasn't her own fear, that she wouldn't mind elaborating on. 'Here's an idea. Imagine your intrusive thought was a fear of a plane falling from the sky onto your house.'

'Oh gee Jasmine, graphic example!'

Jasmine nodded. 'Someone with that obsession might have a daily thing they do to make sure that doesn't happen. A ritual of some kind. Maybe they run the water for exactly 30 seconds in the morning or they look at every corner of the room clockwise.'

'Okay,' Moana said to show she was listening.

'But, when a plane flew overhead, or if someone spoke about flying, that fear would be magnified, and the person might need to do the compulsion again. And then, during the day, they might just think about the planes in the sky and realise they hadn't done their compulsion for a while so they do it again, for good measure. So, you can see, that there is no easy answer to how often or how long. But for most people, they lose a couple of hours a day to OCD.
'

'Is that how much time it takes up in your day?" Moana asked.

Jasmine hadn't told Moana her actual fear, but here in the car, in the dark, it felt like she could keep sharing.

'Probably not for me at the moment, it would be less frequent. I currently have Superstitious OCD – or sometimes it's called Magical OCD,' she hesitated, fiddling with the edge of her sleeve.

'Magical OCD sounds pretty good. All subcategories should sound that good,' Moana said with her usual humour. 'Tell me about it.'

'Okay, so... Superstitious OCD is basically a type of OCD where your brain convinces you that certain thoughts or actions can somehow control things — like the plane falling from the sky example. It's not about believing in lucky socks – it's deeper than that. It's this awful pressure, like you're responsible for keeping the universe in balance with tiny rituals that no one else sees.'

She hesitated, then added quietly, 'For me, I'm terrified of crossing the river. Part of me truly believes that if I stay away, I'm keeping everyone safe, including myself. Logically, I know that my going over it doesn't affect the structure. But OCD doesn't care about logic. It only cares about keeping you afraid enough to obey.'

And Jasmine always obeyed.

Moana nodded slowly, her expression softening. 'That must be exhausting – to carry that thought.'

Jasmine nodded. 'Well, I do a pretty good job of just avoiding it,' she laughed.

They sat in silence until Moana spoke again.

'Are you telling me you've never crossed the river to Duck Island Ice Cream Parlour!?'

Jasmine laughed. She loved that Moana could make light of a difficult situation. 'Nope, but you can buy it from the supermarket on the west side.'

'Not all flavours!' Moana said, laughing. 'Now, let's get you home; you probably have some sheets or towels to colour code before bed.'

Jasmine laughed, although she realised she quite liked the idea.

Chapter Seventeen

What if I get food poisoning?

Jasmine quietly flicked off her shoes at the door of her flat, rubbing her feet, which had been in the same pair of shoes for more than fifteen hours. Moana gave a soft toot of the horn as she reversed from the driveway, making Jasmine smile.

As she tiptoed to her room, she saw Joel asleep on the couch in the lounge. *He really should just move in,* Jasmine thought as she passed him.

Even though she craved sleep, she couldn't go to bed without removing her make-up. She went through her nightly routine of face cleaning and teeth brushing before crawling into her bed. *Ah, bed is bliss,* she thought as she spread herself like an angel right in the middle of it.

Her mind reflected on the conversations of the evening and the stories she heard. She felt a sense of hope, knowing people like her were being supported by the people she met that evening. Although it had been exhausting, she felt good.

As her mind drifted from thoughts of the meeting into distorted dreams, she heard her phone buzz with a message. Reaching to switch it off, she saw it was from Noah.

You back from Auckland?

Yep, just back now.

I finished the diary tonight. What the hell! Tokanui!

Yeah. I was gutted too.

I want to know more. Chat tomorrow. Swing by at lunch?

That will be good. Joel will be with me.

So, Noah knew about his grandfather's mental condition; Jasmine wondered whether that knowledge might shift the way Noah saw him. The reaction would offer a glimpse into how he might respond to *her* truth if she ever found the courage to share it.

She had a session with Dr Kris tomorrow night where she would lay it all out and make a plan.

She fell asleep quickly, her last thought, hazy and dreamlike, was of Noah in a snowstorm, looking in every corner of a field.

***

When she rose in the morning, her two friends were already up. In the kitchen, she found Paige ready for work and Joel immersed in coffee and toast-making while still dressed in his boxers.

'Nice couch?' Jasmine asked.

'It was good enough; I dangled my legs off the end,' Joel said.

'Thanks for being a friend and looking after Paige,' Jasmine said, handing Joel his t-shirt from the floor.

'No way,' Paige exclaimed, 'he wasn't looking after me. He had too much to drink and couldn't drive.'

'Yep, that's why I stayed,' Joel said, winking at Jasmine.

Jasmine grabbed a banana and headed for the door. 'See you at work, Joel – Paige, see you tonight.'

As Jasmine drove to work, she thought about her lunch "appointment". It might lean toward tough conversations about Ben, but it would be nice to see Noah again.

She had repeatedly replayed their kiss in her head, analysing every moment.

What if the kiss was just a one-time thing? Did he even like her, or was he just polite? What if this was something he did every week with a different girl? What if he was actually trying to scam her for money?

Medusa loved spinning doubts. Jasmine pushed back, refusing to let the thoughts progress.

When she arrived at work, she was greeted by Moana, who was holding a small bunch of flowers.

'I've just been on such a high since last night,' Moana said, her voice filled with pride. 'I feel like I can do this, and it's not the end of the world.'

Jasmine felt a glow inside, 'I'm so glad. We can discuss ideas anytime, or I can even speak to Caleb if you think it would help.'

Moana hesitated, her smile softening. 'Like you, he's pretty private about it. But maybe, when he's ready.'

'Of course,' Jasmine said gently. 'I get that.'

They exchanged a few more words, and Jasmine tucked the flowers into a jar on her desk.

Later that day, Jasmine walked with Joel to meet Noah at a café near the river, but just out of sight of a bridge. They grabbed takeaway containers to go to Garden Place, to the chair that Joel and Jasmine frequented. Jasmine was apprehensive to hear Noah's thoughts on the diary.

'It really hit me by surprise. I wasn't sure what I was reading at first,' Noah admitted. 'No one mentioned it to me. I guess it was a secret.'

'Did your dad talk about Ben much?' Jasmine asked carefully.

Noah sighed, 'Not really, other than to say where he had grown up and that he had been sick at the end of his life. But I thought he meant body sick, not mind sick. I guess he was protecting Grandad, or himself.'

Joel nodded, his expression thoughtful. 'That's how shame works, doesn't it? It silences people. I know I've kept things to myself just because I was too embarrassed about how others might react.'

Jasmine responded as well. 'It's hard to open up when you think people might not understand.' She hoped she was planting a seed that Noah might recall at a later time.

She continued, 'That generation grew up in a world where mental illness was hidden away, sometimes literally. But things are changing, and the fact that you want to understand more is huge.'

Noah continued, 'It makes me sad for Grandad, that he didn't have the parenting experience he planned. He seems so caring in the diaries. The whole ending left me feeling dissatisfied.'

'Yes!' Joel blurted out. 'That's how I feel, I'm hoping you are going to fill in some gaps for us.'

Noah smiled, his hand brushing Jasmine's as it rested on the seat. Neither of them moved, the small connection sparking a flutter in her stomach, the kind that she welcomed.

Joel caught Jasmine's eye, giving a fun wink with a knowing smirk.

Noah nodded. 'I can't fill in the gaps, but I think we should talk to Aunty Rose to find out more. Hopefully, she will be comfortable speaking about it.'

'Would she be open to it?' Jasmine asked, her curiosity piqued.

'I think so,' Noah said. 'She's in her eighties, but she's sharp as ever. I'll call her and see if she's up for a visit. You can come if you want,' he directed the comment to Jasmine.

Joel chimed in before Jasmine could respond. 'That sounds promising. Where does she live?'

His question would allow Jasmine to reply, knowing which side of the river the visit would be on.

'Not far from here, near the lake,' Noah responded flippantly, not understanding the importance of the question.

Jasmine quickly responded, 'I'd love to. Do you think I could take a list of questions, like, what happened to Albert, where did she go to school, and did Evie ever have a car?'

'Yep. And I can answer some of those things. Shall I tell you about Albert?'

'Ooh, tell us about cute little Albert. What happened to him?' Joel asked. Then he added, 'He was one of my favourite characters in the book,' speaking as if it were a fictional series he'd read.

Noah smiled, not sure if Joel was genuine or mocking. 'Albert, who everyone called Blue, was a bit of a wildcard.'

'Shouldn't he have been called Red?' Joel asked, 'with his red hair.'

'Don't know.' Noah continued, 'As you read in the diary, when he was about 16, he left home. Dad always said it was because of him being born.'

'Classic rebellious teenager,' Joel said, shaking his head.

'Well,' Noah continued, 'he wasn't heard from for about five or six years. The family didn't know if he was alive or dead. Then, they read a report in the paper about a red-headed New Zealand man called 'Blue' who drowned in Sydney Harbour. Same age as Albert.'

'Oh no,' Jasmine gasped. She hadn't anticipated the shocking end to Albert. 'Evie never mentioned it.'

Noah quickly shook his head. 'No, it was a big coincidence. One day, out of the blue, excuse the pun, he showed up. Just strolled back into their lives like nothing had happened.'

Joel sighed. 'Where had he been?'

'In Australia or in a bit of trouble, or both,' Noah admitted, grinning.

'Oh, how did Evie cope with that?' Jasmine asked.

'I'm not sure. You can add it to the list of things to ask Rose. But Nana looked after Albert's son, Albie, for a few years.'

'Evie must've had a huge heart,' Jasmine said, shaking her head. 'Raising her own kids, fostering babies, and taking in her grandson?'

'She did,' Noah agreed. 'Albert turned out all right, though. He became a big figure in the New Zealand unions. He was quite the talker. Whenever he visited, Dad would take him to the movies just to have a break.'

Jasmine laughed, picturing the scene. 'Well, he always liked the movies in the diaries. Maybe that tactic was hatched when he was a child.'

'Ha. Maybe you're right,' Joel said, nodding at the idea. 'Well, now we know what happened to that cute little boy.'

Noah nodded, seeming happy that the two were so interested in his family. 'Hey, maybe we can find some of his old Union speeches in the archives. I bet they'd make for a great read.'

Joel groaned. 'More reading? Noah, you're turning into Jasmine.'

Jasmine liked that the two of them seemed to get along. She knew Joel didn't have many male friends. Even in a world where everyone claimed to be accepting of all sexualities, the truth was that men were often hesitant to befriend him.

Joel excused himself with a grin, citing a meeting but clearly giving them space. He winked at Jasmine as he left, nodding his approval.

'So,' Noah began sheepishly, 'I've been thinking about our date the other night.'

'Oh, was it a date?' she joked, though she was relieved to hear him say it.

Noah laughed. 'I thought so. I was wondering if we could do it again.'

Jasmine smiled. 'Well, it sounds like we already have one planned.'

Noah furrowed his brow, clearly puzzled.

'To Aunty Rose's house!' she explained.

'Oh, that's not a date!' he protested. 'I can do better than that.'

'You have no idea,' she said, 'that is exactly my idea of a perfect date.'

'Well,' he grinned, 'I'd better throw in dinner too.'

***

Jasmine couldn't believe how light she felt in her heart as she returned to work. Noah was ticking a lot of boxes for her.

Her mind shifted from her lunch date to preparing for her visit that evening with Dr Kris. She had already let her therapist know she was ready to take the next step, but now she was having doubts. *It's not really necessary to confront it today,* she rationalised. *I've been surviving long enough without crossing the river, so why start now?*

Deciding to distract the therapist with a discussion about Noah, she felt some relief from the idea of having to make a plan to target Medusa.

Dr Kris's office welcomed her with the usual calming scents from the diffuser. Carefully selected paintings of New Zealand landscapes and beaches with toi toi and pōhutukawa trees adorned the walls.

Jasmine exchanged pleasantries with Dr Kris, who seamlessly moved into therapy mode.

'I was so pleased to receive your email saying you were ready to take the next step with exposure therapy,' Dr Kris began. 'Tell me, what prompted you to send that message?'

Jasmine inwardly sighed. *Damn,* she thought. *I've left myself no escape.*

'Um, I just felt it *might* be time,' she said cautiously. 'But there's no rush.'

'Ah-ha,' said Dr Kris knowingly. 'You sent that email pretty late in the evening. What had you been doing that day?'

'Oh, I was just reading about someone who had a hard life who inspired me. But really, it's not the same as me.'

Jasmine was doing her best to deflect, keeping Dr Kris at arm's length. But Dr Kris wasn't about to let her off so quickly.

'Jasmine, I wondered if there was a particular reason why crossing the river has been on your mind. Perhaps you felt you were missing out on something?'

Jasmine hesitated. 'Um, well, there was a time recently when I thought about going over.'

As they talked, neither of them had directly mentioned the word 'bridge,' but the conversation was circling closer and closer.

'Are there times you avoid going *near* the river?' Dr Kris asked.

Jasmine could feel the metaphorical water rising. 'Not really,' she replied, her voice light but unconvincing.

'What about when you're in town? Do you ever walk near the river?'

'No, we usually have lunch in the garden at work,' Jasmine said, again deflecting the truth.

'And would you ever consider walking to the river for lunch?'

'Sure, no problem,' Jasmine said, shrugging again.

'Well, that would be a great start. If we can get you close to a bridge, we can work from there,' Dr Kris said gently.

The word 'bridge' hit Jasmine like a bolt, and Medusa stirred. *Focus,* she told herself.

Dr Kris continued, 'Jasmine, avoidance is just another type of compulsion. It feeds your intrusive thought just as much as repeating words or counting. I'd like to see if you can walk by the river, maybe even under a bridge. Today, let's visualise that as part of our therapy.'

Dr Kris brought up an image of a Hamilton bridge on her computer. Jasmine looked away quickly.

'Jasmine,' Dr Kris said reassuringly, 'we're going to play a game of Bananagrams with this bridge in view. You are safe, and OCD isn't welcome in this room.'

Jasmine nodded to show she understood, while Dr Kris continued explaining how she could overcome it.

'The longer you can go without performing the compulsion, the more your brain learns there's no real danger. Plus,' she added with a smile, 'I've been waiting to beat you.'

Obediently, Jasmine picked out the tiles. On Dr Kris's command, they flipped them over and started. Jasmine focused hard, forming words quickly: *trick, route, point.*

Her mind flitted to Noah, her job, her wardrobe, anything but the bridges. She was amazed at how many things she could think of in one moment. She called "peel" first and kept her focus sharp.

When the game ended and Jasmine was victorious again, Dr Kris laughed. 'If you can beat me during exposure therapy, imagine what you could do in normal circumstances.'

Jasmine smiled. 'I think I work best under pressure; there's a *lot* of adrenaline going through me.'

'And have you managed to avoid your counter-measure?'

'Yes,' Jasmine said with a nod. 'I haven't done it yet.'

'Let's keep it that way for as long as possible,' Dr Kris said. 'Every time you feel the urge, distract and delay. I think if you can get through today without doing it, by tomorrow, it won't seem as necessary. Will you try and delay as long as possible?'

'I will,' Jasmine promised, though she knew it wouldn't be easy.

Dr Kris took out her diary to make some notes. 'I am going to send you a programme to work on during the next few weeks. I think you will find you will start to make some real progress.'

Jasmine nodded. 'I have one other thing to discuss,' Jasmine said, glancing at the clock to make sure she wasn't cutting into the next visitor's time. 'I might be seeing someone, or at least, I have a second date lined up,' she confessed.

Dr Kris smiled. 'Very nice. Tell me more.'

'Well, it's early days,' Jasmine said, shifting slightly in her seat. 'But I wanted to mention it because I know how OCD can sabotage these things, and I thought maybe I should be prepared.'

'That's an excellent idea. Awareness is key. Remember to call a thought what it really is, revalue it so it holds no weight, and then shift to another activity to break the cycle.'

Jasmine exhaled. 'Yeah, I know all of this. It just gets exhausting. But it's good to be reminded.'

'It's great that you have a 'friend' you are interested in. Can I ask where he lives?'

Jasmine looked at her toes and curled them inside her sandals. 'Over the river,' she answered while wondering how therapists always knew how to be one step ahead.

Dr Kris smiled. 'Well, there's an incentive,' she said.

***

By the time Jasmine got home, she was utterly drained from the exposure therapy. She hadn't done her counter yet, and she genuinely hoped she could resist; she needed a distraction.

Her first choice was a walk with loud rock music blasting through her headphones.

Halfway through her walk, her phone rang, deafening her eardrums. She smiled when she saw it was Noah.

'Hey,' he said. 'I'm coming your way after a job on that side of town. Shall we have dinner? Is it too soon?'

Jasmine's spirits lifted. He was the perfect distraction, an attractive one, too. She explained she was almost home and sent him her address. Quickening her pace, she hurried home to shower before he arrived.

When she stepped out of the shower, she heard his voice and the sound of laughter coming from the living room. Paige was already chatting with him.

Jasmine dressed quickly and stepped into the living room, her hair still damp from the shower, finding Noah and Paige deep in conversation. Paige looked up with a mischievous grin.

'Well, I see how it is. Invite someone over for dinner, and suddenly you forget about your flatmate,' Paige teased.

Paige excused herself to her room, claiming she had some planning to finish before school.

'Would you like to order takeout?' Noah asked.

Jasmine hesitated. There were only a few places she trusted for takeout, where she knew the meal was handled professionally. She would *need* to eat from one of those places.

Noah noticed her hesitation. 'Or, we can not?' he said awkwardly.

She smiled while her mind ticked through options, looking for an alternative. 'Ahh, no. I was just thinking that I have some food here that we could use to make dinner. Are you happy with that?'

'Sure, sounds good.'

Jasmine was relieved to have skirted around the issue. She quickly pulled together a stir-fry and noodles while they chatted easily.

The conversation flowed, ranging from funny childhood stories to the quirks of their work lives.

They brushed past each other in the kitchen, each time a little closer. Jasmine noticed how comfortable it felt, as though they had known each other far longer.

After dinner, they sat next to each other on the couch, looking at news stories on Jasmine's phone. Jasmine liked how close they sat, touching hands.

As the evening progressed, so did their affection, with each kiss lasting a little longer than the one before. Jasmine could feel the electricity between them and she felt safe. She tried not to overthink it, to analyse his words and tenderness.

At the end of the evening, Noah stretched and looked at his watch. 'This has been very nice, more than nice. But it's getting late. I should probably head home.'

Jasmine hesitated, not sure what to say. 'If you don't want to go, you could stay. There's the couch or, you know, my room.'

She felt herself blush and tried to shake the thought that they had only recently met.

Noah looked at her, his expression unreadable. 'I'd like that,' he said quietly. 'But I'm thinking I'd like to take a leaf out of my grandfather's book and take things a little slower. Did you notice they didn't have sleepovers until they were married?'

Jasmine smiled. 'Are you asking me to marry you?' she teased.

'No!' he replied, a little too forcefully.

Jasmine burst into laughter. 'I was joking. It's okay. I like that idea too, taking things slow, getting to know each other better.'

He nodded. 'I mean, I'm tempted, but let's not rush.'

'Okay, that sounds great,' she said, feeling impressed. She didn't want to rely on physical distractions to avoid deeper feelings.

'But,' Noah added with a grin, 'I'm definitely up for a little more kissing here on the couch.' He reached up and held her face like Jasmine was the most precious person he had seen.

Jasmine smiled. 'Sounds like a good distraction, I mean decision.'

Chapter Eighteen

What if I need a Thyroidectomy?

Jasmine's daily routine had a good rhythm to it.

Noah visited in the evenings, or they met in town, with the exception of the weekends and nights he had his daughters stay.

Lunchtimes were spent with Joel, who was recruited as Jasmine's official support person for her exposure therapy, a job that he took very seriously. After lunch, they would venture towards the river to carry out the planned sightings of the bridges. Jasmine felt confident with Joel by her side and appreciated that he saw its importance.

Following the programme from Dr Kris, Jasmine started by going to the edge of the river, by the city shops that overlooked it. She tried to find beauty in the flowing water and allowed herself to acknowledge that the bridges would be within her sight if she walked a little further.

She and Joel discussed mindless topics; he would come prepared with distracting questions like, "If bread were a form of currency, which would be worth the most?" or "If you had to go without one of your five senses, which one would you give up?"

Jasmine was pretty sure Joel was using his time at work to come up with the ideas.

After a few days of this step, Jasmine felt ready to move closer to putting the bridge in her sights.

Joel, ever faithful, was there, speaking to her through the experience. Her eyes flicked up the river and back to her feet, allowing just a few moments to face her demon in full view. She gritted her teeth and held her jaw against the compulsion, resisting the urge to whisper the reassurance in her head.

Joel continued to be a human distraction, giving monologues about films and actors and his in-depth ranking of every James Bond.

'You're doing so well,' Joel said, encouraging her along. Jasmine concentrated on making the anxiety shrink.

As the therapy intensified, she started walking towards the bridge, with Joel at her side, practising square breathing. Joel pretended to be a birthing coach.

'In through the nose, out through the mouth,' he chanted in a soothing, dramatic whisper as people walked by. 'Breeeeathe through it, darling.' He would then giggle when people were out of earshot, 'I love this,' he said.

'I'm glad someone's having fun,' Jasmine said.

At the end of two weeks, she was ready to walk under the bridge and even gazed up at it. She had started to say the word. It was never easy, but each time, the anxiety lessened.

She wondered why Medusa had chosen this: with all the things in the world, why was this her 'thing'?

It's not going to be my thing for much longer, she told herself. She felt the therapy was working and knew she would conquer. Increasing her therapy sessions with Dr Kris became another weapon in her arsenal.

'Exposure therapy works because you're rewriting the story your brain tells you about fear,' Dr Kris said in their session. 'And you're doing exactly that.'

***

Noah was unaware of her bridge-focused exposure therapy sessions and still seemed to have no idea about Medusa. Jasmine made a point of suggesting venues on the west side of the river and avoided his invitations to his home, always quick to offer an alternative. The time spent with him was perfect; she always felt natural around him.

Noah arranged a visit to Aunty Rose, and Jasmine was genuinely excited. When Noah pulled into the driveway, Jasmine was already waiting.

'Ready to meet my favourite aunty?' he asked as she climbed into his work ute. 'Or should I say *officially* meet her, since you've already *met* her in the diaries?'

'Yep, I just have to make sure I don't bombard her with questions. She might not like some little upstart arriving and knowing all this stuff about her family.'

'She'll love you,' Noah said as they made their way toward the lake area. Jasmine admired the older homes, noting that Rose lived in a neighbourhood similar to the one she had grown up in.

Soon, Noah pulled into Rose's driveway.

'Right, quick recap,' said Noah, 'her husband died about six years ago and her kids are scattered around New Zealand and the world.' As they approached the front screen door, Noah added.

'Oh, and she's cat-crazy. The cats aren't allowed outside, so don't let them escape.'

'Great,' Jasmine whispered nervously. 'Now I'm even more worried. I'll be the know-it-all who let the cat out.'

The door swung open, revealing Rose. Jasmine's first thought was how vibrant she looked for her age. Her hair was white, holding a hint of the red hair Evie had spoken about.

'Hello, hello!' Rose chirped. 'It's so good to see you.'

Jasmine followed Noah into the house, catching sight of two large ragdoll cats sitting on their own chairs like royalty.

'Please, sit down. Would you like a drink? I have lime or ginger beer,' Rose offered.

'Ginger beer for me, please,' Noah said, settling into a chair with a familiarity that showed how at home he felt.

'Me too, thank you,' Jasmine added politely.

As Rose disappeared into the kitchen, Noah called out behind her, 'I noticed your front steps are a bit wobbly. I'll come by one day and see what they need.'

'Oh, would you?' Rose said with genuine gratitude. 'That would be wonderful.'

Jasmine scanned the room while they chatted. It was filled with character; grandfather clocks ticked softly, a china cabinet housed delicate dolls, and a well-worn dining table hinted at lively family gatherings of the past.

Rose returned, placing glasses of ginger beer in front of them. 'There you are,' she said, sitting down. Jasmine was impressed by her energy and grace.

The conversation flowed easily as Rose updated Noah on her grandchildren, flipping through a photo album of their latest adventures.

Eventually, Noah shifted the conversation to the diaries. 'So, I told you how I met Jasmine, who found Nana and Grandad's diaries,' Noah began.

'Yes, you mentioned that. How interesting! I didn't even know they existed.' She turned to Jasmine. 'Where have they been all this time?'

Jasmine was ready. 'We're not entirely sure, but they were donated to the council archives within the last ten years. The note on the box said they'd been found in the roof space of a house, presumably Evie's.'

'Well, I never,' Rose said, clearly astonished. 'How fortunate they've found their way back to us.'

'I brought them for you,' Noah said, pulling the diaries from his bag. 'I've finished reading them, so it's your turn.'

'Oh, how exciting!'

'The diaries end in 1950 when you would have been about ten?' Noah said.

'That's a shame that there's nothing later. We were pretty naughty kids – maybe she didn't want to document our antics.' Rose laughed.

'You were naughty?' Noah asked.

'Oh, yes. Poor Mum. We ran wild, doing our own thing. It was great fun, but we must've been an embarrassment.'

'Can we ask you some questions? There are a few gaps I would like to fill?' Noah asked.

'Yes,' Rose said with a little hesitation. Jasmine wondered if Rose was suspecting some difficult questions.

Noah shifted in his seat. 'The diaries speak about Grandad going to Tokanui.' Noah stopped. He hadn't asked a question but made it obvious the following response should be from Rose.

'Oh, that. It was no big deal,' Rose answered. Jasmine could tell that even after almost 80 years, it was a big deal.

'Dad never mentioned it, and I was shocked,' Noah explained. 'What I can't understand is why Grandad went there.'

'I actually don't know *why,*' Rose stated, 'but I know that he became difficult to live with. He became kind of...,' she paused, looking for the right word, 'paranoid? Or perhaps a hypochondriac?'

Jasmine felt uneasy about the conversation. Perhaps Ben was more like her than she thought.

Noah pressed for more answers. 'But, there's no sign of that in the diaries. What brought it on? Was it to do with the war?'

'No, no,' Rose answered, 'It was all to do with that operation when he had his thyroid removed.'

Jasmine recalled the operation mentioned in the diary.

Rose continued, 'Basically, if you had your thyroid removed back then, you could go a little nuts. Nowadays, there's a pill to keep you balanced, but Dad just lost his marbles.'

'Aunty, I don't think we talk that way anymore about mental health,' Noah said, laughing at her frankness.

'Oh fiddlesticks, everyone is so woke these days,' she said, laughing, 'no one knows what the other person is really saying.'

Jasmine smiled, discreetly touching her neck to check that her thyroid felt normal.

Rose continued. 'If society is so PC, why are redheads still discriminated against?' she added, giving Jasmine a fun wink.

Jasmine laughed out loud, snorting her ginger beer.

Noah brought the conversation back, although Aunty Rose looked like she had enjoyed the diversion.

'So, he had the operation and then went to Tokanui. What was that like for you, to visit?'

Jasmine listened with keen interest as Rose continued with her Dad's story.

'We'd take the bus to Tokanui. Mum and Thomas would be motion sick, so it was never a great day. Thomas had anxiety about that place for the rest of his life. He couldn't drive through Te Awamutu without a knot in his stomach.' Rose seemed to stop herself from dwelling on the negative.

'But I was fine. I actually have fond memories of those visits. Dad was always proud to show us his garden and the work he had been doing.'

Jasmine felt brave enough to contribute to the conversation. 'We saw some drawings in the diary that he sent you both. They are quite special. There are poems he wrote too.'

Rose nodded. 'I remember those. We loved getting the post from him.' She stayed quiet for a few moments, and Jasmine wondered if Rose remembered the day someone put a cruel note in the mailbox. But looking at her face, Jasmine decided Rose was remembering only the good moments.

'Eventually, my Aunty Hazel brought him to live with her in Auckland. She said someone as sensitive and kind as Dad shouldn't be treated like that.'

Noah glanced at Jasmine, his expression sombre. 'I can't believe Dad never talked about any of this.'

'Well,' Rose continued, 'Thomas was probably embarrassed by Dad. I think he worried he might grow up to be just like him,' she explained. 'I suppose it's hard for a child to reconcile those feelings.'

'What was it like when he came home?' Noah asked.

She paused and smiled. 'Ah, Dad was such a gentleman and always called me "dal". And even though he didn't work, he had some chores to do. He oiled our bike chains every Saturday without fail. And then he polished our shoes. I always had a good bike and polished shoes.'

'He sounds wonderful,' Jasmine said.

'Oh, he was,' Rose agreed. 'He had a brilliant mind, too. Also, I used to ask him for things that Mum said no to. He didn't even know what I was asking for but he always said yes.' Noah laughed, 'Aunty, that's terrible.'

'I know!' Rose grinned.

Noah looked at his watch. 'That's a lot for today. Do you want to take a break from storytelling?' he asked.

'Gosh, no. This is the most fun I've had all week. But let's have some biscuits, and I'll find some photos of Mum and Dad.'

Rose wandered to the kitchen, and Noah raised his eyebrows to ask Jasmine if she was still okay. She gave him the thumbs up.

She loved it.

***

Rose returned to the room with a plate of Griffin's biscuits and a bowl of peppermint lollies.

'Oh, peppermints?' Jasmine commented, smiling.

'Is that interesting?' Rose asked, genuinely curious.

'Oh, there's a moment in the diary with your mum. I'll let you read it,' Jasmine responded, not wanting to give away spoilers.

'Oh yes, Mum loved peppermints. She always had a bowl of them, but they were rationed out.'

Rose disappeared briefly, returning with a shoebox of photos. 'These all need sorting out someday, but they're named on the back.'

Jasmine looked through the photos. She had the urge to move into archivist mode and use archival gloves with acid-free envelopes, but for now, she carefully handled the corners of each photo. The images showed Evie with Rose and Thomas, often with a cat in the background. Evie was always smiling, her arms around her children. The absence of a father in the photos spoke volumes.

'She was very beautiful,' Jasmine remarked.

'I suppose so. I only ever saw a mum who was working hard, with red hands raw from scrubbing washing,' Rose said.

'Would you like me to scan these for you so you can have them digitally?' Jasmine offered.

'Oh, could you? That would be great. I'm not sure what I'd do with them next, but then the kids could have copies,' Rose said, pointing to a photo on the wall of her children.

'It would be my pleasure,' Jasmine replied warmly.

Jasmine picked up a photo of the home, with the three of them on the front veranda and the children dressed for school. The faces of the children were bright and happy, with no sign that their early years had been tough.

Rose chuckled at the photo, 'That was Thomas's first day at school. I walked him to the bus and made him get on the wrong one. I'm not sure why; I just thought it would be funny.'

Rose was forming a picture in Jasmine's mind of the difficulty Evie had in bringing up two mischievous children.

Jasmine turned to another photo, this time of Ben with Rose. Ben looked considerably older than he had looked in any of the other photos, but Rose looked youthful. Jasmine assumed this photo had been taken after Tokanui.

'Did Ben ever receive the medication he needed?' Jasmine asked, her tone hopeful, wishing for a happily-ever-after ending.

'He tried it for a while, about twenty years after the operation. By then, he said the "real world" was too overwhelming for him, and he stopped.'

Noah nodded. 'That sounds difficult. It must have been so hard for Nana.'

'It was,' Rose nodded. 'But she coped. She used to say, 'I committed to: for better, for worse, for richer, for poorer, and in sickness and in health.'

Jasmine smiled. It wasn't the first time she had heard Evie's mantra, but she never tired of it.

Rose continued. 'She rode her bike to the hospital most days to visit him during those last few years, when he moved out of the house. She was 70 by then.'

It was confirmed. Evie didn't have the happily-ever-after ending that Jasmine, Joel and Paige had hoped for. Jasmine had dreamed that, magically, Ben had come back to his former self and that he and Evie lived out their twilight years hosting neighbours and riding bikes. It was a sad reality to face.

Rose sat back in her chair, a fond smile spreading across her face. 'You know, there were two moments in my life that stand out, when I saw the Ben that Evie met, the brilliant Ben.'

Jasmine leaned forward eagerly, 'Please, tell us.'

Rose nodded, looking pleased to share the insights. 'The first one was when I was about nineteen. Dad was unwell at the time and bedridden. A friend of Mum's, Mrs Parata, came to visit and popped in to see Dad, who was in bed.'

'It's so good that people used to visit them so much,' Noah interrupted.

'Oh, they always had people coming in. It's not like these days; I haven't seen anyone all week,' Rose said, with loneliness in her voice, giving Jasmine the resolve to visit again soon.

'Anyway, Mrs Parata and Dad were chatting in no time, but I couldn't believe my ears, they were speaking te reo Māori!'

Noah looked up, intrigued. 'He spoke te reo Māori?!'

'I know!' Rose said, her tone rising with amazement. 'I had no idea. Nineteen years of my life, and I'd never heard him speak it before. But there he was, carrying on this deep, fluent conversation as if it was second nature.'

'Where did he learn it?' Jasmine asked.

'Well, apparently, when Dad was young, his family lived on the Waima River Valley in Hokianga, way up the top of the country. His father built a schoolhouse on the farm, and *my* grandmother taught the children from the area on the farm. That's where Dad learned it, with the Māori children from the surrounding areas.'

'That's incredible,' Noah said.

Rose smiled. 'He was always quick to interpret Māori place names, explaining their meanings. He'd say things like, "That means the place where the clear stream runs between two hills." I never questioned it.'

Jasmine nodded, 'That's so interesting. What was the other moment?'

Rose smiled, 'It must've been around 1960, and up the road on our street, there were these two teenage girls who had a horse they kept in a paddock. One day, the horse got out and started tearing up and down Nixon Street. It was chaos. People were chasing it, shouting, trying to corner it – but it just became more agitated. Even the girls couldn't calm it down.'

'Oh no,' Jasmine said, already feeling the tension.

Rose grinned. 'Dad watched from his window, and finally, he decided to do something about it and walked out. This is the man who hardly ever left the house. He started making these horse noises, soft and calm, as he walked toward it. You wouldn't believe it, but the horse just melted into his arms.'

Noah grinned. 'That's cool.'

'Yes. He talked to it the whole time, stroking it and guiding it back to the paddock like it was nothing. Everyone was stunned. Once the horse was safely back, he shut the gate, walked straight home, and went back to his room as if nothing had happened.'

'Where did he learn his horse skills?' Jasmine asked.

'His sister told me that he was a brilliant horseman when he was young,' Rose said, her voice tinged with pride. 'Apparently, he used to ride his horse up the steps and into his bedroom in the sleepout of his farm, grab something from his dresser, and ride back down. It sounds crazy, but she swore it was true.'

'Wow,' Noah said, 'it's hard to believe when all I saw were photos of him looking old.'

'Well, yes, unfortunately, it is still the same today,' Rose said, 'there's always more to someone than you see.'

Jasmine imagined Rose had already figured out Jasmine's secret. She calmed her thoughts and continued listening.

'Mum lived another seven years and continued to bike everywhere until the day before she died. She had even taken soup to a neighbour and then she collapsed and later died in her sleep at the hospital.' Rose had a quiver in her voice, and Jasmine worried they had asked too much of her.

'Well, I think we've troubled you long enough,' Noah said, taking the cue.

'It's been so good,' Rose said, 'come again, and by then, I will have read these,' she said, patting the diaries.

Jasmine reached into her bag and pulled out a small gift. 'I know it's a little strange since we just met, but I have something for you.'

'Ooh, I wonder what it is,' Rose said with delight.

'It's not too exciting,' Jasmine said, downplaying the gift. 'But the archivist in me saw an opportunity.'

Rose unwrapped the package, carefully folding the paper as she went. Noah, now standing beside Jasmine, put his arm around her, touched by the thoughtful gesture.

Rose, having opened the gift, studied it with curiosity. It was a framed print of a pencil-drawn vase. 'I've seen this before,' she said. 'Is this drawn by my dad?'

'Yes,' Jasmine replied, a little embarrassed by the attention. 'I scanned some of his drawings, and I thought this one made a nice piece of art.'

'Well, I never!' Rose exclaimed. 'I will treat this with respect and treasure it.'

She stood up and winked at Noah. 'She's a keeper.'

Jasmine felt herself blush, hoping she hadn't overstepped the mark.

'You know,' Rose said thoughtfully, studying the artwork, 'this reminds me of another box of treasures I have. Come with me.'

She led them down the hallway, where bookshelves lined the walls, stacked with folders and ring binders. Her gaze swept across the shelves and landed on a few ring binders.

'Ah, here they are. If you're interested in reading, I also have these letters from Evie – she used to write to me every week when I was living with the family in Wellington during the 1970s. They're probably a bit boring, but if you think you'd like them, you could read them.'

Jasmine's eyes lit up, and she gave a small, excited jump on the spot. 'Oh yes! But only if you're comfortable sharing them.'

Rose shrugged. ‘I can’t imagine Mum would have written anything too personal. You’re welcome to borrow them – I trust you,’ Rose said with a warm smile. Jasmine felt an unexpected sense of honour at having so quickly gained favour with Noah’s aunty.

‘I promise we will take care of it all,’ Jasmine said, pointing to Noah.

Rose smiled, ‘Perhaps it will make good bedtime reading,’ she said, giving Noah a little wink.

‘Aunty!’ he said, laughing with her.

Jasmine took the box of letters from Rose, promising to return with the scanned photos and letters. Jasmine cradled the new items with care.

On the drive back to her place, she and Noah laughed about Rose and her subtle mischief.

‘Yeah, I get the feeling that she and Dad were pretty difficult to bring up. There are reports of them being in trouble with the police and the neighbours,’ Noah confirmed.

‘Poor Evie,’ said Jasmine thinking about Rose and Thomas tearing up and down Nixon Street.

‘I can’t wait to update Joel and Paige,’ said added, referring not only to the new reading material but also to the insight into how the 1940 baby from the diaries had turned out.

Chapter Nineteen

What if a tiger escapes?

It was the beginning of autumn, with a crispness to the morning air that signalled it was time for the leaves to start turning. Jasmine was heading to the zoo to meet Noah and his daughters – it would be her first time meeting them.

She planned her day by choosing playful, youthful clothes and packing peppermints and snake lollies as icebreakers. Aria and Morgan were being dropped off to go with her – their presence would help take some of the focus off Jasmine.

Aria and Morgan arrived in their usual state of organised chaos, chatter spilling over as they bounded into the house. They carried with them the letters Jasmine had posted, proof that her plan to maintain contact had worked. There were no pressing questions about her absence, only curiosity about the day ahead.

It had been a few months since she and Noah started seeing each other. Their connection had grown quickly through long conversations and a shared curiosity about each other's lives. They tried to see each other each day when he was free. On the days he spent with his children, he and Jasmine messaged each other frequently.

They also enjoyed passionate moments, at times leaving her frustrated. She admired Noah's patience in taking things slowly.

Paige joined them for the zoo trip, and the small group drove to meet Noah and his girls. Jasmine's stomach fluttered with nerves at the thought of the meeting. She reminded herself they were just little girls, not Maria von Trapp's crew, from *The Sound of Music*, plotting to prank her.

Still, she wanted to make a good impression.

Noah pulled into the zoo parking lot in his ute. Jasmine could see two curious faces from their car seats. She allowed him time to get them out of the car before approaching.

'Jasmine, I'd like you to meet my treasures, Jade and Sienna,' he said proudly.

The girls clung shyly to Noah's legs, peeking out cautiously. Jasmine crouched to their level and smiled. 'Hi, it's so good to meet you! I love your names. Remind me, who's Sienna, and who's Jade?'

'I'm Jade,' one of them said, stepping out a little. Sienna stayed hidden behind Noah's legs.

Jasmine introduced the girls to Aria and Morgan, and soon, the children were skipping together.

They made their way through the zoo, stopping at enclosures and pointing out their favourite animals. Jade quickly became attached to Jasmine, asking questions about everything she saw. Sienna was quieter, often walking alongside Noah but darting forward to join her sister whenever something caught her eye.

Paige was on aunty duty, shepherding Aria and Morgan, who giggled and darted from one exhibit to the next. The zoo was alive with the buzz of families and laughter.

Jasmine pushed all the dangers to the back of her mind. There was a lot of trust given to the staff to ensure enclosures were locked and dangerous animals secured. She felt uneasy at the tiger enclosure where just glass stood between her and the dangerous cats. She shuffled the party along, looking forward to arriving at a less threatening enclosure.

The girls seemed sweet, curious, and full of life. When Jade slipped her sticky hand into Jasmine's, she felt a warmth that dissolved her nerves, but tried not to think about what made the hand sticky. They stood together, laughing at the antics and spotting hidden monkeys.

While they watched the monkeys swing and roam the enclosure, Jasmine noticed one of the male monkeys moving toward a female monkey nearby, who was grooming herself. Jasmine could see he was looking for a mate.

Trying to distract Jade, Jasmine pointed towards the trees, asking her to spot a hidden animal. But quickly, Jade asked, 'What's he doing?' and pointed to the excited monkey. Jasmine looked at Noah for help, and he pointed back at her, 'She asked you,' he whispered.

'I'm not sure,' she answered. But it wasn't the end of Jade's educational enquiry.

As the monkey approached the female, he gently touched her arm and sniffed her fur. Jasmine pointed out birds in the trees to Jade, trying to avoid more questions.

Then the female paused, glancing at her mate before turning slightly. Before Jasmine could redirect Jade's attention, the two monkeys were moving in a way that left little doubt about what kind of monkey business was happening.

'What are they doing?' Jade squealed.

Jasmine quickly pointed to Noah, 'Why don't you ask your dad?'

Noah barely blinked. 'That's how monkeys make babies,' he answered calmly.

'Oh,' Jade said, nodding as if that explained everything before turning her attention back to the enclosure.

Paige sidled up beside Jasmine, laughing. 'Tough first-day conversation.'

Jasmine exhaled, rubbing her temples. 'Eek, talk about awkward. I wasn't prepared with an answer.'

Paige kept laughing, 'I loved watching you squirm.'

'Well,' Jasmine added, 'At least someone around here is getting some loving.'

The two giggled like schoolgirls. 'He's still taking it slow?' Paige asked.

'Yep,' Jasmine sighed and moved on from the enclosure.

'I respect that,' Paige said.

'Me too. Doesn't mean it's easy,' Jasmine stated. 'What if he's just not that into me?'

Paige scoffed, 'Don't think like that, we can all see that he adores you. And he wouldn't have you here meeting his kids if he wasn't into you.'

'I guess so.' Jasmine said.

***

As the afternoon rolled around, the group started making their way toward the exit. The kids were slowing down, visibly worn out from the excitement. Noah walked ahead with Aria and Morgan, while Jasmine trailed behind with Jade and Sienna, who were each clutching tiny stuffed animals from the gift shop.

As they reached the car park, Noah turned to Jasmine. 'Would you like to come with us to drop the girls off at their mum's? You could see their other place – it's not far over the river. Paige could take Aria and Morgan home.'

Jasmine hesitated. She could feel the challenge in the offer: over the river.

'I think I'll head home with the girls. It's been a big day,' she said, keeping her tone light.

Noah tilted his head, studying her reaction. 'You sure?'

'Yeah, I'm sure,' she said, plastering on a smile. She didn't want to ruin the day by explaining herself now. 'But will you come over afterwards?' she asked.

'Yeah, see you then,' he responded.

The drive home was quiet, with Aria and Morgan looking sleepy from the outing. In Jasmine's mind, it had been a success. She hadn't embarrassed herself in front of Jade and Sienna, and she had spent time with her nieces.

Best of all, the tiger hadn't escaped.

Once the girls left, Jasmine and Paige dissected the day, both agreeing that Noah's daughters were kind. 'Just like their dad?' Paige said.

Before Jasmine could respond about her feelings for Noah, the sound of a car pulling up outside drew their attention. Moments later, Noah walked through the door, carrying a bag of groceries.

'I thought I'd bring dinner,' he announced, holding up the bag. 'After that zoo trip, I could use a home-cooked meal.'

Paige winked at Jasmine and whispered, 'Yep, just like their dad.' Then, to the whole room, she added, 'I'm meeting Joel for a movie, so I'll go get ready and be off.'

Noah unpacked the bag of chicken, vegetables, and a packet of noodles on the kitchen counter. 'Stir-fry, okay?' he asked.

'Perfect,' Jasmine replied, joining him in the kitchen.

They worked side by side, reliving the day and what the girls had said about Jasmine. She felt flattered that they had thought she was "cool". The easy conversation continued through dinner, and Jasmine found herself mulling over just how deeply she had fallen for Noah.

After dinner, as they cleaned up, Noah leaned against the counter, watching her rinse the plates. 'So,' he started, 'why don't you ever come to my house?'

Jasmine gulped. It was time to fess up and take the consequences. She knew she couldn't delay it longer, and part of her had anticipated this conversation after her refusal to go with him to take his girls home.

'Shall we sit down?' she asked. She could see worry instantly on his face and knew she would have to explain things quickly to minimise his worry.

'I do have a reason. I haven't told you, because – well – it might be a deal breaker.' She had Noah's full attention.

'The truth is, I haven't been to your house yet because...' Jasmine paused. She could see the agony on Noah's face and perhaps even a defensiveness, protecting himself from what would come next. '...I have a fear of bridges, making it difficult for me to cross the river.'

Noah's face relaxed. 'Oh phew, is that all? I thought you were going to tell me you are secretly married.'

Jasmine stopped, 'What?'

Noah laughed, 'I mean – *you* said it could be a deal breaker. My brain went straight to worst-case scenario. Sorry. Bit of a leap.'

Jasmine smiled. She knew what it was like to take a thought to the nth degree, and his comment had allowed for a short break in the focus on her.

'So, is my fear of crossing a bridge a deal breaker?' she asked.

Noah took her hands and interlocked his fingers with hers.

She laughed, 'That's so old-couple-hand-holding.'

'Yep, and I don't mind. I also don't mind your fear of bridges. Honestly, I'm relieved.'

Jasmine felt a calmness settle over her and found herself getting a little braver.

'Okay. So, there's more,' she admitted.

'You're married to *two* people?' he teased.

This time, she ignored the comment.

'It's probably an understatement to call it a fear. The reason I have this fear is because I have something called OCD,' she said, tailing off towards the end of her sentence.

'Okay,' Noah said. Jasmine could see he was choosing his words carefully. Her heart was sinking. This moment could be the end of the relationship.

'What does OCD look like in your life?' he asked sensitively.

Wow. His question was insightful and caring.

Taking a deep breath, she began explaining her history, how she had come a long way and how OCD had shifted over time from one obsession to another. She explained that even though bridge-crossing was her main obsession, she had ongoing small battles with OCD – to keep things safe.

She explained that her life was best when there was little change and no spontaneity. 'I can over-analyse a conversation, find danger in the safest space and ruminate on it.'

She paused. It was enough of a confession.

'So, is it a deal breaker?' she asked again.

Noah smiled at her and held her hand firmer.

'Is my baggage from a divorce a deal breaker for you?' he countered, and before she could answer, he added, 'Or what about me having two kids? Is that a deal breaker?'

Jasmine shook her head, but protested, 'It's not the same, though.'

'Or what about how I count the buttons on the remote while I watch TV, or search for lint in the corners of my pillowcase?'

Jasmine laughed, 'That's kind of the same.' The tears began to fall, as she felt his kindness.

'This is a little off track,' he said, 'but I remember a poster on the back of our toilet door when I was growing up – not sure why it was there, but Dad always liked that stuff. It was titled Twelve Rules To Live By, written by Robert Louis Stevenson. Do you know it?' he asked.

Jasmine shook her head. She was surprised where the conversation was going and that Noah was about to quote a writer.

'I kind of memorised it. One rule that comes to my mind right now is: Don't borrow trouble. Imaginary things are harder to bear than actual ones.'

Jasmine allowed his words to tick over in her mind.

Imaginary things are harder to bear than actual ones.

Noah continued, 'I never really understood that one until right now. I can see that "imagined fears",' he said, raising his fingers in air quotes, 'are harder to bear than real ones.'

Jasmine nodded. She felt Noah's compassion and interest. At that moment, she realised she loved him. It was an emotion she had felt for some weeks, but she had kept it at bay, knowing that she couldn't allow that feeling until he knew the real her.

He leaned closer, holding her gaze. 'Do you remember what Nana Evie said? She married for "better or worse, for richer or poorer, and in sickness and in health," and she stayed.'

'I love that quote,' Jasmine said, now sobbing. And then, to lighten the moment, she added, laughing, 'Are you trying to ask me to marry you again?'

This time, Noah got the joke and brushed over it. 'From the first time I saw you on that video call, I knew I wanted to know you. Not only were you beautiful, but smart and kind.'

'You could tell all that from a video call?'

Noah continued, ignoring the interruption, 'I'm in this for the long haul, and OCD isn't going to get in my way. I'll just have to think of a way to get you over to my house. Maybe a zip line or helicopter?'

Jasmine laughed through her tears, holding his hand tightly. 'I'm working with my therapist to cross the bridge. I'm making headway. Even saying the word "bridge" doesn't scare me now like it used to.'

'I'd like to help you wherever I can,' Noah said, his voice reassuring.

Jasmine looked up at him, 'I think I'm in love with you, Noah Burdekin. How did you come into my life?'

He laughed. 'I came from a book, remember?' He gently brushed the tip of her nose. 'I love you too,' he said, kissing her tears and her mouth.

'Right,' Jasmine said, taking a deep breath to calm the adrenaline still racing through her. 'Thanks for the talk. This has been really good for my soul. And while we are laying everything out, I have a question.'

Noah smiled, 'Okay,' he added suspiciously.

'How is it that the monkeys are sleeping together and we are not?'

Noah burst into laughter. 'Well, I'm not sure if what we saw today counts as *sleeping* together. It looked like it was over and done with pretty quickly.'

Jasmine smiled. 'Do you think it's time for us?'

Noah's smile faded into something more serious, more careful. 'I just don't want to mess up what we have,' he said quietly.

'Agreed,' she whispered. She reached for him, pulling him closer, and kissed him.

He responded with a kiss that deepened slowly. When they finally pulled apart, Noah rested his forehead against hers and said, almost shyly, 'Shall we?'

Jasmine nodded, her heart steady. 'I would like to.'

Noah scooped her into his arms and carried her down the hall.

Chapter Twenty

What if there is asbestos in the building?

Jasmine woke slowly with the sunlight streaming through the curtains and the comforting weight of Noah's arm draped over her waist. She felt content and reflected on an evening that had been worth the wait.

For a moment, she allowed herself just to enjoy the stillness. But soon, her mind started buzzing. She had an idea.

She quickly got up and brushed her teeth, then hopped back into bed, waiting for Noah to wake.

Noah stirred, blinking as Jasmine propped herself up on one elbow. 'Morning,' she said.

'Morning,' he murmured, pulling her closer. 'How'd you sleep?'

'Great,' she replied. 'You?'

He just smiled, and they lay in silence for a few minutes before Jasmine broke it.

'I have an idea,' she said, her voice excited.

Noah climbed out of bed, 'Hold on, let me use the bathroom and brush my teeth too.'

'I have a new toothbrush for you on the bench,' she called out, laughing at herself. *Of course you do.*

When he returned, she submitted her idea. 'The weather's good. How about a little road trip? We could visit my parents in Te Awamutu and drive by Tokanui while we are there.'

Noah laughed as he took the opportunity for a joke. 'Your parents?' he asked. 'I stayed one night, and now I have to meet the parents?'

'They're not scary,' she said with a grin. 'And I think they'd like you. Plus, I'd like to see where Ben was. It's hard to imagine what he went through without seeing the place.'

Noah nodded thoughtfully. 'Alright. Let's do it. But you'd better give your parents some warning about me. I don't want to take them off guard.'

'Don't worry, they already know about you; I've been sharing info for weeks.' Noah flashed a smile, looking more flattered than worried.

***

Jasmine drove towards her hometown of Te Awamutu. She pointed out landmarks as they went, sharing snippets of childhood memories.

Rather than pulling into the street of her family home, they passed through the town and headed towards the abandoned site of Tokanui Hospital, pulling up on the main road at the entrance, which was blocked by a closed gate.

They stood on the road, taking a moment to observe the surroundings. They had driven into farmland, into remoteness and isolation.

The air smelled of farms – dirt, animals, grass, fertiliser – all mixing into an outdoor-smell that left no doubt you were far from civilisation.

The houses along the narrow road looked tired. They sat opposite the old entrance to the disestablished hospital. Smoke rising from chimneys gave evidence of life and habitation.

'These houses belonged to staff, if I remember correctly,' Jasmine explained. 'It was quite a community – with a superintendent and the family living here, along with the rest of the staff.'

'Hmm,' Noah said, unsure what to make of it. 'Interesting view, watching people come and go from the hospital.'

They strained their eyes to find the hospital buildings, but the hedges were so overgrown that only dots of rooflines were visible.

'Let's go in,' Noah said, opening the car door as he stepped out. Jasmine quickly noted the hazard signs on the gate, including warnings of prosecution.

'I don't know,' she paused, doubting her decision. 'There could be asbestos in the buildings, or toxic mould. Plus, there are probably security guards.'

He looked at her. 'Is this my first moment with OCD?' he asked, half-joking but curious.

'No,' she answered defiantly, 'it's just the first one you've recognised! And, it's just good sense.'

'I've got you,' he said. He reached his arm out, and she couldn't resist. She took a deep breath and made her way towards the entrance.

'Okay, but first sign of danger, and I'm turning back.'

They climbed over the barricade and wandered down the old driveway. Remnants of Tokanui Hospital began to emerge through overgrown trees and weeds.

In its day, the site must have been extraordinary with state-of-the-art buildings, ring roads crisscrossing the grounds, and self-sufficient facilities like a laundry, farm and nurses' quarters.

Now, it was worthy of a movie set for a horror film – derelict.

'It's huge,' Jasmine said, glancing at the sprawling layout ahead of them. 'There are so many buildings – like a city. It's not what I imagined.'

Noah nodded, his eyes scanning the grounds. 'There must be at least 70 buildings, and look, an old swimming pool,' he said, pointing towards the distance where the empty pool was just visible.

'It's certainly a long way from anything. There would be no easy way to leave,' he added.

'He must have felt so far away from home,' Jasmine said, referring to Ben.

She sensed the high emotion of the moment and questioned whether it had been a good idea to bring Noah here.

As they approached one of the main dilapidated buildings, they spotted a rusted sign lying on the ground. It had been part of an old information board.

Noah picked it up and read aloud: 'Opened in 1912... built on 80 hectares... self-sufficient in its early days with its farm and bak ery... served patients from as far as Gisborne and New Plymouth.'

He let the sign drop with a dull thud. 'Some of these patients probably never saw their families again. I'm glad Nana, Dad and

Aunty Rose visited, even though it must have been overwhelming.'

'I'm glad we don't care for people this way anymore,' Jasmine muttered. 'Just locking people out of sight.'

They stepped through the overgrown gardens to the edge of a building, making their way to a window.

Jasmine thought that if it weren't a window to an asylum, she would have liked its style – the kind suited to a villa adorned with beautiful furniture and stylish lace curtains.

The bottom half of the frame held a large piece of glass that could slide up in the frame, allowing ample fresh air, or even enough room to climb out. The top part had wood crossing vertically and horizontally, creating small boxes of light.

As she peered inside, she saw long reflections from the sun, in the pattern of the window, resting on the thin, worn carpet.

She gasped.

The room was a stark contrast to the window's potential.

Rows of empty, rusted metal beds lined the space, and doors with padlocks on the outside hinted at confinement. A single wheelchair sat in the corner, twisted and holding no resemblance to comfort.

Was this the window that Ben had looked through, longing for home?

Was it the window that gave him some light to write poetry and draw pictures?

Did he love the window for the hope it offered – or hate it for the confinement it gave?

Was it a window that Jasmine would have been confined to look through if she had lived in another era?

She shuddered.

'Wow,' Jasmine said softly, once she had taken in the full view of the room. 'I must be naive. I imagined Ben living in the comfort of his own room, not with a room full of people.'

Noah frowned. 'Yeah, either that or he was locked in one of those rooms,' he said, pointing to the padlocked cubicles.

Jasmine recalled something in Ben's poems. She pulled out her phone, flicking through the photos she had of his writing. Scrolling through the words, she found what she was looking for.

'These words from Ben's poems make sense, here, in this space.'

> Give me the hope that
> through
> That fog's thick curtain
> The sun will bring a strong
> light new
> A hope! Strong sure and cer-
> tain

Noah nodded, 'Yeah, he was looking for something to give him hope, even if it was just the sunlight.'

He sighed and turned away, 'It's hard to stomach.'

They moved towards another building with the whole window frame missing, broken and pushed inside. Jasmine and Noah leaned through the gap it left behind.

The room held two old baths that sat in the middle of the floor, fitted with restraints and covers. Sinks hung crookedly from the walls, their pipes exposed like wounds.

On the wall hung a sign: *Clean bath after individual use.*

'Oh no,' said Noah, stepping back. 'That's actually sickening. Were people restrained in the bath?'

Jasmine looked at him, 'I shouldn't have brought you here,' she said softly, but Noah didn't answer. He turned and walked away, his hands clenched into fists.

She ran to catch up with him and saw tears of frustration brimming in his eyes.

Noah shook his head. 'No, it's fine. It's good to face it. Now I know why Dad never mentioned it. Why would he? Why would he ever want to remember this place?'

He kicked the shrub in the garden, as if it had something to do with the decision to keep his grandfather here.

Jasmine thought of Jenny in *Forrest Gump,* throwing rocks at her childhood home. She picked up a rock and threw it. It felt so good.

Noah copied, yelling and swearing at the building.

'Ah, that feels better,' he said, breathing hard.

Just then, they heard the sound of a car approaching. A security vehicle rounded the corner of the hospital's ring road, its lights flashing.

'Run!' shouted Noah, grabbing Jasmine's hand.

They bolted off the path, through a paddock and across the grass, reaching a fence that they clambered over quickly. Noah boosted Jasmine up, then scrambled over behind her like a billy goat.

They weaved through old pathways and around concrete bollards, finally reaching the road and the safety of their car.

Once inside the vehicle, they sped away, Tokanui Hospital shrinking in the rearview mirror.

When they both had a moment to catch their breath, Noah started laughing. 'I need to either laugh or cry,' he said.

'I can't believe I did that,' Jasmine said, giggling.

'We escaped Tokanui! If only Grandad had been so lucky,' Noah added.

'Thanks for taking me,' he said, holding her hand. 'Although it's a bit of a strange date.'

She giggled, 'It was tough, but I'm kind of glad I've seen it. It fills in some of the gaps for us. It just wasn't what I hoped to find. I guess he wasn't off at a resort.'

Noah nodded, 'True.'

They made their way towards Te Awamutu town, putting distance between themselves and the hospital.

'So, what's the rest of this date going to be like?' Noah asked. 'Will there be a need to run away from your parents' house?'

Jasmine giggled. 'Ah, yes, just you wait.'

***

Cliff was waiting at the door as they arrived, his arms crossed, and he had a curious look on his face.

'Well, well. Who's this?' Cliff called out as Jasmine and Noah climbed out of the car.

'Dad, this is Noah,' Jasmine said, rolling her eyes at her father's theatrics.

'Noah, nice to meet you. I'm Cliff,' he said, shaking Noah's hand firmly. 'So, what do you do?' He launched straight into the inquisition.

'I'm a builder,' Noah replied.

'Ah, good trade. Hard work, though. You have your own business?' Cliff asked.

'I do, yes. Just me and an apprentice at the moment,' Noah said.

'Keeps you busy, I bet.'

As they approached the door, Cliff paused to turn to Noah. 'Please remove your shoes – this house is a no-shoes-inside place.'

Jasmine whispered to Noah, 'I forgot to tell you, Dad has a bit of OCD. It's in the genes.' Noah nodded, looking a little worried that he might offend Cliff.

She quickly gave him some tips. 'Just wash your hands for dinner, don't double-dip your food and leave your shoes at the door.'

Inside the house, Jasmine's mum greeted them with a warm smile. 'Welcome, Noah. I'm Gaye – it's so lovely to meet you,' she said.

They settled in the living room, Cliff's questions continuing to flow as they drank together.

'So, how'd you two meet?' he asked.

Jasmine jumped in before Noah could answer. 'Through work, sort of. Noah's family history ties in with some diaries I've been archiving.'

'Diaries?' Gaye asked, intrigued. 'Whose diaries?'

'His grandfather and grandmother's diaries,' Jasmine explained.

'And who said you would never meet anyone in the archives?' said Cliff.

Jasmine nodded, giggling.

Cliff continued, 'You've been reading them, Noah?'

'Yeah. It's been eye-opening,' Noah admitted. 'I never really knew much about my grandfather before.'

Cliff leaned back, considering this. 'Well, I'm impressed that you care about your family's history. That's rare.'

Jasmine smiled, and Noah looked proud. 'I'm just trying to catch up. Jasmine's done all the hard work.'

Jasmine enjoyed sharing Noah with her parents. The conversation flowed well with Cliff and Gaye asking lots of questions, and Noah trying his best to impress them with the answers.

As Noah and Jasmine prepared to leave, Cliff pulled Noah aside. 'You treat her well, alright? She's one of a kind.'

Noah nodded solemnly. 'I will. You have my word.'

Back in the car, Jasmine looked over at Noah. 'Survived the inquisition?' she teased.

'Barely,' he said with a grin. 'Your dad's intense – I mean, he started the questions before I even went in the door. Your mum is great, though.'

'He's just thorough,' Jasmine said, laughing.

Jasmine had noticed how hard Noah worked on impressing Cliff. She overheard snippets of conversation about the stock exchange and volunteer work.

While in the car, she thanked him. 'I noticed you tried really hard to impress Dad. I appreciate it.'

'It's all good. I'm sure I'd have some doubts too if my daughter's boyfriend arrived on the scene with kids and possible baggage,' he admitted. 'I want to show him that I'm all in.'

Jasmine couldn't help the smile that spread on her face.

'Sooo,' she said, dragging the word out, 'you're calling yourself my boyfriend now?'

'Of course!' he said, laughing as he reached for her hand.

'I'm glad we came. Thanks for bringing me,' he said.

'Thanks for coming,' she replied.

'Now,' he said, eyes twinkling, 'are we heading home to yours?' But I could do with a change of clothes and some toiletries.'

'I've got spare toiletries, and as for clothes, we could wash them tonight. They'll be dry by morning.'

'Perfect,' he said with a wink.

'To my house it is – although Joel and Paige will probably be there. It could be a second inquisition before bed.'

'I'm keen,' he grinned.

Chapter Twenty-One

What if I cause a catastrophe?

The days fell into a regular pattern. Jasmine and Joel used each lunch hour to fight with Medusa, wearing her down and diminishing her power. Jasmine made incredible progress, now regularly walking under the bridge and even standing there, listening to the cars pass above.

When Noah wasn't with his daughters, he was with Jasmine at her house. Most weekends were spent with the four of them going places. Jasmine loved the family time and adored how Noah treated the girls. She could see it was full-on, but it was still rewarding.

This coming weekend was an opportunity for the two of them to go away together. His daughters were at a cousin's birthday, and Noah was free. Jasmine loved planning where to go and what to do. She was at her desk, wishing the hours to go by quickly, when Moana entered the office.

'Caleb baked again. Triple chocolate cookies this time,' Moana announced, placing a plate on Jasmine's desk. 'I figured you wouldn't mind being a taste tester. It's part of his therapy, using ingredients in the kitchen that are also used in the science lab.'

'Oh, so these are sulfuric acid-based?' Jasmine asked, half joking.

'No, just baking soda and vinegar if you can believe it – plus chocolate and sugar,' she answered.

'Thanks, I'll take one for morning tea,' Jasmine said, wondering if she would actually eat it. 'They look amazing. Tell him I said he's spoiling me.'

'I will,' Moana said with a laugh, sitting down in one of the chairs and leaning in for a whisper. 'He's doing so well, Jasmine. I can't thank you enough for encouraging us to start the therapy.'

Jasmine smiled. 'That's great to hear. How's he managing it?'

Moana's face softened. 'Better than I could have hoped. He's still anxious, of course, but he's pushing himself in ways I never thought he could. The other day, he went to an Open Day at a high school. We knew that the science lab would be part of the tour, so we made a plan in advance, and there were no surprises. One month ago, we wouldn't have got him to the school grounds.'

'That's incredible, Moana. You must be so proud of him.'

'I am,' Moana said, her eyes glistening with emotion. 'And it's thanks to people like you who've helped me understand what he's going through.'

Jasmine shook her head. 'You give me too much credit. Unfortunately, I'm just experienced in these things.'

Moana nodded but then hesitated, her expression shifting to something more serious. 'Actually, there's another reason I came to see you today, and it's about that experience you have.'

Jasmine tilted her head. 'What's up?'

'Well, I've been thinking,' Moana began, her voice measured. 'When we went to that support group in Auckland, I realised how much it helped me to talk to other parents who understand what it's like. And I started wondering, why don't we have something like that here in Hamilton?'

'That's a great idea,' Jasmine said immediately. 'There must be so many parents and families who would benefit from that.'

'I think so too,' Moana said, her enthusiasm growing. 'But here's the thing, I don't think I can do it on my own. I was hoping you might help me. Maybe even lead it?'

Jasmine was caught off guard. 'Me? Moana, I don't know, I'm not an expert.'

'I can find an expert, I want someone with experience. You understand OCD in ways most parents don't. And you've been amazing at helping me understand everything with Caleb. That's all anyone would need to start.'

Jasmine leaned back, her thoughts racing. 'I don't know if I'm the right person for something like that. What if people ask questions I can't answer?'

'I'll have a counsellor there too. You'll be fine,' Moana said confidently. 'We could even use the council's library as a venue.'

Jasmine considered it, imagining a group of people sitting together, sharing stories, supporting one another. It wasn't so different from what she and Moana had done for each other.

'The library, huh? That's actually a great idea.'

Moana leaned forward, her eyes shining with hope. 'Will you do it? With me? Even if it's just a trial run?'

After a long pause, Jasmine nodded. 'Okay. I just can't say no to you. No wonder you work in HR, persuading people to do jobs.'

Moana let out a breath of relief, her smile wide. 'Thank you, Jasmine. I know this will make such a difference for so many people.'

Jasmine smiled back, 'Alright, let's go to work. We have a support group to plan, and the first person I will recruit is my mum.'

'Great idea! It will be so helpful to showcase someone who has brought up a child who turned out okay.'

'Okay?' Jasmine smiled, 'If you say so.'

***

Jasmine continued working while thinking about the plans for the support group. She jotted down ideas for the first two meetings, planning how to connect the parents safely while allowing the children to keep their anonymity.

She slipped down to the archives to grab some files and used the time to let her mind evolve the ideas. The quiet of the dungeons allowed her to be in planning mode.

Jasmine jumped with a fright when Noah appeared at the dungeon door; she hadn't heard his footsteps in the corridor. Once the surprise passed, she smiled, pleased to see him.

And then she saw his face, something was wrong.

'Noah? What's wrong?' she asked, moving towards him with concern.

He stepped inside, 'I wanted to check on you if you had heard the news,' he said, his voice tight. 'There's been a shooting. In Christchurch at two mosques.'

Jasmine froze, 'What? How bad is it?'

'Bad,' Noah replied, his hands trembling slightly. 'Dozens of people... killed, they are saying up to 50.'

Before Jasmine could respond, Joel appeared, his usually animated face subdued. 'I came to check... You left your phone,' he said simply.

The three of them sat down at the small table, and Noah rested his elbows on his knees, staring at the floor. Joel scrolled through his phone, reading aloud the unfolding reports.

'They're calling it the darkest day in New Zealand history,' Joel said, his voice barely above a whisper. 'Dozens of people were in prayer.'

Jasmine's heart clenched as she listened, imagining the grief and terror that had unfolded in what should have been a place of sanctuary. 'How could this happen in New Zealand?'

Noah nodded. 'It doesn't feel real. This is supposed to be one of the safest places in the world.'

They sat in silence. No words were good enough.

Jasmine looked at her hands, clasped tightly in her lap and then, standing up, she announced, 'I'm crossing the bridge tomorrow.'

Noah and Joel both turned to her, startled. 'Um, that's not what I was expecting,' Noah said gently.

'I'm sick of bullies. Bullies with guns, bullies with power and I, well, I live with one in my brain, and it's time to stand up to it,' Jasmine said firmly.

'Medusa, you are out of here,' she added, tapping her forehead.

Noah smiled at her, 'Okay. Let's swap a romantic getaway for a fight with a bully. I'm in!'

Jasmine felt a flicker of determination ignite inside her, more substantial than she had ever felt before.

Tomorrow, she would face *her* bully and take back some control.

***

The group of friends gathered at the house that evening. The weight of the day's events pressed down on all of them. They felt helpless, unsure how to be of any real support to the terrorised community. Usual activities like watching TV felt superficial and disrespectful.

They discussed the plans for tomorrow. Even though Jasmine had bravely made the announcement, she still had no idea how to go against the very thing that had kept her feeling safe for the past few years.

'I still think we should strap you into a life jacket,' Joel said, making his contribution to the strategy. 'You know, just in case.'

Jasmine shook her head. 'As much as I like the idea, I think it's a no.'

Jasmine looked at her three friends, softening at Joel's offer to be helpful. 'Do I need to do this?' she asked, hoping they might talk her out of it. But before they answered, she continued, 'Yes – no – yes.'

Noah nodded, his expression serious. 'Alright. Let's figure this out. First, which bridge?'

'Fairfield,' Paige suggested without hesitation. 'Shortest one with high sides. Less exposure.'

Jasmine agreed. 'Okay. That makes sense. And which car are we in?' she asked, needing to visualise every part of the plan.

'My ute,' Noah said firmly. 'It's big and it'll feel safer for you.'

Jasmine nodded as she heard Medusa's voice: *Not safer. It has further to fall.*

'What else?' she said, pushing through the noise.

Joel raised a hand. 'Breathing coach, reporting for duty.'

'And music,' Paige added. 'I'll pick something that will distract you.'

Jasmine laughed despite herself. 'So, Joel's on breathing, Paige is on music, Noah's driving the tank... and me? I'm just sitting there, trying not to lose it.'

'You're doing the most important part,' Noah said softly.

'Do I need a blindfold?' Jasmine asked, half-joking but also half-serious.

'No way,' Joel said immediately, 'it'll look like we're kidnapping you.'

'It's also counterproductive,' Paige said. 'You need to see it, Jaz. That's the whole point.'

Jasmine sighed. The battle lines were drawn, and Jasmine had a small army on her side.

'We will all be fine,' Noah said, his voice steady. 'Just remember we are fighting against that bully in your brain.'

Jasmine noted that Noah was a quick learner and considered that he might be reading OCD help books on the side.

'Once I cross over, I might never come back.'

'Good,' Noah said with a grin. 'Because then you can stay at my place.'

Paige made a dramatic gagging noise. 'Don't ruin the moment, Noah.'

Jasmine sat down on the couch and looked at her friends who would help her cross the bridge – literally and metaphorically.

'Alright,' she said, exhaling deeply. 'Tomorrow morning. Fairfield Bridge.'

Noah reached over and took her hand. 'See ya Medusa.'

As she prepared for bed, with all three of her friends staying the night, she was grateful for the support. She always assumed it would be too difficult to explain OCD to someone. But, here they were, all supporting in the way she needed and without eye-rolling or scoffing. That in itself was a success.

While Noah showered, Jasmine knocked quietly on Paige's door, aware of Joel sleeping on the couch in the lounge, just metres away.

On entering the room, Jasmine sheepishly asked Paige a favour. 'Can you bring this with you tomorrow without anyone noticing? I think I feel a little better just knowing it will be in the car.'

She handed Paige the *Team Jasmine* life jacket. Paige smiled, 'Sure.'

'I mean, I don't mind if the others see it, but I am trying to minimise people knowing just how extreme I can be.'

'I get it, I'll be discreet.'

'Goodnight, and thanks,' Jasmine said, leaving the room.

During the night, there was an incredible downpour of rain. Jasmine lay awake, imagining the overly full river flowing swiftly.

Jasmine's thoughts swirled like the water:

Why am I doing this? What will Noah think? What if he leaves me? What if I cause a catastrophe?

Her thoughts swirled endlessly until, finally, she drew on what she had recently advised Moana. *You have to push back. Take the ground back. Be in control.*

And Jasmine wanted control.

Chapter Twenty-Two

What if the bridge falls down?

When Jasmine woke in the morning, the rain had ceased, and to her surprise, the brown grass, dry from a long summer, already had a tinge of green and a sign of survival.

The kitchen smelled like coffee and toast when Jasmine made her way there. Noah, Joel and Paige were chatting about basic topics like the weather and car diffuser smells.

While Jasmine managed some Marmite on toast, she let herself prepare.

Cobham, Victoria, Claudelands, Whitiora, Fairfield, Pukete.

Cobham, Victoria, Claudelands, Whitiora, Fairfield, Pukete.

She managed to recite her ritual in her head while smiling and nodding, multi-tasking of sorts. She knew that today wasn't the day to resist her counter-measure, 'That will come later,' her therapist advised.

Today, she just had to face her obsession head-on.

'Let's go,' Noah said once the dishes were cleared, and there was no reason to stay.

Jasmine looked around the room, hoping for a legitimate delay.

Sensing her tactic, Noah added, 'The sooner we go, the sooner you win.'

She nodded and could feel emotions brimming in her eyes and chest. 'It's not going to be easy,' she said as her one final declaration.

The friends piled into Noah's truck. Jasmine sat in the passenger seat, her hands gripping her lap tightly. Joel and Paige settled into the back, their chatter light and deliberate in an effort to keep the atmosphere as normal as possible.

'Alright, team,' Joel said, leaning forward between the seats. 'Breathing coach here. Jaz, let's start with a big inhale for four counts. Ready? One, two, three, four...'

Jasmine obeyed, filling her lungs and holding her breath before exhaling. As the truck rumbled closer to the river, her chest felt tighter, her pulse louder.

Paige started the music. 'I have chosen something a little upbeat and old, but it had the message we want.'

She started blaring, *I'm Gonna Get Along Without You Now.*

Jasmine smiled for the first time that morning. The idea that Medusa could be treated like a bad ex, someone she'd outgrown, someone she could say goodbye to with just the right amount of sass, felt good.

It felt possible.

Noah glanced at Jasmine. 'You okay?'

She nodded quickly, though her stomach churned. 'Yeah. Just keep driving.'

As they approached the Fairfield Bridge, its distinctive arches came into view. Jasmine's snakes rattled in her head.

You shouldn't do this.

Your friends will be hurt.

She pushed back on the thoughts.

I am safe.

It's just OCD.

Go to hell, Medusa.

I am in control.

She began to sing out loud. Joel immediately picked up on it, and joined in.

'This is just like carpool karaoke with James Corden,' he said, trying to distract and defuse all at once.

Jasmine gripped the door as the truck began approaching the bridge.

'How many seconds do you think it will take to cross?' she asked, hoping for more distraction.

'Well, that probably depends on how fast I drive,' Noah joked. 'Permission to break the law and speed?'

'Probably not,' she managed to answer.

'In that case, I think it will take ten seconds to cross. Just ten seconds.'

The car turned left onto the bridge, crossing the river that Jasmine hadn't crossed for years.

'I can't look,' Jasmine whispered, shutting her eyes tight.

'Open them,' Joel said gently. 'Remember, you're safe.'

She opened her eyes slowly, her heart raced, and she could feel the thoughts swirling in her head. The arches passed one by one, and with each span, Jasmine felt relief that she was getting closer to the other side. Her breathing steadied, and her grip on the door handle loosened.

And then, just like that, they were over.

Jasmine exhaled a shaky breath, her eyes welling with tears.

Joel let out a loud 'Yahoo!' from the backseat, throwing his arms in the air. Paige joined in, clapping. Jasmine laughed, the sound bubbling up from somewhere deep inside her. Her friends' reactions were equivalent to her winning gold at the Olympics.

'Can you pull over?' she asked Noah, who immediately obliged, pulling into a side street.

Jasmine opened the door, took a deep breath, and then vomited in the gutter.

'Oh dang, girl, wasn't prepared for that,' Joel said. 'Should have brought a bucket.'

Noah laughed. 'Let it all out.' He handed her his water bottle, which she drank from before pouring the rest over the mess in the gutter.

She bent over, catching her breath, and quietly let it all out in a whisper.

Cobham, Victoria, Claudelands, Whitiora, Fairfield, Pukete.

Cobham, Victoria, Claudelands, Whitiora, Fairfield, Pukete.

When she was composed, she asked, 'Can we take a photo? I need to send it to my mum.'

They gathered around Jasmine's phone, showing the street sign in the background, and pushed send with the words, "Victory against Medusa".

'Now that we have you here, we have a full day planned, starting with Duck Island ice cream,' Noah said, quickly keeping her distracted.

'Ice cream? In the morning?' Jasmine asked, her smile widening.

'It will be good to replace some of the contents from your stomach,' he joked, pulling back onto the main road.

During the car ride, Jasmine felt like a celebrity, a university graduate, or something equally grand.

They made their way through Hamilton East, on streets that Jasmine hadn't seen for a few years. She noticed some houses had been demolished and replaced with apartments. She saw familiar haunts that she and Paige had frequented when they were students.

She used the view to distract her mind from what she had just done.

Noah pulled up outside the famous Hamilton ice cream parlour. Jasmine chatted away, explaining that she had watched a video showing a whole apple pie crushed into the ice cream.

The chatter helped her push the thoughts away.

Inside, Joel insisted on tasting nearly every flavour before settling on a scoop of salted caramel and coconut. Jasmine went for the apple pie, two scoops.

The group sat outside on a picnic table.

'You crossed a bridge and ended up at Duck Island,' Joel said, raising his cone like someone making a toast with a glass.

'And no one got hurt,' Jasmine said.

Not yet, she heard Medusa.

She ignored it and pushed on.

'What's next?' she asked.

'Next, my love, is that you get to come and visit Nixon Street,' Noah said as Jasmine clapped.

'Ew, when did she become *my love?*' Joel groaned.

***

Jasmine stepped out of the truck, feeling the warmth of the sun on her face. Noah led the way up the short path to the house, his excitement evident as he pointed out things of interest on the footpath and gate.

Joel and Paige followed, with Joel pretending he was the presenter for a home and garden show.

'Isn't the house amazing, Jaz?' Then, in a low whisper, he told her, 'You would fit in here quite well.'

The exterior of the house was unassuming but full of character and a charm that matched the diaries. Jasmine ran her fingers lightly along the wooden railing of the veranda.

'This is it,' she whispered, 'where it all happened.'

'Come on, let's go inside,' Noah said, unlocking the door and holding it open for everyone.

Stepping inside, Jasmine was struck by how well the house had been preserved. The hardwood floors creaked softly beneath her feet, and the air carried a faint, earthy scent that reminded her of old books.

She couldn't help but imagine Evie bustling about the kitchen, Ben sitting by a window with one of his notebooks.

She chose to remember the early years when Albert was at school and the younger children had just been born. Her fingers brushed against the handles of the doors, the same ones Evie must have touched countless times.

'These doors,' Jasmine said, her voice reverent, 'Evie touched these.'

'For fifty years. And probably cursed at them,' Noah said. 'You know how temperamental old doors can be.'

Jasmine tried to soak in every detail. Noah led them outside to the garden. Jasmine's eyes immediately went to the old copper, now a centrepiece in an outdoor BBQ area.

'That's where they used to boil the laundry,' Noah explained. 'Now it's part of the BBQ setup.'

Jasmine ran her hand along the rim of the copper. 'Evie's hands would've worked so hard over this.'

Noah nodded. 'And I'm sure you want to see her treasured grapevine,' he said, motioning toward a sprawling vine that climbed along a trellis.

'She was so proud of these grapes. She used to pack them up and send them by train to her family down south. I'm not sure if you noticed her mention the vine regularly in the diaries.'

Jasmine plucked a grape, washing it at the outdoor tap before popping it into her mouth. It was sweet and tasted better than anything store-bought. She smiled. 'They're perfect. Are you telling me this is the original vine?'

'Yep, preserved all these years,' he replied.

Paige was exploring the garden, poking her head into every corner. Joel, leaning casually against the trellis, chimed in.

'I bet they used basic slag to fertilise these grapes. That's probably why they're still alive.'

Noah groaned. 'That joke is never going away, is it?'

'Not while I'm here,' Joel said, grinning.

Before they moved on from the vine, Noah stopped Jasmine near the trellis.

'I've been saving this for the right moment,' he said, pulling a small pot from beside the vine. It had a bow around it and held a grapevine cutting, already showing signs of life.

Jasmine was touched. 'You grew this for me?'

He nodded. 'Well, I propagated it. It's a little piece of Evie's garden for yours. I thought you might like it?'

She hugged the pot to her chest. 'It's perfect. Thank you, Noah.'

He smiled, looking pleased with himself. Jasmine and Noah wandered further into the garden and around the house. The old pathway wound past the bedroom windows.

'Is this where your dad, Thomas, slept?'

'Yes, his room used to be part of the veranda until they closed it in to make a bedroom. It still slopes. And Rose's room is the girls' room when they stay.'

'It's just so bizarre to be here ninety years later. It's more amazing than I imagined,' Jasmine said, doing a 360-degree turn to take in everything at once.

'If I close my eyes, I can almost imagine I live here,' Joel said dreamily.

Paige snorted. 'You *almost* live with us. Make up your mind.'

'Fair point,' Joel conceded. 'But a guy can dream.'

Noah clapped his hands. 'Alright, on with our day, we have more plans.'

'Ooh, what's next?' Jasmine asked, enjoying the reward of the day.

Noah smiled, 'We are going to visit a certain two nieces who are busting to see their aunty.'

Jasmine beamed – it was just as she had hoped.

They piled back into the truck, Jasmine holding the grapevine carefully. As the car travelled towards Chartwell, where her nieces lived, she felt pure joy at being able to visit them and introduce Noah to Bree and Todd.

***

They pulled into the driveway of a modern home that had a simple rock garden with miniature flax and ferns. The house was a contrast to the almost 100-year-old home they had just left.

Jasmine gave a friendly knock on the door and was thrilled when Morgan peered through the window. At the sight of Jasmine, she pulled the door wide open and jumped into her arms.

Within seconds, Jasmine was rushed into the house and marched through the rooms. She called out to Bree and Todd, 'That's Noah, introduce yourselves.' She was glad he was confident enough to care for himself.

'Come!' Aria insisted, pulling Jasmine down the hallway. 'We've got something to show you.'

The two girls took her into their bedroom, where Aria dramatically lifted the lid of a brightly decorated box, revealing an assortment of letters, each carefully stacked and preserved.

'We kept them all!' Morgan said proudly, beaming up at her aunty. Jasmine recognised her own handwriting on the envelopes.

'You two will make excellent archivists one day,' she said proudly, stroking their hair. It felt so good to be in the same room as them.

Morgan nodded seriously. 'We have a system to keep them in order.'

Aria added, 'And we re-read them. The one about your neighbour's cat sleeping in your bed during the day is our favourite!'

Jasmine laughed. 'That was quite the saga.' She took a moment to glance over the letters again, grateful for the idea from Evie and Ben to connect with her nieces.

Morgan smiled, 'You haven't visited in ages.'

Jasmine hesitated for a fraction of a second before mustering an answer. 'Well... I was a little nervous about crossing the bridge.'

The girls exchanged a glance and nodded as if this made perfect sense in their childlike logic.

'Bridges are kinda scary,' Aria agreed. 'But you made it!'

'I did,' Jasmine said, touched by their unwavering acceptance. 'And I'm happy I did.'

Morgan clapped her hands together. 'Okay! Now you have to stay for lunch!'

Jasmine let out a mock sigh of defeat. 'Oh, well, if I have to.'

The girls cheered and grabbed her hands again, dragging her back toward the living room, where the adults were deep in conversation. Jasmine just sat and listened while braiding the girls' hair. It was contentment in the fullest sense.

After socialising with the family, Jasmine knew she had to make the return trip. She had started to dread the thought as she sat and listened to the conversation, her nieces at her feet like puppies.

She could tell the anxiety wasn't as heightened as the first time, but it was still there. She couldn't avoid much longer, she *had* to go home.

The friends prepared to leave, picking up their items and dragging out the goodbyes.

At the door, Jasmine felt a hand take hers and she turned to see Bree standing next to her. Bree leaned in and whispered, 'I'm proud of you Jaz. You truly are amazing.'

Jasmine was happily surprised and just squeezed her sister's hand. 'I'll be back again,' she said.

'When you can make it, we will be excited to see you.'

The group used the same method of crossing, breathing, music, and distraction to reverse the trip home.

Paige said from the backseat, 'You're practically a professional bridge-crosser now.'

Jasmine nodded. *If only it were that easy.*

But, she appreciated her friend's supportive comment.

When they reached Jasmine's place, she turned to Noah. 'I think I could manage to do it again next week.'

'Absolutely,' he said as he helped Jasmine carry her new grapevine inside.

Chapter Twenty-Three

What if someone dies on my watch?

Autumn moved into winter, with the friends maintaining an excellent rhythm of evening antics and quiet weekends.

Jasmine regularly challenged herself to cross the bridge, usually with Noah supporting her. She hadn't crossed by herself yet, but she knew she would get to that stage.

Joel was out more often now that Lucca had become a permanent fixture in his life. Paige often tagged along as a third wheel for either couple, her company always adding to the friendships.

On a particularly wet day, Jasmine drove home from work as fat, relentless raindrops pelted her windscreen, overwhelming the wipers. She was relieved to pull into her driveway and smiled when she saw Paige's car already there.

Dashing through the downpour, she reached the front door, drenched within seconds. Laughing, she flicked off her wet outer layers and called out to Paige, asking if she'd been caught in the same downpour.

No response.

Jasmine knocked on Paige's door and found her curled up in bed. The floor around her was littered with several tissues, scattered around a rubbish bin.

'Are you sick?' Jasmine asked, concerned.

Paige shook her head and turned toward Jasmine, revealing swollen, tear-streaked eyes.

Jasmine's heart clenched as she jumped to the worst scenarios. Was it Joel? No, she had just seen him at work. Paige's family? Her job?

Years of navigating her own crises had taught Jasmine how to respond. She sat gently on the edge of the bed and rubbed Paige's back, knowing she would share when she was ready.

Paige thrust her phone toward Jasmine. A news story showed on the screen. Jasmine scrolled through it, her stomach sinking as she took in the details. A six-year-old girl had died in Hamilton. The report was vague, but it was clear the child had received deadly injuries at home, and a stepfather had been arrested.

'Do you know her?' Jasmine asked softly.

Paige nodded, unable to speak.

'Is she from your school?' Jasmine asked, still rubbing Paige's back.

Another nod. Then, through a choked sob, Paige managed, 'In my class.' She pounded her chest in frustration. 'In my class!'

'Oh, Paige, I'm so sorry.'

'How did I not know?' Paige's anger heightened. 'How did I miss the signs?'

Jasmine searched for the right words. 'People are very good at hiding what they don't want others to see.'

Paige shook her head. 'She was so sweet and quiet. I thought she was shy, but maybe she was scared. I never saw a bruise or *anything.*'

She dissolved into sobs again, and Jasmine held her, crying with her and for the girl, for all the children who the adults let down.

The sound of the front door opening made Jasmine excuse herself to intercept Joel before he could burst in cheerfully. She met him in the hallway, explaining the situation.

Joel's expression sobered instantly. 'What can I do?'

Jasmine bit her lip. She didn't know. There was no fix. 'Just comfort her.'

Joel nodded and stepped into Paige's room without hesitation. Jasmine watched as he climbed onto the bed beside her, wrapping her in his arms. She could hear him making soft, shushing noises, stroking her hair like a parent soothing a child. His large frame engulfed Paige, giving the appearance of protection.

If only it would be that easy, Jasmine thought, knowing it would be a pain in Paige's heart that would last a lifetime.

Jasmine slipped into the kitchen to make a soothing drink for Paige. She wanted to throw something to release her frustration. In the absence of a rock, Jasmine picked up the tea towel and whacked it on the bench as hard as she could, swearing under her breath. She heard a car pull up on the road and looked to see Noah's truck, the rain still pelting down. Meeting him at the door, she tried to explain, but as soon as the words left her lips, she broke down sobbing again.

To her surprise, Noah's eyes welled up, too. 'What shall we do?'

It was the same question they all had. *How can we help?*

A few minutes later, Joel emerged from the room, his own eyes red. 'She's asleep,' he said quietly, his voice filled with the same tenderness as a father watching over a child.

Silence stretched between them before Joel finally asked, 'Will she recover?'

'She will,' Noah said after a moment. 'But it will change her. It will change her for life.'

***

Jasmine took the next few days off work, staying at home with Paige, who slept a lot.

When she seemed especially lost, Jasmine offered to read from Evie's letters, the ones written to Rose. Jasmine hadn't read them, but now seemed the fitting time to be comforted by Evie.

Jasmine was glad for the excuse to delve back in time with Evie. She opened the box full of letters. They were flat and typed on thin, almost see-through paper.

'Typed! Any of us can read these treasures,' Jasmine announced. 'And it looks like we start in summer 1976, 13 February,' Jasmine read aloud.

'Wow, we jumped almost thirty years.' Paige said.

Jasmine was happy to hear her voice – and her interjection.

'Yep, thirty years, and she's still in the same house. I believe the letters start just after Ben moved into full-time care at the hospital.' Jasmine said, giving context to the letters.

Dear Rose

I found out that your Northener train gets to Hamilton Station at 5.10 am. I am enclosing $2 for you to get a taxi, as I don't have a car to meet you. This is just a little, but please take it as if I were able to meet you. You will wonder where you are when you step out of the *train. The new station is situated in a very quiet area and is rather puzzling.*

Jasmine glanced up at Paige, who had shifted slightly but was still listening. Jasmine continued, reading Evie's careful details about the journey and preparations for a party.

'She was always thinking of everyone else,' Paige murmured.

Jasmine nodded. 'Even in the little things, like sending two dollars for a taxi.'

Paige managed a small smile, and Jasmine took it as a sign to keep going. She selected another letter, this one dated 11 March 1976.

Dad is very well at present and loves the picture you sent of the horse. He asked me not to give the foal hot milk as it would kill it. It showed his love for horses and his lack of understanding. I placed it on the wall of his room and it seemed to please him.

She continued to read, the two of them enjoying time in a different decade and listening to Evie's familiar voice. She still mentioned the weather and washing, as well as trips to town and escapades on her bike. She spoke of visits to Ben in the hospital and spoke of him with fondness.

Jasmine unfolded a short note from 1976 that was still in its envelope.

This is just a short note, mainly to let you know that I will be taking grapes to the Road Services tomorrow a.m. to go on the train. I do hope they will arrive in good condition. Even if grapes are cheap in Wellington, I'd like you to have some from home.

'Ahh, the grapevine is still strong in the 1970s,' Paige laughed, and Jasmine was relieved to hear the sound from her friend. The letters had a calming impact on them both.

She continued reading.

24 November 1976
Today, Dad said, 'If I have to go in the long box, don't tell the children. Just say I have gone for a long holiday.' It made me feel awful when he said that. He has never said anything like that before.

Paige let out a shaky breath. 'That's awful,' she said. 'She deals with so much. How did she cope?'

Jasmine paused to reflect, 'She probably shows us the most positive things in her writing. I'm sure there were moments when she was low.'

Paige nodded. 'She seems to have a backbone of steel.'

Jasmine continued to read.

Molly came to visit today – she's almost 40 years old, which is so hard to believe. I remember her being with Ben and me as our first foster child. Ben remembered, too, when I told him. She came with her mum, Mrs Taylor, who still lives close by and has stayed in contact with me all these years.

Mrs Taylor never had more children. I think the emotional strain was just too great. Molly doesn't remember being with me, of course, but I remember her. Her visit left me with much to ponder.

Paige nodded. 'Aww, our first foster baby back after 40 years. That must have been satisfying for Evie.'

Jasmine reached for another letter. 'Shall I keep reading?'

Paige nodded, leaning her head against the couch. 'Yes, please. Surprisingly, this is *my* Balm of Gilead.'

I worked at the Save the Children shop today, and what a busy day it was as we prepared for Christmas. I didn't even have a chance to stop for lunch. We took $600 for the day. By closing, I could feel it in my legs and slept well that night.

'How old is Evie in these letters?' Paige asked.

Jasmine quickly worked it out. 'About 70.'

'Good effort with volunteering in a shop at that age. No surprise it's for a cause saving children.'

'I agree,' said Jasmine, wary that they were getting into a sensitive topic for Paige.

'Read on,' Paige said, clearly grateful for the distraction.

December 1976

On Sunday, I had all the family here for Christmas tea. I didn't think I could manage it this year, but Thomas's girls came for the afternoon. They made lettuce salad and all the trimmings, cutting tomatoes like flowers.

They also prepared the fruit salad and whipped cream for trifles, which I had made before going to church. I cooked the lamb on Saturday night after tea. It was all lovely, and we just wished you could have been here too.

Thomas cut the meat and did all the dishes. There were ten of us in total. Albert arrives on Sunday, and we will have Christmas dinner with Thomas's family.

Didn't we have a lovely time last year when we had it at his house with two little ones in highchairs?

Thomas says he's coming to collect me for a day and a night while they're at Raglan. I will enjoy spending time there and hope to go fishing. I love fishing – that must be where Thomas gets it from.

Paige interrupted, smiling. 'Isn't this just the best letter?'

Jasmine scanned the letter again. She could see what Paige meant – this letter had everything they had loved about the diaries.

'First, it's another Christmas *with all the trimmings*. The tomatoes are cut like flowers, her tiny house is full of descendants she never thought she'd have, and we learn she *loves* fishing at Raglan – our beach. Not to mention, she still goes to church and makes trifles,' Paige said. 'She's *our* saint; we are so lucky to know her.'

Jasmine nodded. She could just visualise the tiny dining room, ten of them crammed in with no one excluded. Just Ben would be missing – another Christmas without him at the table.

'Read on,' Paige said, pulling her blanket up around her chin.

And so Jasmine read. She read about Albert and Maple visiting, with Albert doing "quite well now".

Jasmine continued to 1980.

You will be wondering why the letter is written on Wednesday. It is to let you know that Dad is very sick. I had a call from the hospital yesterday afternoon telling me he had been vomiting all day and was very weak.

Thomas took me up. Dad didn't have any voice. We went up again in the evening, and by that time, his temperature had risen, and he did look ill. I managed to give him a little orange drink with glucose, which I had taken up. When I asked Dad if he wanted more drink, he whispered, 'Too right,' and at the finish said, 'Ka pai'.

Those were the only words that were hearable. But you can see he is still with us. I will ring you if necessary.

Jasmine saw that the following letter had jumped a few weeks and suspected it was the news of Ben's death. She felt teary as she approached the letter, even though the death had occurred almost 40 years earlier.

March 1980

It's been a strange time since you all returned to Wellington. I find myself thinking of things to tell Dad or take to him, and then I remember. But as you suggested, I am trying not to grieve too much, as we know he will be happy to be free from that sick body he has carried for so many years.

I think about how peaceful he looked when it was all over. It was wonderful to have Thomas and you with me – I feel we are very close. Having Albert with us was also very good.

Everyone has been kind to me; even now, the phone hardly stops ringing. Aunty Maple went home yesterday. Last night, I had a horrible nightmare. I woke up crying and yelling. I was sure glad to find it was just a dream.

Today, I sorted through all of Ben's things that came back from the hospital. I washed everything and am taking them back on Tuesday.

I am giving Ben's cardigans to the ward to use for anyone who might need them. I've taken his dressing gown to be dry-cleaned.

The bereavement notice will be in the newspapers on Saturday, and I've sent a letter to Knox Church thanking the minister and the ladies for their kind visits to Ben.

Jasmine stopped reading. It was too hard. She looked at Paige, who had silent tears streaming down her face.

'She's lost her lobster,' Paige mumbled through her tears.

Jasmine bit her lip and nodded.

'Read on,' Paige whispered.

And so Jasmine continued, letting Evie's grieving but healing words stretch across time, offering comfort to Paige's broken heart.

Chapter Twenty-Four

What if there's an oil spill?

The healing was slow, and during the next few months, Paige seemed to return to her old self, although she often spent time alone in her room. Jasmine occasionally heard Paige speaking on the phone and frequently typing on her computer. Joel suspected Paige had a secret boyfriend, but Jasmine couldn't agree.

The friends trod carefully around her, giving her healing time.

Jasmine's bridge-conquering was well in hand. She had almost put that snake to rest. It seemed that Medusa had gone into 'hibernation'. Apart from OCD's safety reminders, she had no intrusive thoughts dictating to her.

But she knew it wasn't a time to be complacent.

Medusa would slide back if given any crack.

Moana had done an excellent job of establishing a support group in Hamilton. She'd found families who wanted to attend and recruited both Gaye as a mentor and Dr Kris as a counsellor to speak at the first session.

Jasmine felt a little worried about admitting to people in her own city that she had OCD. As the first meeting approached in September, Jasmine received a message from her mum.

Shall I print in colour or black and white?

Black and white will be fine. Thx

Bit nervous but looking forward to it.

Me too. Noah's coming. Hope it doesn't frighten him away. LOL

I don't think that man will be frightened away. Lots of love to you too.

Jasmine laughed at her mum's interpretation of LOL.

Moana stopped by Jasmine's dungeon.

'I'm just checking on tomorrow night and our schedule,' she said, handing Jasmine an itinerary. Jasmine scanned down the page, spotting her name next to the introductions.

Moana continued, 'I'm just wondering if we should ask the parents if they want to have an outing with the kids so they can get to know each other.'

As Jasmine thought about how that would work, Moana added cheekily, 'Although we might need a lot of hand sanitiser.'

Jasmine smiled. 'I think it would be good to have the kids meet, but let's meet the parents tomorrow first. And remember, not all OCD thoughts involve hand sanitiser,' she said, winking.

'I know, I was being satirical. I just wanted to show you how much I have learned,' she said.

'I think you might be the next speaker,' Jasmine suggested, hoping she might be let off the hook.

'I'll see you tomorrow night,' she said as she left the room quickly.

***

The following evening, Noah, Jasmine, Moana and Gaye met at the central library early enough to clear tables to the side and create a friendly environment with chairs in a half circle. Gaye brought homemade ginger slice and arranged it beautifully beside the cups and drinks Moana had organised.

Families soon trickled in, some on their own, some in twos or even threes, with aunties and grandparents in support. Jasmine was impressed to see how many people wanted to help a loved one.

Moana welcomed everyone and explained the group's purpose, reminding them that it was a safe space to talk and that stories shared should stay in the group. She explained that tonight's speakers would be Dr Kris, followed by Jasmine, who would introduce herself.

She then introduced Gaye, explaining that she was the mother of an adult with OCD who had years of experience and was here to be a mentor. Jasmine could see everyone nodding and smiling at her mum while Gaye beamed. Jasmine was glad she was doing this, for her mum more than for herself.

Dr Kris spoke well about managing expectations.

'When you have a new situation, you need to prepare. Your children will struggle with unpredictability because they live in a world where they need order and control. When your child seems resistant to go for dinner or to the movies, you must ask yourself why that might be. There might be something about the venue or the people that is a trigger, so make a game plan,' she explained.

'Isn't that just babying the condition, giving in to it?' a parent asked.

'I can see why you ask that. It is important not to give in to it. But having a game plan isn't the same as giving in. There's a fine line.'

Jasmine could see the parents were scribbling notes or nodding to each other. Lightbulb moments and questions were coming from those realisations. Before long, it was her turn to stand. Just as she had in the previous group, she boldly explained that OCD was a part of her life. She ran through some examples she had experience with, including moral, fear, and superstition.

Next, the parents started sharing, and each story had its heartbreaking account. One parent cried as she shared how her young adult son was afraid of oil spills from cars and that if he saw oil on the road or in the car park, he insisted on cleaning it. It became so bad that he started doubling back to check a spot he saw on the road to see if it was oil. He had to leave his job because he was always late. 'How can I help him?' she asked, 'I'm sure there is no way forward.'

Jasmine took a deep breath. 'That's hard, and I would recommend getting professional help to work through some steps. But don't give up. Even what seems impossible to overcome can become possible. Let me share my most recent fear as an example.'

Jasmine then laid out her fears of the bridges and her compulsions. She included the panic attacks and how she couldn't even hear, see, or speak the word 'bridge'.

She paused, 'Now that I have told you how deep my intrusive thought was, do you think I could or would ever cross a bridge?'

'No,' they all said, shaking their heads.

'Do you think I needed to cross it?'

She saw some shrugging their shoulders, and finally, one person said, 'I guess not. Not if it causes that much anxiety.'

Jasmine nodded. 'And that is how OCD wins – fear,' she said calmly. 'With help from some good people, including my therapist, I crossed the bridge, and I now do it regularly.'

She heard some of the parents clap, and she saw others cry.

'People with OCD have to fight back. It takes so much effort, which is where *you* are needed. OCD is a bully, and the best way to remove a bully is to stand up to it.'

Moana called the evening to a close. She promised to set up a chat group to ask each other questions. Everyone lingered, enjoying the ginger slice and conversation in a safe place.

Gaye came up to Jasmine and smiled, 'It's so good. I wish I could've come to one of these.'

Jasmine nodded, feeling validation for sharing her thoughts with strangers.

Noah was a social butterfly, meeting people and listening to them.

Moana nudged Jasmine, 'He's a keeper. I mean, is he perfect?'

'He snores,' Jasmine said, laughing. 'But to be honest, he can probably benefit from support too. I'm not going to be the easiest of girlfriends.'

Noah made his way over to the pair, 'Man, I had no idea how bad some of these situations are. I mean, that's a lot for people to deal with. And it seems there isn't a lot of help from the health system,' he said, scratching his head. 'I might try to see how I can help more. I kept thinking of Grandad. I wish he had someone to help him.'

Jasmine could see that Noah's willingness to help was part of a mission to right the wrongs of his grandfather's situation, and she understood that.

Moana, Gaye, Noah, and Jasmine left the building and locked it as they went.

'That was great,' Moana sighed. 'We did good!'

As Noah and Jasmine hopped into his ute, he asked, 'Your place or mine?'

She giggled at his corny line. 'Can we do mine, please? I want to keep an eye on Paige. She's doing well, but something's up.'

'Good call,' Noah said as he reversed the ute.

On the way home, they unpacked the evening. Noah had been impressed with Jasmine's presentation and continued to learn more about the complexities of OCD. 'I'll be back for the next one,' he said, smiling.

When they arrived home, Paige and Joel were waiting for them. Jasmine thought Paige looked more like herself than she had in a while and happily accepted her offer of a hot chocolate.

As Noah and Jasmine discussed the evening's highlights, Paige placed their drinks on the coffee table. She chimed in with all the right noises about their meeting, but she took a deep breath when the conversation died down.

'I have *news*,' she announced.

Jasmine studied her friend, noticing the way she was beaming. Maybe Joel was right – maybe there *was* a secret man in Paige's life.

'I'm just going to blurt it out,' Paige said. 'But please, I don't want anyone telling me all the reasons why I *shouldn't* do this.'

Jasmine's mind raced. Was Paige about to announce she was moving to Alaska?

Paige cleared her throat and straightened her shirt. 'I'm going to foster a child,' she said.

Noah started clapping, Jasmine cried, and Joel laughed.

'So you *don't* have a secret boyfriend?' Joel asked.

Paige frowned. 'What? No, I haven't had time for that.'

'Well, you've been doing something secretive,' he said defensively.

'I've been having endless meetings, completing *hundreds* of forms, and getting vetted, but it's finally been approved.'

'Wow, Paige, this is huge news!' Jasmine said. 'When will it start?'

'I've asked to foster a young child so maybe when one is born. I hope by starting while they are young, I can make a difference early.'

Jasmine teared up. 'Does that mean you won't be my flatmate?' she asked, knowing the question was a little selfish.

'Probably not. I'm sorry,' Paige said gently. 'That's another thing, I'm looking to buy a house.'

'Dang. Any more life-changing announcements?' Joel asked, still processing the swiftness of the news.

Paige smiled at him. 'Well, either of you can move in with me – once you pass the police vetting,' she laughed.

Jasmine tried to soak it all in.

Paige's expression softened. 'You know, it was Evie who gave me the idea,' she said, glancing at Noah. 'Look at all those children she looked after. Didn't you say it was more than 100? And she was doing it before she even became a mother.'

Noah nodded, clearly proud of his grandmother. 'She would be proud of you.'

Paige grinned. 'And I don't know if I'll be a mother. I think I have a lot to give, so I want to do it. If someone significant turns up in my life, they will have to be all in with me and my children.'

Joel nodded and then made a dramatic sound. 'Well, since we're all sharing life-altering news, I guess it's my turn.'

Paige whipped her head around, 'What?'

Joel smiled. 'I'm going back to uni. I've decided to do a Master of Counselling.'

There was a beat of silence before Jasmine grinned. 'Joel, that's amazing.'

Paige's jaw dropped. 'Since when have you wanted to be a counsellor?'

Joel shrugged. 'I guess it's been creeping up on me for a while. Social media has started to feel too superficial, you know? Then I looked at what Jasmine was doing with the support group, and I thought that's real. I was a little jealous.'

He gave Jasmine a small smile. 'I don't know, I just think I could be good at it. And I want to do something that actually matters. I kept thinking about Ben and how he didn't receive the help he really needed.'

Noah nodded approvingly. 'That's awesome, man. You'd be bloody good at it.'

Joel exhaled, clearly relieved by the reaction. 'There's just one catch.'

'Uh-oh,' Paige said. 'Here it comes.'

'I'm going to be a broke student again,' Joel admitted. 'So if anyone knows of somewhere cheap to live that doesn't involve sharing a flat with first-years, let me know.'

Paige grinned. 'Well, I do have a house to fill. And, you know, police vetting is a breeze.'

Joel groaned but was obviously chuffed at the idea of being part of Paige's new set-up.

Jasmine glanced around at her friends, their lives shifting and reshaping.

***

Later that night, as Jasmine and Noah curled up in bed, their discussion turned to the changes.

'Next year, things will look so different,' she mused. 'Paige will have kids. Joel will be studying. I find that hard.'

Noah ran a hand through her hair. 'Maybe we'll be living together,' he said thoughtfully.

Jasmine lifted her head to look at him. 'At your place or with Paige, Joel and the kids?'

He smiled, 'My house. It makes sense, doesn't it?'

Jasmine didn't reply straight away. The idea of moving in together had crossed her mind, but hearing him say it made it real.

'Maybe,' she said. 'Although I don't think Ben and Evie would approve of us living there without being married. And I'm not sure how I feel about that.'

Noah laughed, pulling her closer. 'You're probably right. Just think about it, okay?'

Jasmine let the idea settle in her mind. She would take her time, but one thing was certain, the year 2020 was going to be very different to 2019.

Chapter Twenty-Five

What if there's a pandemic?

Spring rolled into summer. Paige prepared for her change in life by house hunting and completing parenting courses. She had secured a home that she would take over in February, giving Jasmine a short timeframe to decide whether to move in with Noah.

Joel tried to cram in as many hours of work as he could before becoming a broke student while continuing to see Lucca, the hot-headed sparky, who had turned out to be incredibly sweet.

Jasmine and Noah celebrated their first Christmas together, including being with her nieces and his children, giving Jasmine what she considered the best Christmas ever.

For New Year's activities, the two of them went on a camping trip in the far North, where Ben had grown up. Noah complained that it was the geekiest holiday he had ever had. They had visited cemeteries and old addresses from electoral rolls.

Even though he made fun of it, Jasmine knew he loved it. Seeing the farm and river where Ben grew up gave context to his drawings and poetry, adding another layer of understanding.

Jasmine's final day of holiday was spent with Noah at her parents' house. She set the table for dinner while her mum bustled about in the kitchen, talking about the progress of the kids in the support group. Gaye thrived in the role, and the parents leaned on her for advice. It had been Gaye who had organised a visit to a science lab for Caleb, carefully arranged and monitored, so he could start high school next month.

They discussed the plans for the year.

'Is there any news on when Paige will receive the children?' Gaye asked.

'Yes, there's a baby due in April that will likely come to her and maybe even the baby's older brother, who is in temporary care.'

'How wonderful that the children will be going to Paige, but also, what a tragedy for the mum.'

'Yeah, the programme Paige is in works with the families to try and reunite them. And Joel,' Jasmine added, 'I think he's just as invested in this as Paige. He's done the training and is now qualified to be a foster parent, too.'

'That'll be good for his studies – they'll make quite a cute couple of parents. Things are really changing, but it's exciting.' Gaye added. 'Joel is also going to help with the support group as part of his training.'

Jasmine nodded. She was proud of where her friends were in their lives.

'And what about you? What will you do when the children arrive?' Gaye asked carefully.

'I'll just wait and see,' Jasmine said, smiling. 'I have a few months, and I hope it will be obvious what to do. I might stay with Paige, move in with Noah or get my own place.'

'It's great that you are so flexible about it. Medusa never would have allowed that in the past,' Gaye said knowingly.

Her mum was right. A year ago, she would have needed to answer all the 'what ifs' of uncertainty. But now?

The snakes of Jasmine had been silenced.

Jasmine spied her two favourite men in the garden, walking around and discussing the plants. It made her happy. She went out to join them, catching the end of their conversation.

'You're going to love the tomatoes this year,' Cliff said as she approached. 'Look at that colour already – deep red, full of flavour. You can't buy tomatoes like this in a store.'

Noah nodded appreciatively. 'You have a great setup here, Cliff. It makes me want to get into gardening myself. I guess a bit of dirt under the nails never hurt anyone.'

'Dinner's ready,' Jasmine called, interrupting their discussion before it veered into how potting mix could cause Legionnaires' Disease.

At the table, they settled into their meal, enjoying Gaye's lamb salad and bruschetta.

'Have you seen the news about that virus spreading in China?' Gaye asked over the dinner table. 'They're calling it... what was it? Corona?'

'Yeah, or COVID-19, I think,' Jasmine said, glancing at Noah for confirmation.

He shrugged lightly. 'It seems to be just in China.' Trying to play down the news, he added, 'These things come and go. We've seen it before – bird flu, SARS. It never amounts to much here.'

'I saw them testing people on a plane before flying?' Gaye said. 'It looked like something from that movie we watched, Contagion?'

Cliff added, 'We're an island. Things like that don't spread here.'

Jasmine let her dad's words linger.

He was wrong.

Even as an island, the country was connected to the rest of the world, and that virus might just make its way here.

She felt Medusa's snakes rattle.

In the car on the way home, she asked Noah what he really thought about the new virus. She could see him hesitate.

'It's hard to know what is media hype and what is concerning. I think it will probably play out to nothing, but I'm watching it. And you probably shouldn't,' he said wisely.

Jasmine nodded. 'I won't read anything.'

***

Jasmine and Noah's first anniversary approached. They picked up Jade and Sienna to join them at an anniversary dinner. Both girls were entirely at ease with Jasmine, chatting and joking with her as if she had always been part of their lives. They selected a little family burger bar; it wasn't exactly fancy, but it was perfect for the girls, which made it perfect for Jasmine.

The girls brought notebooks and coloured pencils, happily immersed in their own little world, and Noah used the time to honour the occasion. Taking Jasmine's hand, he said, 'Happy anniversary.'

She smiled, squeezing his hand gently. 'It's been a great year.'

He continued, 'Did you notice we have a few similarities to Evie and Ben?'

Jasmine nodded. Joel had pointed it out to her a few times.

Noah continued, 'For example, he was seven years older than her and lived on Nixon Street. I'm seven years older than you and live on Nixon Street.'

'Right,' Jasmine replied, catching on. 'He was a father, and you're a father,' she said, nodding toward the girls.

'Exactly,' Noah said with a grin. 'They met at work, and we met *through* your work.'

'I hadn't thought of that one,' Jasmine admitted. Then, with a cheeky smile, she added, 'He had a mental condition, and I have a mental condition.'

'Unnecessary comparison,' Noah countered, though he was laughing. 'Ben liked gardening, and I'm *going* to like gardening.'

Noah's expression softened as he continued. 'And they got married.' He paused, letting the statement linger.

Jasmine raised an eyebrow, wondering why he was steering into her usual territory of marriage jokes.

Noah leaned down to whisper something into Jade's ear. Her face lit up with excitement. She quickly whispered to Sienna, and together, the girls placed a small box on the table in front of Jasmine.

Her heart flipped as she stared at the box, trying not to jump to conclusions. Noah held her hand tighter and slipped onto his knee. 'I know it's been only a year, but it was good enough for Ben and Evie, so I think it's good enough for us too. Shall we get married?'

Jasmine's eyes brimmed with tears as she traced the delicate band and the modest art deco setting with small diamonds set in a square. 'It's beautiful,' she whispered. Looking up at Noah, 'Yes, Noah. My answer is yes.'

Noah slid the ring onto her finger, his grin wide. The girls clapped and laughed, and the room erupted with cheers. The waitress quickly delivered complimentary drinks. Strangers from other tables came over to admire the ring and offer congratulations.

When the chaos died down and Jasmine had time to catch her breath, Noah added, 'FYI, the girls want to decorate the cake.'

'Deal,' Jasmine said, glancing at Jade and Sienna, who were bouncing in their seats.

'Can we choose your dress too?' Jade asked.

Noah grinned, ruffling Jade's hair. 'Don't scare her off now. We'll leave the dress decisions for another day.'

Jasmine held her hand out, looking at the ring. It looked so authentically art deco. Could it be Evie's?

Noah answered her question. 'Aunty Rose took a shine to you and gifted me Evie's ring. I had to get it restored, but it's now yours.'

Jasmine felt the emotion overwhelm her. She cleared her throat. 'I have to call people.'

'Oh, I already spoke to your mum and dad, so they might kind of know.'

By the time they left the restaurant, the pair had called Jasmine's parents, Bree and Paige, who all gave equally excited yelps and congratulations. They left a message for Joel, who didn't answer his phone, but pretty soon, the reply came through.

> Sitting in the movies with Lucca. Can't talk. Congrats! I'm already thinking of what to say for my bridesmaid's speech.

***

The following day, Jasmine woke to a flood of text messages from friends and family responding to the photo she and Noah had shared. Jasmine's heart felt surprisingly calm. The "what ifs" hadn't even started coming.

Jasmine started wedding preparations immediately with a plan to marry by the end of the year. She made appointments for dress fittings, cake testing, venue hire and hairdressers.

But the world began to shift.

News of the virus grew louder each day; the world was changing faster than anyone could keep up. Overseas, reports of COVID-19 dominated the headlines, including overwhelmed hospitals and cities in lockdown with mass burials. She followed the news obsessively. Despite promising herself she'd step back, Medusa wouldn't let her.

Preparation is key, she told herself as she stocked both Noah and Paige's pantries with an assortment of supplies: milk powder, pasta, flour, and cocoa.

Joel teased her. 'Are you opening a 1950s baking club?' he'd asked.

But Medusa was thriving, and for once, Jasmine let her.

New Zealanders keenly watched the hard-hit countries, tracking their responses and bracing for what would inevitably come. It seemed only a matter of time before their small country down under would follow others into some form of lockdown and restrictions. There was an uncertainty that Jasmine had never felt before.

Uncertainty was a breeding ground for OCD.

The online conversations in Moana's support group ramped up, with parents sharing stories of their children's heightened anxieties. Jasmine tried to be helpful, offering reassurance and advice, but she knew that if things continued as they were, the "what ifs" filling the group chat would soon become realities.

***

At the end of February, the inevitable news arrived – New Zealand had its first confirmed case of COVID-19.

Panic swept through the country and through Jasmine's mind.

She and Noah sat on the couch, watching the news in silence as reports poured in. Noah switched off the TV, tossing the remote onto the couch with a sigh.

Jasmine turned to him. 'What's going to happen?'

'There's talk about a full lockdown,' Noah said. 'Closing the borders, shutting businesses, everyone staying indoors.'

'How will that even work?' Jasmine asked. 'What about schooling and incomes?'

'I don't know,' he admitted. 'But it might come down to the cost of lives being lost outweighing the cost of businesses, rightly or wrongly.' He took her hand and gave it a gentle squeeze.

Then, without preamble, he said, 'Let's get married *next week*.'

Jasmine blinked. 'What?'

He held her gaze, steady and sure. 'It's not what we were thinking, but I want to go through what's coming next with *you,* in this house. And I know you want to be married *before* you move in, so let's do it. Next week.'

Jasmine opened her mouth, then shut it again. The idea was so sudden, so different from what they had envisioned. But the more she thought about it, the more she realised it made perfect sense.

'How?' she asked. 'Can we even obtain a license that quickly? And a venue?'

'We'll do it *here*,' Noah said simply, pointing around the room. 'Just our closest family. Weddings are already being cancelled because they're considered super-spreaders – this is the perfect excuse for a small gathering.'

Jasmine hesitated, then smiled. 'What would I wear?'

'I'll provide the venue and license,' Noah grinned. 'You sort out the clothes. And remember, you have a designer sister who can adjust anything.'

Jasmine bit her lip. 'Mum still has her dress. I've always liked it – it wouldn't take much to alter.'

'We'll do a BBQ – I can handle that – and buy a cake from The Cake Box. Oh, and I know a Bishop whose house I worked on. He'll do the ceremony.'

Jasmine looked at him. Her heart raced. 'Are we really doing this?'

'If you want to.'

'I *really* do.'

***

The following week flew by in a blur of preparations. True to his word, Noah handled the food, ordering premium meats while Jasmine and Bree worked on altering Gaye's wedding dress. It had held up beautifully over the years – a simple but elegant gown with delicate lacework. Bree adjusted the fit, adding a few modern touches without losing the vintage charm.

It was a beautiful day for a wedding. Bree and Todd arrived first, with Morgan and Aria in tow.

Cliff and Gaye arrived wearing masks. It startled Jasmine at first, but she understood.

'I never thought I would wear a mask to my daughter's wedding,' Gaye said, half joking, but Jasmine could read her worry.

'Well, this is a perfect event to kick-start isolation,' Cliff added.

Joel arrived after collecting Jade and Sienna. He was keen to take on his unofficial role as 'Uncle Joel.' The girls stood with Morgan and Aria who giggled with excitement.

Paige came in her jeans with a daisy tucked behind her ear. As she arrived, she announced with a wink that her gift was a 1-litre bottle of hand sanitiser.

Jasmine had always imagined getting married on a beach or in a picturesque garden, but as she stood in the backyard of Nixon Street, she realised she wouldn't have had it any other way. Jasmine felt it was exactly right, surrounded by the people who mattered most.

Noah looked as calm and steady as ever, though she caught the tiny flicker of emotion as he stood to make his vows.

'Jasmine, most people use a dating app to meet people, but you did it the old-fashioned way – stalking.' Everyone laughed as

Jasmine nodded. 'What a blessing it was that you came looking for me – well, you sent your friends first.'

'Just as well!' Joel yelled.

Noah continued, 'I soon learned that you are smart, funny, quirky and super organised. You are brave and caring. I promise to be the calm when your thoughts are a storm. And to never take for granted how lucky I am that you found me, both in the archives and in life.'

Jasmine looked at the four little girls in the room. They were beaming and proud and mirrored how Jasmine felt. She took a breath and shared her vows.

'Noah, you are a person who builds. You build houses, you build decks, and you even build bird houses for your girls. I've watched you build people up. I see you building a life with me, brick by brick. And even when some of my bricks are a little wonky, you just work out a way to make it work. I look forward to building the future together, and with Sienna and Jade. I can't predict what life will throw at us. But, for better, for worse, for richer, for poorer, in sickness and in health.'

As the couple kissed, the girls squealed with a mix of disgust and joy. Instantly, Jasmine felt little arms around her legs.

Looking down, she saw pairs of eyes staring up at her, eyes that accepted her, eyes that wanted her in their life.

***

When it was time for speeches, Joel went first, raising his glass with a mischievous grin.

'I'd like to take full credit for this union,' he said. 'Because if I hadn't made Jasmine read me Evie and Ben's diaries, then she never would have met Noah. So, really, this is *my* love story.'

The guests laughed.

Cliff and Gaye followed, speaking through their masks. 'Jasmine, you've always been fiercely independent, and that's something we've admired. We are excited for this new chapter and we'll be here for you. Well, we will probably be locked down somewhere for a while. But after that, we will be here with you.'

Paige wiped a tear from her eye before raising her glass. 'To Noah and Jasmine, the builder and the archivist.'

One by one, the guests left, knowing they might not meet again for some months. It was a strange feeling, as if Jasmine had really moved away to a new city or a new life.

But she knew, with absolute certainty, that she was exactly where she was meant to be.

Chapter Twenty-Six

What if the snakes come back?

Just three weeks later, Jasmine and Noah sat in fear as the New Zealand Government announced a nationwide lockdown order.

People had 48 hours to stock up on food and figure out their living situations. For Jasmine, the announcement stirred a mix of emotions she'd never experienced – validation for her cautious tendencies and a deep-seated fear of stepping into an apocalyptic reality.

Paige's job as a primary school teacher would move to online classes, an idea that was as unexpected as it was daunting, especially while she waited to hear if she would receive foster children. She hoped for the best but worried about children stuck in unsafe homes during lockdown.

Joel's university course would also move online. Jasmine could handle some collections remotely, but without access to physical archives, her work would be limited. And Noah, a small business owner, was facing the financial worst of it.

The night before lockdown, the group gathered for a video call to do a welfare check on everyone. Noah explained that his daughters would stay with their mother during lockdown. 'It's for the best,' he said, though the fear on his face was unmistakable.

Jasmine squeezed his hand. 'We'll call them every day and write emails.'

'Yeah, Lucca is considered an essential worker, so he'll be doing electrical emergencies. I might have to cut the power to the house to see him,' Joel said with sadness.

'It's going to be tough, but I'm glad you two have each other,' Jasmine said, looking at her friends on the call.

Later, she checked in with her parents and Bree, making sure they were okay. She reassured them that she and Noah were settled at Nixon Street and joked that Joel and Paige, now sharing a house, would either come out of lockdown as best friends or sworn enemies.

After the calls, Jasmine and Noah had one last errand. They set off for Aunty Rose's house.

As they pulled into the driveway, they spotted her silhouette in the window. By the time they reached the door, she had already opened it, wearing a mask and standing a careful distance away.

'We've come to take you to our house, to be in our bubble,' Noah explained, his tone firm but kind.

Rose hesitated, her hand resting on the doorframe. 'Oh, I couldn't impose. And I have the cats. I'll be okay here.'

Noah frowned, shifting his weight as if preparing for a more extended conversation. 'No, it could be weeks, even months. Do you even have food for that long?'

She tilted her head, considering his question. 'Well, I have enough food for the cats and for me for about two weeks. And then I can go shopping.'

Noah glanced at Jasmine, who stood quietly at his side. His voice softened. 'I won't force you, but I strongly encourage you to join us. Dad would want me to have you. If he or Mum were alive, they would insist.'

He paused, bracing himself before adding, 'The cats can come too.' His lips twitched, betraying his reluctance.

'And I have your box of letters to read with you,' Jasmine said, hoping to add a carrot of incentive.

Rose's eyes darted between Noah and Jasmine. The mention of the cats seemed to pierce her resolve. She sighed, her fingers drumming on the doorframe before she nodded. 'Okay. Let me pack.'

Jasmine and Noah entered the house, using the hand sanitiser that Rose had set by the door. The new smell of sterilisation lingered in the air as they moved through the house. Catching the cats proved more of a challenge, with one darting under the couch and the other scrambling to the top of the bookshelf.

Eventually, they had created a pile of belongings at the front door.

'Can I come back to check on the house?' Rose asked.

'I don't think so,' Noah explained, 'I believe we can't drive around without a purpose.'

Rose shook her head. 'I thought it was crazy days in the 1960s, but this is something else.'

As Rose stepped out of the house, cradling a nervous cat in her arms, she paused on the porch. 'I feel like I've been evicted,' she said, her voice trembling.

'Try to think of it as a holiday,' Noah said, not knowing how to really offer comfort to a situation that was unfamiliar to them all.

***

As they pulled into the driveway of her old family home, Rose peered out the window.

'Well, this is a twist I didn't see coming,' she said. 'Back to Nixon Street after all these years. Let's hope it's not haunted.'

'There she is, that's the fun aunty I know,' Noah joked.

'Oh, Thomas and I had the best ghost stories in this house. We used to stay up late, against Mum's wishes, and see who could scare the other one the most. I do believe I won that competition.'

Jasmine helped Rose unpack a small bag and set up an area for the cats. Rose made herself a space in the spare room. As the two women worked to make the room feel like home for an uncertain length of time, Rose began to reflect.

'Jasmine, did you know that this room used to be the bathroom?' she said, glancing at the high ceilings and panelled walls. 'Although when I lived here, there was never a toilet in the room. That came later.'

Jasmine smiled. 'You'll be glad there's an inside toilet now.'

'If there wasn't, I would have stayed at my own house and faced the isolation,' she joked. 'Here's a memory for you – even when Dad was unwell, he would always come with me outside as a guard when I went to the outhouse. I hated going out there, but he'd be my watchman. He never complained, day or night.'

'That's a nice memory,' Jasmine said, 'he must have been a dedicated father.'

'And that room over there,' Rose continued, pointing to the large lounge that they would use to watch TV and play games, 'that's where Dad used to sleep. Well, not just sleep – it's where he lived for more than twenty years – reading and thinking, sometimes shuffling out for a meal.'

Jasmine sat on the bed, letting Rose reminisce while soaking in every moment. She saw the irony, for Rose to now be locked inside, in the place her dad had lived in isolation from the community.

'Do you know, I stood at that window and watched him calm a frightened horse. Why did I watch from inside? Why didn't I go out and celebrate him?' Rose became emotional. The toll of leaving her home and the uncertainty of lockdown was breaking the usually strong woman.

'Perhaps it was the safest place for you to be,' Jasmine offered.

'Perhaps. I probably should have told Dad I was proud of him that day.'

They sat in silence, Jasmine unsure what comfort to offer. Her eyes shifted to the window – the one that had been Ben's view of the world for more than twenty years. It matched the one Jasmine had peered through at Tokanui.

Same style.

Different confinement.

Rose continued after a moment's pause.

'Did I tell you that when I was an adult, my doctor came to make a house call on Dad? It was the first time he had met Dad, who was by then in his 70s. I was so worried about what Dr French would think of my dad. But, later, he told me, "What a terrible waste of a brilliant man. One little pill a day, and his life could have been so different".' Her voice softened. 'I try not to dwell on the what-ifs, though. He was who he was, and he loved us deeply.'

Jasmine nodded. It made good sense to ignore the what-ifs.

Rose smiled gently. 'There's no changing the past. I can only hope he and Mum are happy together now – and that he's sane. Well, as sane as any of us are.'

Jasmine responded with a smile. 'At the moment, I think we've all gone mad.' She began lining up a bunch of masks on the dressing table.

'Now,' Rose said, shifting her tone, 'I hope I can get that old Singer sewing machine working. Mum used to have it running perfectly in the old days, and I've watched some great videos on how to make masks from old pillowcases.'

Jasmine smiled, doubting the machine would ever work, but they'd give it a shot. After all, they had plenty of time.

***

Life in lockdown took some getting used to. Weeks blurred together. One rolled into two, then a month. The memory of life outside lockdown began to fade. Staying connected with loved ones became a deliberate effort. Daily check-ins required purposeful coordination, and it seemed as though the entire world had suddenly mastered Zoom calls and Messenger groups.

Joel and Paige sent videos of their increasingly ridiculous dance challenges, keeping everyone entertained. One particular number ended with Joel knocking over a lamp. 'It's interpretive,' he declared in the group chat. 'Symbolic of the downfall of the world through Covid.'

Noah spent his days working on the house, fixing odd jobs he'd ignored for years.

'At this rate, the place will be ready for a magazine shoot,' Jasmine said.

'And I'll be broke,' Noah replied.

Though his smile softened the words, she knew he was worried about income and how long he would be unable to work.

Rose became part of the household effortlessly. She and Jasmine experimented with recipes Evie might have made, often with mixed results.

Despite all her efforts, Jasmine noticed obsessive thoughts creeping into her life, with Medusa gaining momentum.

Jasmine had never struggled with contamination OCD before, but now she found herself sanitising her hands constantly and she started turning the tap on and off more than once as she washed her hands, counting to five, which seemed a good, safe number.

Lying in bed one night, with one of Aunty Rose's cats sleeping at her feet, she confessed her thoughts to Noah.

'I don't blame you for feeling that way,' he said quickly, 'I'm thinking of adopting OCD myself.' Then, realising she was serious, he leaned on his elbow and added softly, 'I didn't want to say anything, but I saw on the news that compulsions have really spiked for people with OCD. It makes sense. Society's basically telling them to do everything they'd spent years trying not to do. The whole reason to fight it has disappeared.'

'I saw that too. And the fallout from this for those people could last for months. Any good ground won will be lost,' she said, worrying. 'I mean, people are telling us to wash vegetables with bleach and not to handle groceries for three days after buying them. People *without* OCD are doing that. It's going to escalate, and I might just get caught up in it.' Jasmine felt disheartened; she had come so far in the past year, and this could be a setback.

'What would you tell the people in your support group?' Noah asked.

'They've been reaching out,' she said. 'I've told them to do the basics: resist, delay, and do something different – basically trick OCD. It's easier said than done, though.'

'Let's do it together,' he suggested. 'I could put a timer by the soap so you can see how long you can go without using it.'

'That's actually a great idea. We could make it into a little competition. Maybe I'll even tell the support group parents about it and let the kids have a go.'

'See? You're helping already,' Noah said with a smile.

Jasmine hesitated for a moment, then admitted, 'You know, Noah, this is what life is like for me. There's no off-switch for OCD. There's a simmer switch, and maybe even moments where I can disconnect. But, I just have to keep working at it.'

Noah squeezed her hand. 'And you are. Look at you – you turned an obsession upside down and pushed it out of your life. And when another one comes along, you'll do it again.'

Jasmine exhaled, feeling the weight of it. 'I feel so helpless watching people relapse, and I just wish I could explain it better – help them the way I've learned to help myself.'

'You've explained it pretty well to me,' Noah said. 'I went from knowing nothing about OCD to feeling like I understand it.'

'I've had a lot of practice,' she admitted with a faint smile.

Noah sighed and shifted on the bed. 'At least you're doing something meaningful. I'm just sitting here while work dries up.'

Jasmine placed a reassuring hand on his arm. 'When this is over, people will still need their homes fixed. You'll have work waiting for you. Bars and restaurants, on the other hand, they'll never get those nights back.'

'I know,' he said, his voice heavy. 'It's just the uncertainty.'

They lay in silence for a moment before Noah spoke again. 'You want to help people understand OCD, right? Why not write a book about it? Use a character with OCD to tell the story. You have time now.'

Jasmine thought about his idea. Could she do it? Should she do it?

'Maybe. I'll think about it. I need a plot, and I don't have much imagination.'

'Ha!' Noah laughed, 'Don't tell me you don't have an imagination. Isn't OCD constantly making up scenarios?'

She smiled. 'That's a pretty loose interpretation.'

'See? You're already teaching me. Write about it.'

That night, Jasmine's mind buzzed with possibilities. Unable to sleep, she got up and tiptoed down the hall, the floorboards creaking. She remembered about Aunty Rose's stories about how impossible it was to sneak in late at night without being heard and now she could believe it.

She went into the lounge where there was a desk set up by the window.

By Ben's window.

She started to scribble ideas that flowed out from her, from a place she didn't even know existed. She wrote down her fears, thoughts and obsessions through the years. She noted characters who could be in her book: Ben, Tokanui, Caleb, her parents, people in the support group and herself.

In the morning, she woke, finding herself slouched in the chair next to the window. She stretched, trying to straighten her back. Noah was in the room waiting for her to wake.

'Morning, sorry to bother you, but it's time for the daily call with the outside world.' She nodded and patted down her hair.

Joel's video camera was propped on the counter while Paige stirred something on the stove. Cliff and Gaye were bickering about the phone angle, with their nostrils dominating the screen.

Rose sat in the background, occasionally chuckling at the conversation. Noah was on a separate call with his daughters, who proudly showed off new crafts.

It was a new kind of routine, one that none of them had seen coming.

Once the calls ended, Jasmine leaned back in her chair. She felt a quiet excitement blooming inside her, like something big was about to happen.

Noah came over and rubbed her shoulders. 'So, what's the plan for today?'

She smiled up at him. 'I'm going to attempt to write the first chapter of a book about someone with OCD.'

'Ooh, can I be in it?' he asked.

'Maybe, depending on whether it's horror or romantic fiction.'

'Hopefully romantic fiction,' he said, laughing.

'Actually,' she said thoughtfully, 'with your permission, I think I want to write about your grandparents.'

'That would be perfect,' Noah said.

Before Jasmine could begin typing, Joel reappeared on the screen, balancing a cup of coffee in one hand and what looked like study notes in the other.

'What's up? I thought you would be back to breadmaking,' Jasmine asked.

Joel sighed dramatically. 'No rest for the future *Doctor* Joel.' He waved his study notes in front of the camera. 'I've just been offered a placement for my counselling training. It's part-time, so I'll still be working and studying. Of course, I have to wait until lockdown is over.'

Jasmine beamed. 'Joel, that's amazing!'

'And terrifying,' he admitted.

Paige appeared behind him, peering over his shoulder and holding up her phone.

'The baby is born,' she beamed. 'It's a boy and he arrives here tomorrow.'

For a moment, no one spoke, and then Joel squealed. 'We're having a baby!'

For the first time in lockdown, Jasmine felt the genuine loss of connection. She was locked away from her friends and wouldn't see the baby.

'I'm so excited for you guys. I can't wait to meet him online.'

She reminded herself that things would go back to how they were, eventually.

After the call, Jasmine popped herself in front of the computer screen, hoping it would unlock some inspiration.

Rose popped her head into the room with a cuppa. 'Tea for the writer,' she said, setting the cup beside Jasmine. 'Noah told me your plans; I expect a starring role, of course.'

Jasmine laughed, realising that Rose would, in fact, have a starring role.

She turned back to her screen, hoping her words would help someone.

She smiled as her fingers moved over the keyboard, unleashing years of her experiences and Ben and Evie's stories onto the computer screen in front of her.

She began her first chapter: *Most people worry about big things. I could worry about anything.*

Author's notes

This novel weaves together strands of truth and imagination. Some elements are inspired by the lives of real people, while others are entirely fictional, created to carry the story forward.

OCD portrayal – All examples of obsessions and compulsions are grounded in real experiences, though they are fictionalised through the characters.

Characters – The characters of Jasmine, Paige, Joel, Moana, Caleb, Noah, and Dr Kris are inventions for the novel.

Family story – The story of Ben and Evie's lives is drawn from real history. Names, letters and certain details have been changed to protect privacy. Aunty Rose's story is based on fragments of family accounts.

Ben's writings – The diary extracts are adapted from his original notebooks, with some abridgement for length. His poems, letters, and drawings were preserved from his time at Tokanui.

Evie's writings – She never kept a diary; the entries in this novel were written to capture her voice and to tell a story of the time. They are inspired by the many letters she sent to her family, with some adapted for narrative flow.

The grapevine – The grapevine is real, and a cutting continues to grow in the author's home today.

About the author

Suzanne Miller is a New Zealander passionate about helping others understand the complexity of OCD. Born and raised in Palmerston North and now living in Hamilton, she was inspired to write *What If? What If?* after her own experiences navigating the challenges of anxiety and compulsive thinking within her family.

She holds a tertiary qualification in Business Communication and has a love of history and family history. As a mother of four, Suzanne sees family life as one of her most meaningful works. She is a creative person at heart, and also enjoys sewing, crocheting, and cardmaking.

What If? What If? is her debut novel.

Questions for discussion

Which characters experience isolation, and how are they best supported?

How can we better support people living with OCD, both personally and as a society?

What might the window on the cover symbolise throughout the novel? How does it reflect both hope and confinement?

How did the OCD information shape the way you respond to or support someone who lives with this condition?

How does Jasmine's OCD both hinder and help her in life?

Compare how different characters supported Jasmine. In what ways were their responses helpful or perhaps unhelpful?

What lessons from the past impacted Jasmine and her friends? How did these lessons shape their choices?

Which scene or moment stayed with you the most?

If you could speak to one character, who would it be, and what would you ask them?

Printed in Dunstable, United Kingdom

81321325R00178